PASS
INTERFERENCE

Book #6 of the Connecticut Kings Series

Christina C Jones

warm hues creative

D1711248

the savior, the family, the friends,

the betas, the readers.

without y'all, where would i be?

One.

April 2018

She had a thing for making me wait.

And damn if I didn't just go along with it, every single time, because as certain as I was of who the fuck I was… it was, unquestionably, a privilege for me to be there. If we were talking about identity, shit… I knew who *she* was when I was in the early stages of getting to know my damn self. Had spent ample time *getting to know myself* with images of her in my mind.

Sloane Brooks.

Baddest woman alive, and the competition wasn't even *close.*

Hell.

There *was no* competition.

Just *her*, in a category all by herself, which was why I was on her doorstep at one in the morning. I knew she was up, knew she was home, knew she was probably just on the other side of the door, waiting for whatever arbitrary length of time she'd chosen to punish me with this time to pass. She claimed the frustration made the sex better, and I claimed I wasn't doing this shit anymore, not even one more time.

My claim was a lie.

"What do you want?" she snapped when she – finally – opened the door. I'd expected the glass of wine she had in her hand, but her attire… *that* was a pleasant surprise that helped make the wait worth it. The sheer, floor-length robe wasn't concealing a damn thing – blackberry hued areolas peaked with hard nipples were right at eye level for me, practically begging to be tasted.

The height differential dragged my gaze lower – her feet were clad in the spiked Louboutins she'd found on her doorstep a few weeks back – a birthday gift from a not-so-secret admirer. Those heels raised her at least five inches off the ground, and I hadn't yet taken the two last two steps up to her doorway.

Now that the door was open, I did, pulling my gaze up to meet her eyes.

"My pussy," I told her, fighting the urge to grin as she pulled her bottom lip between her teeth.

With the front door still open, and her eyes locked on mine, she unbelted her robe with one hand, using the other to keep her wine glass level. She lifted the glass to her mouth for a sip as she propped a hand at her side, keeping half of the robe tucked behind her.

"*Your* pussy, huh?"

With one hand at the base of her neck, I kept her where I wanted as my mouth descended onto hers, savoring the sweetness of wine on her lips and tongue. I pulled her in further – licking and exploring as my fingers crept upward, to the base of the silky, colorfully printed scarf she wore to protect her hair, and then underneath. Instead of scolding, or complaints, my fingertips against her scalp provoked deeper moans, even when I dug into her carefully fashioned twists.

I pulled back from the kiss, just enough to smirk against her lips.

"Yeah. *My* pussy."

Her throaty, sexy giggle only made my dick press harder into her stomach before she backed away from me, turning to saunter down the hall, offering me yet another view to admire. "Where have you been?" she tossed over her shoulder as I stepped fully inside, closing and locking her door behind me. "You taste like you've been drinking."

"So do you."

She turned back to me, glancing at the wine glass in her hand before she rolled her eyes. "Are you going to answer the question?"

"Arch and Point."

A little smirk came to her face, and she shifted positions, placing a hand on her hip again. "*Oh.* So that's what this is? You go to the strip club for the show, then drop by here to get what they won't give you?"

"I can't believe you managed to say that with a – mostly – straight face," I countered. *Arch and Point* was a high-end club, with high-end talent. But with that face, and that body, nobody was fucking with Sloane and she knew it.

I knew it.

Everybody knew it.

"Just speaking the truth – took a trip to the titty bar for you to *finally* come see me, after neglecting me for weeks."

I chuckled as I ambled toward her, grabbing the silken belt of her robe to pull her toward me. "You just say anything, huh?" I asked. The truth was that I'd been trying to pin her down since her birthday, wondering if the gift had been too much, had been the thing that scared her off from whatever we had going.

Her response to tonight's text had been a pleasant surprise that I hadn't taken for granted, leaving an unofficial team gathering to come straight here before she changed her mind.

"You saying I'm wrong?"

"I'm saying that I've *been* trying to get next to you."

"And *I'm* saying that you haven't."

I frowned. "So tonight is the first night I've reached out?"

"I didn't say that," she smirked.

"So what are you saying?"

"That tonight is the night you said something worth responding to."

Damn.

Okay.

Quickly, I thought back on the things I'd said in an attempt to broach communication with her over the last weeks. Questions about her life, politics, pop culture, etc., all of which had gone ignored – a perceived slight that most men would have taken as an attack on their ego, and a reason to fall back.

Getting Sloane had been a challenge.

It went without saying that *keeping* her would be too.

Tonight though, there had been no real thought put into it, no deeper intellectual meaning. Just an intoxicated, impulsive one-liner, sent off after a fantastic lap dance from a beautiful, flexible woman, that hadn't done a damn thing for me.

"*I need to be inside you tonight.*"

That was all the text said.

And after weeks of radio silence, I got a text back almost immediately.

"I guess you'd better get over here then. – S."

Got it.

"I'm starting to think you only want me for one thing," I told her, prompting a grin.

"And yet, you still have your clothes on."

My hands went to her ass, gripping her through the sheer fabric of her robe as I pulled her against me. I grazed my lips over hers before I kissed her again, deeper this time, until I felt the telltale dip of her strength leaving her knees.

"Hold that thought," I told her, smacking her ass before I walked away, letting memory lead me to her downstairs bathroom to relieve myself and wash my hands – both of which were necessary after a long night out, *before* I indulged myself with Sloane.

Heading back into the living room, I found her perched on the arm of the couch, finishing her wine as she stared into the fireplace, which had already been lit when I arrived. Unable to help myself, I stopped to take her in, as if I hadn't already seen her in her full glory many times.

It was a view that never got old though.

Hooded eyes, full lips, high cheekbones, rounded nose. Velvety soft, deep brown skin. Toned arms, thick thighs. Ample breasts, flat stomach, wide hips, *perfect* ass.

A goddamn dream.

"What's on your mind?" I asked, approaching while she was still seated, stepping right in front of her.

She looked up, and drained the rest of her glass before she put it down. "While I was waiting? Work. Now that you're back... I have every expectation that you'll make me forget what that word means."

I put a hand under her chin, tipping her face up toward mine as I bent to meet her, kissing her again. Her hands went to my shirt, deftly undoing the buttons and then pushing it down over my shoulders before I scooped my hands underneath her, bringing her with me as I sat down on the couch.

My mouth went to her breasts, not even bothering to open her robe before I started lavishing them with attention as her fingers dug into my shoulders. I looked up to find her looking at me, lips parted in pleasure as I tugged her nipple between my teeth, then sucked it to soothe the sting.

I didn't want her *looking* though.

With my hands under her ass, I urged her up onto her knees, then hooked her thigh over my shoulder and the back of the couch. The movement was so quick, so fluid, that she barely had time to catch herself before I dove in, immersing myself in my favorite place.

Sloane's Pussy.

My pussy.

She instantly went for the top of my head, the only place my hair was long enough for her grip. Her other hand went to the couch, digging into the fabric as she let out a loud exclamation of pleasure.

"*God*, Nate," she whimpered as I covered her with my mouth, using my tongue to collect every drop of arousal I could reach, slurping her up. I pushed my fingers into her, making her buck into my face as I lapped her clit with my tongue in measured swipes. Breathing in deep, I inhaled her, pressing my nose into her folds as I savored her aroma, her taste, the tight feeling of her around my fingers, contracting and trying to pull them deeper.

Her breathing shifted, and so did her body, to shallow breaths and a more pronounced rocking of her hips into my face as she rode my fingers. I could feel the tension in her muscles, knew she was almost there, so I focused in – stroked her deeper, faster, sucked harder. This time when I looked up, her mouth was wide open, eyes shut tight, head thrown back.

That's what I want to see.

When she came, it was with both hands gripped in my hair, damn near suffocating me as she kept my face buried between her legs. I had no complaints – I'd gladly drown between her thighs in an attempt to lick her clean, because that's *just* how caught up I was, unashamedly.

But then she reminded me that there was more.

She carefully unhooked her leg from my shoulder, then lowered herself back to my lap to kiss me. While she was there, she easily undid my belt and slacks, freeing my dick with skill that was, in my experience, unmatched.

She stopped the kiss just long enough to look me right in the eyes while she spit into her hand, and then her hands went to work. Pumping my dick and caressing my balls while she lapped her tongue in my mouth, making me harder than what should have been legally possible. She stroked harder, faster, as her body slipped through my hands, sinking until she was down on the floor.

I was *never* fully prepared for the wonder of Sloane's mouth.

A hiss escaped my throat as my dick hit the back of *her* throat, making her let out a hum of pleasure that vibrated through me, all the way to my damn *toes*. She gagged, just the tiniest bit, then immediately recovered, creating suction around my dick like she was trying to swallow me whole as she moved back up to the tip.

And then she *did* swallow me whole.

It went on like that, her making a perfect mess of saliva, and jacking me off, and treating my balls to the talents of her tongue and sucking me to the point of me snatching that goddamn scarf off so I could grip her hair while I stroked into her mouth.

And then she swallowed the natural result of *that*.

By the time she'd climbed back into my lap and sank onto my dick, nothing between us, I was already reassured of my status as a *very* lucky man. But the warmth and tightness of her pussy, the grip of her thighs, the skill in the roll of her hips… all of that was *further* confirmation that this was a damn privilege.

One I had *zero* intention of losing.

I frowned at my hair in the mirror, mentally calculating what I might be able to do to repair the damage done to it last night. I'd spent an hour carefully twisting it, with every intention of a perfect twist-out today.

There was *nothing* perfect about the tangled mess I was looking at now.

Totally worth it.

I glanced behind me, through the open bathroom door, to where Nate was still sprawled across my bed – deliciously nude, and here way past our agreed upon deadline.

This time though, I'd allow it.

I pulled my messy twists back into a bun, which was neat enough for what I needed to do. I was getting ready to dress in my running gear when Nate's wide shoulders filled the door frame. He stepped into the bathroom, stretching his long limbs before he ambled to the toilet to relieve himself.

"You shouldn't still be here when I get back," I told him, once he'd flushed the toilet and moved to the sink to wash his hands.

"I know that, Ms. Brooks," he said, arms crossed as he pressed his hip into the counter, watching me. "You have quite a knack for making sure I understand my place around here."

"Nate…" I stopped, panties in hand, to catch his eyes. "We've talked about this." I dropped the underwear back onto the counter, moving to press a hand to his bare chest. "You *know* you have a special place in my…"

His eyes narrowed. "In your *what*?" he asked. "Definitely not your heart."

"No, but…" I smirked as I moved in closer, let my hand drift lower. "I'll give you three guesses where else?"

I squealed with laughter, biting my lip as he turned me around, bending me over the counter. My laughter quickly shifted to a gasp as he plunged into me from behind in one deep, firm stroke. His hands came up, cupping my breasts as he stroked into me with precision.

"*Shiiiit*," I moaned, my back arching as his fingers pinched and pulled at my nipples.

"One," he grunted, forcing me into a more upright position. My heart was already racing, but started pumping faster as he dragged his hand upward, stopping at my neck to grip me by the throat as he fucked me harder. "Two." His mouth went to my shoulder and he bit down, just enough to send a tingle of pain through me. He pressed his lips there, then urged me back down before he put his other hand between my legs, dipping his thumb into me for moisture. A moment later, his thumb was in my ass, pressing down as he kept his dick moving. "*Three.*"

Hell yes.

As lovers went, Nate was absolute perfection.

Fine as hell.

Big dick, and he knew how to use it.

He – mostly – wasn't too needy.

And he *worshipped* me.

Too bad I have to let him go.

For now though, I was going to enjoy every single moment of him, and every single inch.

When we were finished, I dressed for my run and left my house still smelling like him. I had a full day, and the quickie had already cut into some of my time, so I decided that instead of my usual five miles, three would have to do.

Hopefully, that would put me back on track.

The scenery was part of why I'd chosen this neighborhood, and as usual, it didn't disappoint. The hilly terrain gave me a decent workout, but it was cultivated – and populated – enough that I felt no need to be on high alert, which meant I could let my mind run free.

Today, that was necessary.

Life changing.

Groundbreaking.

Inspiring.

Those were just a few of the terms already being thrown around in reference to a job offer I hadn't even received yet. Not that I wasn't confident I'd get it, but one thing I *wasn't* looking forward to was the circus that would come with it.

And I was *not* the type of woman to shy away from attention.

I *relished* it.

Usually.

I wiped away a brow full of sweat as I powered through the loop that marked the halfway point of my run.

Maybe you should talk to Nate about the job…

Ha.

I dismissed *that* thought as soon as it popped, unbidden, into my head. There were plenty of things I could talk to him about, if I felt inclined. He was well-traveled, well-informed, and well-rounded enough that he could probably speak on any topic I brought up, but *this* topic was off-limits.

Which is why I'd been ignoring him.

Last night had been a moment of weakness.

As I approached my house, I frowned at the flashy black Mercedes G-class parked in my driveway. It wasn't Nate's car – he knew I meant it when I said it was time to go – but it still made my jaw tight to see it. As soon as I hit the door, I went searching for the owner and found him in my kitchen, in my refrigerator, like he owned the place.

"*Garrett*," I snapped, and he looked up, with a mouthful of the strawberries I'd intended to go with *my* breakfast this morning.

"Good morning baby," he said, backing out of my refrigerator with a grin. "You look… *damn*. You went running in that?"

I folded my arms, scowling as he made his way up to me with that goofy ass expression still on his face. "It's a sports bra and running shorts. What's the problem?"

"Nothing. Just wishing I could have seen it. *That* ass in *these* shorts? Ooh-*wee*," he teased, wrapping his arms around my waist.

"Why are you touching me?"

His lips twisted to the side. "You doing me like that? It's a cold world when a man can't even get close to his wife."

"*Ex*-wife," I quickly corrected him, since he – somehow – *loved* to forget that part. "What are you doing in my house?"

He tightened his hold around me. "You *know* what I'm doing here. Heard you've been stressed, so I thought maybe you needed a little… relief. Thought I could help you out this morning."

"Oh you *did*, did you?" I laughed, pushing away from him to grab a bottle of water for myself. "Thought you'd drop off a lil' something?"

"I don't know about *little,* and neither do you." I rolled my eyes as he approached me again, trapping me against the counter. "Don't act like this wasn't the best dick of your life," he murmured into my ear as his hands moved to my ass. "You forgot or something?"

I bit my lip as I looked up, meeting his eyes. Garrett Brooks was, honestly, finer than fine. Once upon a time, he'd been everything to me, with his deep golden skin and curly hair and light eyes – Black 90s heartthrob material through and through, and he'd played me like a damn fool, just like on the sitcoms.

"No. I haven't forgotten that you *used* to be the best dick of my life."

"Wait, what?! I know you haven't been—"

"This looks *cozy.*"

I looked up to find my – *our* – sixteen-year-old daughter, Madison, standing in the doorway to the kitchen with a huge grin on her face.

"Do *not* get any ideas little girl," I warned her, already knowing what that look meant. She'd been on a not-so-secret campaign to get us back together, and still hadn't *quite* gotten the message that it wasn't happening.

It was *never* happening.

"*What do you mean?*" she shrugged, playing innocent as I pushed Garrett off me.

I shook my head. "Don't play. Grab something to eat while I get ready, and then I'll take you to school okay?"

"Oh, no worries mom," she said, stopping beside her father, who was still looking thrown off by my statement. "Dad is taking me to breakfast, *and*... he's letting me drive!"

My eyes went wide. "Letting you—your *Mercedes*?!" I asked, looking at Garrett.

"She has her permit, she'll be fine."

I opened my mouth, then immediately closed it again, swallowing a petty, unnecessary reminder that he'd *never* allowed me behind the wheel of one of his luxury "babies", even after I'd *had* his damn *baby*.

But if he wanted to spoil his baby… it was no concern of mine.

Mads was a good kid. Great grades, good behavior, excellent work ethic on the girls' rugby team at her school, and when she *did* have her episodes of teenaged angst, they were never directed at me.

She deserved something to brag about with her friends – some of whom were already pushing their *own* "G-Wagens" with their fresh new restricted driver's licenses.

"Just be careful please?" I asked, pressing a kiss to her cheek. "And wear your seatbelt."

"Yes," she squealed, practically bubbling with excitement. "I came to ask if I can borrow a pair of sunglasses?" My face must have registered confusion, because she amended, "The Gucci aviators."

Oh.

Of course.

Why would she need to ask permission for the ones I'd grabbed at Target?

"I'm about to see you in a Mercedes wearing Gucci sunglasses on Instagram in about an hour, aren't I?" I asked, bringing a sheepish grin to her face.

"*Maybe*?"

"Get the glasses girl," I granted, shaking my head. "And they'd *better* find their way back to my room when you're done with them."

"*Thank youuu*!" she shrieked, giving me a quick kiss on the cheek before she raced off. I smiled after her, sending up a silent thank-you of my own for the life I had, of which that little girl was a huge part.

"Okay so let's talk about this," Garrett spoke up, reminding me that he was there.

I groaned. "Can we not? There's *really* nothing to say. Aren't you dating some Instagram model or something right now?"

"She's a sports reporter," was his dry response, and I raised an eyebrow.

"*Is* she?"

"Yes, but that's beside the point."

My face wrinkled in confusion. "*How*?"

"We decided to cool things off."

"She found out you were screwing somebody else, didn't she?"

"What? *No*," he insisted. "That's really what you think of me?"

"Why would I think anything else?" I asked, then took the last swig of my water. "You've been a hoe since the eighties, and my silly ass *married* you. You really are great in bed though, I'll give you that," I told him, with a pat to his arm as I started off.

Instead of letting me go, he grabbed me, pulling me close to him. "I am a changed man, Sloane. Why don't you give me a chance to show you that?"

"Because I am *not* your type anymore and you *know* it. You like twenty-year-old "sports reporters", remember?"

He sucked his teeth. "*Please*. I'd pick your fine ass any day, and you know it. Coming in here all sweaty, with these little shorts on." He leaned in, with his mouth to my ear. "If Mads wasn't here I'd spread you open right here in this kitchen... lick *all* this sweat off you," he told me, squeezing my ass for extra effect.

I laughed as I pushed him off, not wanting him to feel my hard nipples... or smell Nate on me. "I need to take a shower."

"Is that an invitation?" he asked, already pulling his arm out of his shirt until we heard Madison's footsteps coming down the stairs. I took that as my opportunity to escape, kissing my daughter goodbye before I headed up the stairs to my bedroom to get myself together.

I still had to get to that meeting.

As strongly as I'd proclaimed myself to not be nervous, my heartbeat was roaring in my ears.

Just be cool, Brooks.

Ha.

Much easier said than done, when I was the only woman in a room full of men whose decision today would determine the next step of my career.

Head coach, assistant head coach, offensive coordinator, offensive assistants, director of pro personnel, director of player personnel, general manager, assistant general manager, president, and owner. All were in attendance, and all were, currently, looking at me.

Waiting.

"So what do you say, Brooks?" Eli Richardson asked me, from the head of the table. "You ready to make Connecticut Kings history?"

With squared shoulders and my head held high, I nodded. "Yes sir."

My words prompted a wide, warm smile across his face as he stood, rounding the table with his hand extended. "In that case… welcome to the team."

I stood from my chair and shook his hand – sealing my fate. Of course I'd understood the gravity of this, how completely unheard of it was. But it wasn't until I clasped hands with the owner of *the* professional football team that it *really* hit me.

I'd done it.

I'd become the woman that sixteen-year-old me had daydreamed about in front of the TV. She'd advocated for girls to be allowed on her high school team, and made it happen. She'd done it again a few years later, in college. A few years after that? She took her talents to the semi-pro leagues.

Once I was derailed by injuries, I went back to my college, where they gladly offered a position on their coaching staff. Since then, I'd been *Coach Brooks*, helping lead team after team to championship titles.

This jump to the NFL though… this was different.

This was *new*.

I'd always been a fan, from the moment my Daddy sat me on his knee while the game was on, so we *both* stayed out of Mama's way, to give her some time to herself. I knew the players, knew the rules, knew the politics of it all.

And now… I was there.

I'd made it.

"Congratulations Brooks," Kyle Underwood, the offensive coordinator said to me as he and the coaching assistants gathered around. "Heard things about you."

"All good, I hope," I told him, accepting the hand he offered.

"Absolutely. You've made a notable difference with the wide receivers at BSU, which is something to be proud of. With that said… this isn't college football. This is the big leagues – arrogant, grown ass men with big egos and bigger salaries. You're in for a challenge."

I stood a little straighter. "Well, I've never been one to back down from those, so it's fine by me. All I need to know is when we get started."

Underwood nodded. "That's the type of attitude I like to hear. The draft is this Friday, and we'll hold rookie camp to get the new recruits acclimated to the pro playbook. Study up between now and then. We'll be watching."

I held my tongue, fighting the urge to inform him that telling me to study was unnecessary – I'd be ready when I needed to be, no question. Instead, I nodded, and then after quick introductions and encouraging words from the rest of the room… the meeting was over.

Just like that.

"Ms. Brooks!" Eli called as I stepped out, and I waited for him at the door. "Walk with me for a moment," he insisted, and I fell into step right beside him.

"What can I do for you?" I asked, biting back a fresh wave of nerves. "You're not already having second thoughts, are you?"

He laughed. "No, not at all. But you might, after you hear what I have to say."

I stopped moving, which prompted him to as well. "Please. Just tell me what you have to say."

"Of course. As you know, there aren't many women in the NFL, in *any* capacity. And the number of Black women is even lower."

I nodded. "Yes, I do. I understand what a big deal my hiring is."

"Right. And… as such… I'd like to capitalize on it. Cover stories, TV interviews, podcast appearances, the whole nine."

My eyebrow went up. "So… you want to use me as a PR project for the team."

"Yes," he answered, with no hesitation, which I appreciated. It showed he respected me enough to not bullshit me. "My question is, will it be a problem?"

"Not at all," I shrugged. "You see this face, don't you? The camera *loves* me, and I love it back."

"Sounds like there shouldn't be any problems then," Eli laughed. "The PR team will be in touch after the season starts."

I nodded. "I'll be looking forward to it."

Eli extended his hand again, and I accepted, for one more shake. "Once again Ms. Brooks… welcome to the team."

He left me there in the hallway, and I took a second to just look around, still in quiet awe that I'd made it this far. There had been – and still would be, inevitably – so much bullshit to contend with, but none of it had defeated me.

I was *here*.

And nothing could take it away from me.

"Well, well, *well*. If it isn't Sloane Brooks, in the *flesh*."

Unbidden, a smile came to my face at the sound of Nate's voice – a smile I wiped off before anyone, Nate included, could see it. I turned to face him, and instantly got annoyed by how damn good he looked.

It really should be a crime.

"What brings you to my neck of the woods?" he asked, gesturing at the office space around him – the Kings' organization corporate headquarters.

"Employment. They offered me the job today, and… I accepted."

"*Congratulations*," he said, looking genuinely proud as he extended his hand.

"Thank you," I told him, returning the gesture. "I'm very excited about it."

"Excited enough to feel like uh… celebrating?" he still hadn't released my hand, and took the opportunity to give it a squeeze to make sure I didn't miss the subtext of his words.

With a little sigh, I pulled my hand from his as I glanced around, making sure we were the only ones in the hall. "Actually… about that… you *do* know we can't—"

"Don't say it. *Don't* say it," Nate insisted, shaking his head. His lips were still curved, and there was a smile in his eyes, so I knew he was just playing.

Mostly.

"We had fun," I said, getting closer to him, but staying far enough that it wasn't overtly inappropriate if someone rounded the corner and saw us. "Didn't we?"

Reluctantly, he nodded. "Yes, we did."

"Okay. So *now* I set you free, to use everything I taught you on some pretty young thing, who you're gonna give a pretty ring, and some pretty babies."

He gave a slight shake of his head. "You already know how I feel about that."

"And *you* already know how I feel about this."

We'd had this discussion, when I first offered my name for the position. Nate and his sister Cole shared the *Director of Player Success* position in the Kings' front office. Since Cole was engaged to one of the players – Jordan "The Flash" Johnson, superstar wide receiver – on the offensive side, she worked with the defense, leaving the offense to Nate.

Which was where *our* conflict came in.

I didn't think, for even a moment, that Nate would try to use our relationship to influence the way I coached, or treated the players. What I did worry about was the *appearance* of impropriety. I had to consider the impact on the team, on the players, on my reputation if I *ever* wanted to get hired anywhere else, or survive past my first season with the Kings.

Imagine being a woman, getting your dream job in the NFL, only for it all be messed up because you were sleeping with the team owner's much-younger-than-you son. It was a PR nightmare just waiting to happen, and I could already see the headline.

"Connecticut's Cougar Coach caught cuddling CEO's child!"

I'd *never* live it down.

"We're going to have a *great* season," I told him, patting his hand – a completely underwhelming gesture, but the best I could do considering our current surroundings.

"Indeed." He gave me a little nod, then turned away to continue towards his destination. "Congratulations again."

There was an unexpected twinge in my chest as I watched him walk away, missing some of his usual swagger. I knew his feelings for me had developed beyond our little affair, into what had to be a minor crush. Nate was only thirty years old, while my last birthday had put me at forty-three.

He *had* to know there was no future between us… *right*?

Instead of prolonging the conversation with a reply, I turned the opposite way, to leave. My day wasn't done yet – groceries, getting Madison's uniforms from the dry cleaner. I was still a mother, still had a household to run, despite my renewed status as *"Coach Brooks"*. Even at college level, coaching had been a strenuous job – mentally, emotionally, and physically, so I could imagine how my workload was about to increase, dealing with a professional team.

Finding balance had been hard enough already. But when it came to fulfilling dreams, sacrifices were part of the game. Everything got pared down, and simplified, so football was what you lived and breathed. Anything else was a distraction, and you had to make hard decisions, deciding what was and wasn't important enough to give your attention.

You had to choose.

Necessary distractions – family, health – I would just have to work around. Unnecessary? Those had to go, because I wasn't letting anything keep me from not only doing good at this job, but dominating.

Too bad those *unnecessary distractions* included Nate.

Two.

2014

"You are wearing the hell out of that dress."

I glanced to my left, following the sound of the male voice that had interrupted my conversation with Zora. An immediate grin came to my lips at the sight of what may as well have been a babyface – a very handsome one, but still young.

A face I recognized.

"Nathan Richardson. Finally got the balls to approach me in person, huh?"

He smirked, taking my words as an invitation to move closer, close enough to feel his body heat in the crowded room. "Finally got the *opportunity*. Been had the balls."

"Is that right?"

"Absolutely."

As a server went past with a tray of champagne, he flagged her down, grabbing two glasses. One for me, and one for Zora, before he grabbed a third for himself, giving me a chance to really take him in. Tall and deep brown, wide shoulders, strong features. I met Zora's eyes, long enough for her to shoot me a sly look before she walked off, finding *someone* else to occupy her time while she left me alone with this… *kid.*

"Are you even old enough to drink that?" I asked, watching as he took a sip from his glass.

That boyish grin spread over his face again. "Yes *ma'am*," he teased. "Twenty-six years old… a grown ass man."

"Oh that's adorable that you think so," I told him, taking my own sip. "Twenty-six is far from *grown*."

"Grown enough to make you soak your panties… *if* you're wearing any."

He spoke those words right into my ear, and damn if I didn't feel it right between my legs. His little fine ass was trouble.

"Last week, you posted a picture of me on social media," I started, meeting his eyes. "You said you used to have posters of me up on your wall as a teenager… right?"

He ran his tongue over his lips. "Right."

"What did you used to do in your room at night with the door locked… lotion by the bed…"

He leaned in a little more. "*Used* to do? You must not have seen the pictures from your Sports Illustrated spread yet?"

I laughed, backing away from him to put some distance between us. "I've seen them. I look *good,* huh?"

"You are *bad as hell*," he insisted, getting close again. "I thought I made my admiration perfectly clear."

"Admiration, or obsession?"

"Does it matter?"

I nodded. "Absolutely. What would it look like for me to have an infatuated, horny teenager sniffing around, hoping for a whiff of my pussy?"

"I told you already Ms. Brooks… I'm far from a teenager."

"So you say."

"So you can see for yourself." A tingle of pleasure raced up my spine as he touched me, slipping a hotel keycard into my hand. "What happens in Vegas… right?"

He walked away after that, leaving me standing there with the wet panties he'd threatened. He hadn't even been gone long enough for me to process it when Zora came back, grinning.

"That is *quite* the young tender Ms. Brooks," she gushed. "What was that about?"

I flashed the keycard at her, knowing she'd recognize the logo since this little shindig was at her family's hotel. "Something that is *not* about to happen."

"And why the hell not?" she asked. "You are fine, flexible, and freshly divorced. What exactly is the problem?"

"He's a *baby*," I insisted, rolling my eyes. "What can he do for me?"

She sucked her teeth. "He can keep up. And keep *it* up." she stopped talking, and I followed her gaze to where Nate was now standing with his father – who was standing with Zora's father, and a few other men. "That is no *baby*. That is a… blank slate. Prime for learning."

"Mmmhmm. So why haven't you thrown anything in Trei Norwood's direction?"

"Because that's different. He's practically family."

"Uh huh. Excuses."

"Whatever bitch. We're not talking about me right now – we're talking about *you*."

"And *I* am not screwing a man who used to jack off to my pictures – as a *teenager*!" I hissed, making her laugh.

"Would it be better if he'd been a grown man? Because… you *do* know there was a lotion shortage all around the world the day those Sports Illustrated pictures dropped, right?"

Shaking my head, I drained the rest of my champagne. I *had* looked amazing in those pictures.

"Anyway," she continued, "You act as if he's still a teenager now. He's pushing thirty."

"And *I* am knocking right at *forty's* door," I countered. "Again – what can he do for me?"

Zora dropped her empty champagne glass on a server's tray as they passed, then faced me again, putting her hands on my shoulders. "He can fuck you like he's been dreaming about it all his life. He can *worship* you, like a goddess. He can make you forget Garrett's trifling ass… even if it's just for a night. All you have to do is swipe that card."

I looked away from Zora because I felt eyes on me – Nathan's.

He winked at me, then turned to walk away, disappearing into the crowd.

Presumably, up to his room, where the unknown awaited.

All I had to do was swipe the card.

2018

"Okay I must have the wrong office – can you point me to the one you use for your actual *job?* Thanks."

I grinned as my sister – my *twin* – Nicole didn't even bother looking up from what she was doing to flip me off. Taking a seat in front of her desk, I watched as she referred to some list she had, comparing it against what appeared to be a page full of numbered circles, with lines extending from each one.

"Shouldn't your fancy wedding planner be handling that?" I asked, and finally she looked up, brushing sleek, shoulder-length strands from her face.

"What do you want, Nate? I'm busy."

I frowned. "Damn, I can't just be checking in on my sister, seeing how she's adjusting to our promotion?"

In previous years, our title had been *Assistant* Director of Player Success, and there had been four of us with that title, managing the team. Now, Cole and I shared the new position of simply *Director of Player Success*, splitting the team in two – offense and defense. The other two people had gone to different positions on the team.

"Well, considering that it's offseason, and my guys know I'll string them up by the balls if they fuck up on a day off, I am doing peachy. Don't have much to do."

"So you plan your wedding at your desk?"

"Yes. We are just two months away right now, with plenty to do. So this is what I'm working on. Problem?"

"No."

"Good. Do you think Emma is old enough to be a flower girl, without eating the petals?" she asked, referring to our baby sister.

I twisted my lips, thinking. "Eh… not sure. Maybe have somebody walk with her, to guide her? She just turned two, so I imagine those flowers are going to look pretty appetizing to her."

"True. But it'll probably make for great pictures. Maybe Mel can do it, and that will give her something better to do than just sitting there. You know? Like an actual place in the wedding."

Instead of responding, I chuckled.

"What?" she asked, looking up from her seating chart again. "Why is that funny?"

"Because two years ago you barely wanted to be in the same room with Mel, now you're making sure she has a place in your wedding."

Cole shrugged. "That's true. I guess I realized it was time to grow up… at least for some of us," she added, giving me a pointed look that made me frown.

"Whoa, hold on – are you suggesting that I haven't grown up?"

"Of *course* not, brother," she said, with a syrupy sweet smile that suggested it was *exactly* what she was saying. "You're just… not that serious. Which is fine, as long as you aren't hurting anybody, I just… I don't know. I never thought I'd beat you to the altar."

"Because I beat you at everything else. I was trying to give you a win, and look at you holding it against me!"

She rolled her eyes. "Whatever Nate."

"Don't whatever me, it's not too late for me to pull off a little quarterback sneak, pop up with a wife on you. Put you *back* in second place – your rightful spot."

"The day *you* "pop up with a wife" is the day I eat this desk," she laughed. "Are you even dating anybody? Like *seriously?*"

Immediately, my mind went to Sloane – and how she'd resent the implication that what we were doing extended beyond the bedroom.

"Nah," I shook my head. "Not seriously."

"So what are you waiting on?" she asked. "It's not like either of us are getting younger."

"We're just thirty, Cole. You say that like death is knocking on our door."

She scoffed. "Death may not be around the corner, but my biological clock is starting to sound more like a time bomb. I want a few years with my *husband* before the babies start coming. Look at Dad and Mel – married *ten* years before they decided to have children, and they were so in tune with each other that they didn't miss a single beat."

"So that's what you think is going to happen with you and Jordan?"

"I don't have *time* for that to happen with me and Jordan. I don't have ten years to wait – I can give it two. Three, max."

I nodded. "So around the time Jordan will probably be ready to leave the league."

"Yeah. So he doesn't have to miss anything."

I propped my elbows on my knees, leaving one hand up as a resting place for my chin. "Man… you've thought this all the way through, haven't you?"

"As much as I can. Haven't you?"

That question made me sit back, raking my fingers through the springy hair at my chin.

Nah.

I *hadn't* thought about it.

At least, not in any significant way. Whenever I brought up marriage and babies, it had always been in a joking manner – never something I could foresee for myself. I was happy for my friends and family of course, when it happened to them… I just never saw it for *me*.

"Are you just going to spend your life as a player?" Cole teased, finally closing the folder she'd labeled "*seating*" in her neat handwriting. "Is there really just no woman that can lock you down?"

None that wants to be locked down.

"How did we get on *me*?" I asked, trying to deflect the conversation. "You're getting married in two months, what else do you have left to do?"

"You know *damn* well you're not interested in anything related to this wedding."

"I'm interested in how fine your bridesmaids are, and if they need help getting dressed that morning."

Cole laughed. "They're all either married, lesbian, or off limits to *you*."

"Off limits to *me*, specifically? Damn, what did *I* do?"

"Ronnie Newell, in high school, is *who* you did, Nate, remember that?"

I shrugged, drawing a blank. "You'll have to refresh my memory."

"Gladly. She was my best friend, and you stole her from her boyfriend, then dumped her two days later. She blamed me, told the whole school, so I lost the election for class president."

For a few seconds, I frowned, then sat up straight when the details clicked for me. "*Ohhh*, damn. I did do that, huh?"

"Yeah," she nodded. "You did. And now, you keep your dick to yourself and out of my friends. No exceptions."

"I'm a changed man."

Cole snorted. "We already followed *this* line of conversation, didn't we?"

"And I see we're back, yet you still haven't given me a real reason that you think I'm… immature."

"I never said you were immature, and I don't think that about you. I *do* think you're an asshole, but that's a different conversation. Regarding the matter at hand though… no, I *don't* think you're a changed man. You come here and do your job very well – that's never been an issue for you. But how do you spend your time outside of that?"

I shrugged. "I'm… sleeping. Or with my boys or my family. Occasionally, female company."

"Occasionally?" Cole challenged, eyebrow raised.

"Yes, *occasionally*."

"Then I stand corrected. You *are* a changed man, because you were definitely a hoe before."

I opened my hands. "See? Respect my progress."

Cole laughed. "Sure, Nate. But that one thing isn't enough to change the perception, and as you know…"

"Perception may as well be reality."

"Right. If you're happy with life as is, I'm happy for you, but whether or not it's fair, when the world sees a thirty-year-old man with no serious partner and no kids, they think *perpetual bachelor.* They think you need to grow up."

"Which is bullshit."

She smirked. "Try being a thirty-year-old single *woman* with no kids. At least people just think you need to grow up. For us? There *must* be something wrong. And God forbid you own a cat or two. You may as well sign your *spinster* papers according to these folks."

"Don't be dramatic."

"I will stab you with this pen, don't say that shit to me," Cole warned, knowing I'd only used that word to get under her skin. "It's not dramatic, it's the truth. And you know it."

I sighed. "Yeah, I do. But you're engaged – going to be married soon. You don't have those problems."

"No, I don't. *My* predicament is these damn blogs and their *Bump Watch 2018,* because they swear I must be pregnant already. As if that's the only reason Jordan would want to propose to me."

"Well…" I grinned. "This *is* quite the quickie wedding. Engaged in February, wedding date in June? Don't most people take a year to plan?"

"I'm not most people. And I want to have everything wrapped up before training camp. You sure you can handle the team by yourself for those two weeks?"

I scoffed. "Between our assistants and me, it'll be covered. I can't *wait* to show our father that your job is disposable."

"Don't play with me," she warned, holding up the pen she'd threatened me with earlier. "But thank you for covering for me. And if there's an emergency, you -"

"There won't be," I insisted. "It's handled. You can focus on your wedding, and your honeymoon."

A grin spread across her face. "Thank you, Nate. Your help means a lot to me."

"No point in being twins if I can't bail you out when necessary, right?"

I left Cole in her office with her wedding plans, intending to head to my own. The draft was approaching, fast, and I still had to finish up the generic parts of my welcome package for whoever we got on offense – something Cole must have already done, if she was working on other things. I already had a list of the rookies that the team was considering, but we wouldn't know for sure until after the draft. Then, I could go back through and personalize.

I was almost there when my father's assistant came rushing up the hall, flagging me down.

"Mr. Richardson wants to see you," she reported, so I bypassed my own office to follow her to my father's much larger one.

"Ah," he said, looking up from his desk. "I see she caught you before you left."

I glanced back as she stepped out, closing the door behind her. "I wasn't leaving yet. Had some business to take care of first."

"I'll keep this brief then – Sloane Brooks."

Immediately, my shirt felt buttoned way too tight around my neck. "Coach Brooks, yes. What about her?"

"What do you think? Good hire?"

I raised an eyebrow, surprised that he was seeking my opinion on it, especially *after* she'd already signed the paperwork securing the job.

"Are you asking me as your son, or as your staff?"

"Both," he answered, gesturing for me to take a seat.

I did, then nodded. "Yes, I think so. She had an excellent coaching record at the college level, and she was good at the game herself. She's played the position, so she knows the ins and outs. She deserves a chance to prove herself as much as anyone else."

"And you think your players are ready for this? A female coach… who looks like *her*?"

I chuckled. "Well… honestly, that part might be a little tricky, especially with the younger guys. But she managed at BSU."

"Indeed."

I leaned forward. "What makes you ask me this *now*?"

"Are you or are you not *Director of Player Success*?" he asked, eyebrows lifted. "It occurred to me that since you're the liaison, it would be wise to have you prep these guys – our wide receivers. It's never been an issue before because we've never had a female coach before."

"These guys aren't stupid," I assured him. "And from what I've seen on the field, Sloane is no shrinking violet. There may be a bit of an adjustment, but I think she'll be fine."

Eli nodded. "Good. As you already know… the Kings are in a transitional period. We've been lucky the last two years, even *making* it to the Super Bowl… I'm not expecting lightning to strike a third time. As such… this is the year we evolve, take risks, change the game. You've seen the players we're looking at for the draft – it's a volatile bunch, with a lot of potential."

"Yes, I noticed that."

"And so will the press. They're going to be all over us, especially with the addition of Ms. Brooks. She's not the first female coach in the league, but she's the first *Black* woman. Which means we're traversing uncharted waters. We *cannot* afford a scandal here. Make it clear to your guys, before we hit that field for training camp in July – if it comes to a choice between them and Brooks… we will *still* be the first in the league with a Black female coach, and *they*… will be on the bench. If not looking for a new team."

"Understood."

"Good. Emmanuelle has a new tooth," he said, sitting back as he shifted from business to family. "Bit the hell out of me last night."

I laughed. "That's what she's supposed to do with them, right? You know Cole is worried she's going to eat the flower petals instead of throwing them at the wedding, right?"

"That's a valid concern," he agreed, chuckling. "Either that or refuse to let them go. But we'll get it worked out."

"No doubt."

Not knowing if Cole had mentioned it to anyone but me yet, I decided not to bring up her idea of Mel walking with little Emma. Knowing Cole, all the details of the wedding were probably fluid, and liable to change any day.

"You have anyone in mind to help you catch up to your sister?" he asked, drawing my attention. "We have the wedding now, and then soon after, you know there will be babies."

I shook my head. "I thought having your own would get you off our backs about it, old man."

He laughed. "I'm not on your back, I'm asking a question. A simple one at that – yes or no."

"No," I answered, immediately and honestly. "I'm content to let Cole have this one."

"That's… unsurprising. You never have enjoyed being anchored to anything except this job – reminds me a lot of myself when I was your age."

"You were already a widower with twins when you were my age."

He shrugged. "Fine – give or take a few years. The point is that, it wasn't until I met your mother that I had any interest in being settled. It takes the right one."

"Well… I'll let you know when I find her, how about that?" I asked, standing from my seat in front of his desk. "But until then… I'm good. Why does nobody seem to believe that?"

"Ah. So your sister has been in your ear too, with her soon-to-be-wed wisdom."

"*If* you want to call it that. I need to put these packets together for my incoming rookies – was there anything else?"

My father shook his head. "No, son. That's all."

I got my ass out of there as quickly as I could without *looking* like I was rushing. Between my father and my sister, I was exhausted with talk of my future.

I lived a *great* life, and saw no pressing reasons to change that.

In my office, I got to work finishing up my packets – a task that took less than an hour. As requested, I made sure to make a note about Coach Brooks, giving her bio and coaching record, and even linking to a video of her in action.

Videos I went back to once my work was done.

Woman or not, Sloane was a great choice, and it showed in the way her players took direction from her. They trusted her, *respected* her, and in return, she'd molded several mid-tier wide receivers into players that were dominating now in the NFL.

Jordan Johnson included.

We'd been at BSU at the same time, even though she'd long since graduated. I wasn't on the team – had never felt the urge to play, even though I loved the game. I'd gone for the business degree, with a minor in sports management. She was just as fine now as she'd been back then, on the sideline with her clipboard, hyper-focused on the game, watching for the smallest mistake on either side – looking for whatever adjustments she could make for our team, or whatever weakness she could exploit for the other.

It was sexy as hell.

I knew back then that shooting my shot was beyond pointless. I was a kid at that time, not to mention that Sloane was still married to her high school sweetheart, Garrett Brooks – a linebacker for the

Kings who would've snapped any of us in half for even looking at Sloane too hard.

When she finally dropped his ass though… I felt like it was my time.

I wasn't nervous at all – I was confident, determined. Wanting a woman and not getting her was a foreign concept to me, so when I approached her in Vegas, at an off-season party hosted by the team, it never occurred to me that she wouldn't use the key I'd given her to my room there at the hotel.

But… she didn't.

In fact, with Sloane, it was the *third* time that ended up being the charm, at a BSU alumni event. She'd made me chase her – made me work for it. And *that* little detail made having her so much sweeter.

*But you don't **really** have her, do you?*

There was the other thing I hadn't really expected – to be the one left wanting more. Sloane was… phenomenal. In conversation, in bed, on the field, wherever. She had an energy about her that made you sit up and pay attention, an energy that was… *addictive.*

And she knew it.

It was probably why she kept me at arm's length, constantly making sure I understood that sex was all we would ever have. I told myself that was fine, because I had zero intention of anything beyond that either.

That was a lie though.

It hadn't been at first, but it became that eventually, as fulfilling a childhood crush morphed into feeling like I never had enough of her. I wanted what she wasn't willing to give, and with a woman like Sloane… there was no budging.

I was a boy toy, to her.

Which should've been enough to make me focus my energy elsewhere, on the women – closer to my age – who were vying for my attention. But it wasn't the same, somehow. They never had the same confidence, the same potency, the same … *anything*.

They weren't the woman I wanted.

But the woman I wanted… didn't want me.

Three.

May 2018

It couldn't have been more perfect.

Beautiful weather, a football in my hands, freshly manicured turf staining my fresh white sneakers green. Of course, I'd been on a practice field before – been on *this* practice field before, back when Garrett rocked the royal blue and gold for himself, and I was loyal wifey, ready to cheer him on through anything.

But this was new.

This was… *official.*

This was me, my *job*, to get things in order for these rookies.

Coach Sloane Brooks, reporting for duty.

Damn that sounds good.

Of the oversized roster we'd be starting training camp with, eight of those guys were rookies. One of them, Rutledge Amare, had a *huge* amount of potential coming out the gate – I thought he was a good choice myself, even though there were rumors of attitude.

But, that label got thrown around easily in the football community, *especially* about Black players. All you had to do was not allow yourself to be treated sub-human, and the Good Ol' Boy's club was ready to bring out the pitchforks, branding you "stubborn", or any number of other negative adjectives.

I didn't care about any of that.

I considered every single player a blank slate – I didn't give a damn about your reputation, show me who you are and what you can do *now*. I demanded two things – respect, and excellence. As long as I saw those, we'd get along *just* fine.

From my position beside Coach Underwood, I frowned as I watched Amare and another player, a defensive back named Stroy, run a play. They'd already done it twice, and it was clear from where I stood – a latecomer, who was supposed to be moving into her tiny office, but couldn't keep herself off the field – what the problem was.

Amare – our newest wide receiver - wasn't putting enough power into it.

"Again!" Coach Underwood shouted, nodding to acknowledge my presence from there. I watched, internally cringing as again, Amare phoned it in, not moving fast enough to avoid Stroy – a mistake that in a game, could result in a costly interception.

"You're not exploding off the line!" I called out, tucking the ball in my hands against my hip as I moved up a little.

Amare turned, eyeing me with something that was way too close to a sneer for me to let it ride.

I pushed my oversized sunglasses – *not* the Gucci ones – up onto my head, giving him back the same glare he was giving me. "Is there a problem?"

His eyes narrowed as he gave me another once-over after he'd glanced back, noticing the stares and snickers of the other men on the field.

I knew *right* then, there was, indeed, a problem.

He grinned at me – way too slick – and said, "Yeah. My dick feeling kinda dry. I 'on see nobody else out here who could help. Unless you ready to drop down on ya knees to handle that, you can get the fuck off the field and let me do what I'm getting paid to do."

Oh.

Ohhhhh.

That's what we're doing today, huh?

I returned his grin with one of my own amid the reactions from the others on the field – Coach Underwood included. But I'd already made myself crystal clear to my peers – barring someone getting physical with me, I *never* wanted them to intervene between me and a player.

I was glad to see that request was being respected – Underwood shifted to cross his arms, obviously pissed, but saying nothing as I stepped forward, closer to Amare.

"Considering that sucker ass contract you signed, I *doubt* your dick is much for me to work with, rookie. Besides… your young, dumb ass probably *just* learned how to hold it to even pee." I stepped even closer as his jaw tightened, but his glare didn't waiver. "Instead of talking about the needs of your undersized dick, how about you master this play, and while you're at it – learn my name."

He scoffed. "Ya' name?"

"Yeah. And especially my damn title."

"Which is?"

"*Coach*. Sloane Brooks. As in, Coach Brooks." I smirked as his head immediately swiveled to look past me, to Coach Underwood, for confirmation. I couldn't see the exchange, but could imagine Underwood nodding, prompting Amare's rolled eyes as he brought his gaze back to me. "Mmmhmmm," I purred. "Now… You ready to get this knowledge, or would you rather start with the twenty laps your misogyny just earned you?"

He didn't say anything at first, just stared me down and I stared right back at his ass. It wasn't even that I needed him to back down – I needed him to cut the silly shit and *get to work*.

There was an *Amare* on every incoming squad I coached, without fail – at least this one was a little older than the hormonal college kids I'd gotten accustomed to at BSU. Somehow, it didn't change much though – even once I'd gotten my peers used to what to expect from me, there was always some little sexist bastard who thought *they'd* be the one to put me in my proper place – the kitchen or the bedroom.

It never took very long for them to understand that I was *exactly* where I was supposed to be.

After a tense moment, he took a step back, yielding the floor – the field – to me, so I could do my job.

I nodded.

"You need to *explode*," I explained, as if our previous exchange had never happened, and no beats had been skipped. He was practicing a *Quick Out* – which was a risky play that could have a big pay off if executed well. If executed badly… well… he'd already seen the results of that. "Make the DB think you're running a Go Route. What you're doing instead is picking up gradual speed at the line."

"Yeah, easy for a fanatic to say, but players need to practice to get it," he said – making excuses, as far as I was concerned. "That's what we're doing here. Practicing."

"Some need practice, and some just have it." I looked around, craning my neck to support my *next* point. "And where the hell do you see a fanatic out here?"

"Oh, my bad," he said, in a dry tone. "Let me keep it politically correct – someone who's "passionate" about the game."

I chuckled, then backed away from him, tossing the ball in my hands to one of the coaching assistants. "I'll do you one better."

I ignored his offensive demeanor as I got in position at the line, exchanging a look with Coach Underwood to make it clear what I expected to happen. He gave me a nod, and I turned, ready. As soon as the whistle blew, I did what I *expected* my wide receiver to do.

I exploded off the goddamn line.

Easily, I outmaneuvered Stroy, partially because I was moving fast enough to blow past him, dodging his attempt to bump me before I broke right, catching the pass from the QB stand-in we were using for this mini-camp.

Somehow, I staved off the urge to run in for a touchdown.

Jogging back to where Amare stood, I started speaking before I even made it all the way there. "If you don't explode off the line and you're slow, the DB is going to move slow too. That gives him time to think about your play. And if he's fast…faster than you…" I shrugged, letting him fill in the rest as he stared at me like one of us was crazy.

It damn sure wasn't me.

"You gonna try it again, or start your laps?" I asked, completely unfazed by his stare-down.

I found the restraint in me, somewhere, to not laugh as he spit at the grass… and then jogged off to start his laps.

I wasn't naïve enough to think things would be peachy between us going forward, and honestly… I didn't care.

Respect.

Excellence.

That was all I wanted from Amare and my other wide receivers. I didn't care if he hated my guts. I didn't care if he used anonymous social media to troll me on the internet. I didn't care if he plastered my swimsuit pictures up and down the locker room.

I'd endured worse, from players with less at stake than *these* men, who had to fall in line or risk getting cut during training camp, and losing their million-dollar deals.

They couldn't surprise me, and they couldn't scare me.

I was *that bitch* everywhere else – the field would not be an exception.

Underwood shook his head at me as I approached him, barely hiding a smirk.

"Did you really have to do him like that?" he asked under his breath, as the others moved on to running a different play.

I shrugged. "He was practically begging to be an example, so I made him one. Now that that's over with, we can play some football."

He tugged down the brim of his *Kings* hat, still trying not to laugh. "You go too hard on a young man like that, you'll lose him. Never get his head back."

"Then he can stay lost – somewhere other than this team."

"Damn, Brooks. You're cold-blooded when it comes to this stuff huh?"

"You already knew that," I grinned, patting his arm. "And by the time this camp is over… my rookie will too."

"And *then*, do you know that little asshole had the nerve to call me a *fanatic*?" I took a sip of my wine, then held up a finger. "No wait – he corrected himself. *Someone who's passionate about the game.* Like, get the fuck outta here," I fussed, giving the retelling of my first day with the Kings way more energy than it deserved.

From the grill, Garrett laughed, tipping back his beer to drain the last few swallows with one hand, and flipping the steaks with the other. "You want me to go up and there and talk to 'em for you?"

I gave him the *ugliest* side-eye I could dredge up, which spurred raucous laughter from my guests – Miles and Joan. Miles was a former *King*, like Garrett, and the two had left the field behind the same year to start their sports management firm. He and Joan had gotten married two months after Garrett and I had, and were still happily wed.

I considered it pure luck that I'd been able to quite easily make *good* friends with my husband's bestie's wife. The fact that we'd *remained* friends after the divorce?

A blessing.

"Garrett is out here trying to get his wig split I see," Miles laughed, wrapping his arm around Joan from his reclined position on the outdoor chaise. She didn't say anything, just took a pointed sip from her glass as she met my gaze, because she *already* knew.

I didn't need Garrett doing a *damn* thing for me.

"He's working hard at it, huh?" I teased. "He's already on his second strike for today."

"Wait a minute, what was strike one?!"

My face wrinkled. "Negro, you showed up at my door unannounced, *with* guests, talking about you were cooking a celebration dinner for me. *That* is strike one."

"It wasn't unannounced, it was… a surprise."

"Same difference."

He sucked his teeth. "So you're telling me you *don't* want this premium tomahawk from your favorite little bougie grocery store?"

I sat up a little straighter. "You ordered those steaks from *Eat Clean?*"

"*And* the vegetable skewers, and the wine."

*This **is** a good bottle of wine…*

"I *guess* I'll accept it as a surprise. But it's still a strike."

"You're so damn *mean*," he accused, as I pulled myself up to peek at the grill.

"Yeah. That tends to happen when a woman has to divorce you for being a raging whore."

"*Damn*," Miles chuckled. "Raging?"

"I said what I said," I answered, and before Miles could offer a rebuttal, Joan spoke up.

"Uh-uh," she told him, with a disapproving glare. "You were covering for his hoeing, you don't get to ask questions."

"He never covered for me!"

"I never covered for him!"

Miles and Garrett declared at the same time, both giving off the impression that their denials mattered.

They didn't.

"You didn't tell him to stop though, so…" Joan said, playfully pushing her husband in the chest.

"Will you tell these women how I tried to minister to you?" Miles turned to Garrett, seeking help.

"Yeah, he definitely warned me you were gonna leave," Garrett agreed.

Miles gave a triumphant nod. "*And*?"

Garrett's little grin dropped. "*And* you warned me she was going to kick my ass."

"Not just *your* ass, but…"

"Really nigga?" he asked, looking stressed.

"*Your* ass *and*," Miles just repeated, insistent on getting an answer.

Garrett blew out a sigh. "*My* ass *and* the groupies I "rode in on"." He raised his spatula, waving it in our direction. "But I want it to be on the record that *I* did not get my ass *kicked*. Maybe a light tapping."

I snorted.

The *groupies* in question hadn't been so lucky.

Garrett had been smart enough to lock himself in the bathroom after the first few licks, preventing me from properly going upside his head when I called myself "surprising" *him*, only to find him having quite the good time out of town with not one, not two, but *three* women, none of whom were… *me*. Those broads called themselves jumping on me – a really, bad idea, considering that I was still playing in a community football league at the time.

The whole thing ended with me in handcuffs, mostly unscathed, and *them* – Garrett included – nursing two concussions, a broken nose, a broken wrist, and myriad bruises between them. No charges ended up being pressed, but their monetary settlements got rolled into my divorce judgment, so basically Garrett paid for it.

Not my proudest mome—wait, no, that's a lie.

I wasn't ashamed, at all.

Everybody in that hotel room knew who Garrett Brooks was married to, so as far as I was concerned, they'd earned that ass whooping.

My only regret was having to explain daddy's black eye to Madison, when we sat down to tell her that we were breaking up… even though she told me later that she would've punched him too, even though we'd given her the vaguest possible details.

She *adored* Garrett though, so… it worked out.

As if I'd thought her up, Madison came breezing through the patio doors, fresh from a date with her little boyfriend.

Boy. Friend.

Not *boyfriend*, since her father wasn't into the idea, but somehow didn't understand that calling it one thing didn't mean it wasn't another.

Neither of us cared to argue with him.

"Look at *you*," Joan gushed. "You look so cute and summery. Did you have a good time with the *senior*?" she teased, making Madison grin.

Baby girl had been over the moon with excitement when she came to me, asking if *Langston* could take her to the movies. After the usual research into Langston and his people, her father and I had agreed, and they'd been *friends* for almost five months now, which was a long time for high school. Mads had been a little down because he was getting ready to graduate, but today she was all smiles.

"What's going on?" I prodded. "Something happen?"

"He picked a school," she told us, practically bouncing on her heels. "He's going to stay local for two years, and then go to BSU. He's only staying because his Dad is sick, and he doesn't want to leave his mom alone, but... still!"

I returned her smile, knowing that the chances of their little puppy love lasting were drastically improved by him going to school here in Connecticut. Of course I hadn't shared any of my pessimism with her – she'd experience her first heartbreak whenever it happened, I had no desire to rush it along.

"Well, I'm happy you'll have more than just the summer with him sweetheart, but I hope his dad starts feeling better sooner than later. Is he having a hard time with the chemo?"

Madison nodded, her expression growing strained. "That's why we cut tonight short, so he can sit with him while his mom gets some sleep."

"Early?" Garrett bellowed, stopping the work of taking the steaks off the grill. "It's after nine o'clock!"

Immediately, Madison's eyes shifted to me, like *I* had anything to do with her crazy ass daddy's idea of an appropriate curfew.

"I… my curfew is eleven on weekends…" she stammered, confused. "Right?"

"You're sixteen – ain't nothing but trouble out there after eight o'clock at night!"

I frowned. "That's about what time you rang my doorbell, fool," I admonished, then tipped my head to the side. "So… hmm… I guess you have a good point."

Joan gasped. "Are you calling me *trouble*, Sloane?!"

"Hell yes," I agreed, laughing. "Baby go on upstairs and call your little friends and tell them your good news before you spend all night texting Lang," I told Madison, dismissing her before her father could confuse her any further.

"I wasn't finished talking to her," he scolded me as he turned off the grill and we headed inside, to the dining room.

"You absolutely *were*," I countered. "Why are you giving her a hard time, she's a good kid."

"*She* is, but I don't know that lil' nigga, and I don't know what he has her out in the streets doing."

"What did *you* have girls doing when you were his age?" Joan asked, and the look on his face – and Miles too – said it *all*.

Garrett shook his head. "She can't see that boy again. Absolutely *nawl*."

"Madison is a smart, responsible girl. She's not going to let that boy get her in any trouble, not with rugby, and a driver's license, and my Gucci glasses all on the line."

"Keep that energy when she comes through here with a baby on her hip," Garrett quipped as we grabbed dishes to take to the dining room.

"Wait," Miles chuckled. "How are you leaping from a nine o'clock curfew to a baby, man? Just skip the whole pregnancy, huh?"

"Whose side are you on?"

"*Common sense*," Miles answered, making us all laugh.

It went on like that, shifting away from Madison's little teenage love affair to whatever random topic came up, until hours had passed, and Joan and Miles excused themselves to head home. I joined Garrett in the kitchen afterward, intending to help him clean up – *his* task, even though this was *my* house, since this impromptu dinner party was his idea.

With us working together it didn't take long, but it was still nearly midnight when we finished. And, in a move that surprised no one, once everything was clean, and everyone else was gone, and Madison had fallen asleep on the phone with Langston… Garrett called himself making a move.

"Come here," he told me, pulling me back out onto the patio after I'd poured myself one last glass of wine for the night.

I shook my head, but gave in to his nudging, meeting his gaze as soon as we were outside. "What do you want? It's late, and I have a second day of rookie camp tomorrow."

"I know," he said, wrapping his arms around my waist, and resting his hands way too low on my back. "Earlier, when you were telling us about your day, you seemed like you could use a little relaxation." His fingers pressed in, digging into my flesh in a way that – no lie – felt good. "Why don't you let me give you a little massage?"

My eyebrow went up. "A *little* massage? How does that work, G? Your fingers, my pussy?"

"I could go with that. I like your suggestion, let's do it."

"It was *not* a suggestion, damn fool," I laughed, then bit my lip. I raised my hand, up to his collar, tugging it aside a little. "Maybe whoever gave you this hickey would be down for it though?"

He groaned. "Here you go again."

"Uh, yeah," I agreed, easing out of his hold. "Garrett…" I sighed. "When are you going to let this go? We're great as friends… great as co-parents… we get along. There's minimal fuss around here. Why would I agree to something as foolish as getting involved with you again?"

"What makes it foolish?" he asked, sincerely, and my eyes went wide.

"The *obvious* territory marking on your neck!"

He shook his head. "That's… *nothing.*"

"It's *enough*," I shot back. "It's a reminder of all the little signs that I ignored, and lied to myself about."

Garrett propped his hands on his head. "I'm… a single man, Sloane. Am I not allowed to enjoy myself?"

"You absolutely *are* supposed to enjoy yourself – I sure as hell am."

He frowned. "And what does that mean?"

"It means whatever it meant when it came out of *your* mouth! Or what… you can't handle knowing that someone else is getting what *used* to be yours? *Exclusively*. Not that it mattered to you."

"Don't do that…"

"What, tell the truth?"

"Making it seem like I didn't give a damn about you is *not* the truth."

I let out a huff, then drained the glass of wine I was still holding in one gulp. "You sure had a funny way of showing it."

"And that's my mistake. *That* I will own up to. I fucked up, full stop. But I *loved* the hell out of you, Sloane. Honestly… st—"

"No!" I held up a hand, cutting him off. "No, you will *not* do this. Not tonight, not with that mark on your neck, not… at all. We had a good time tonight with our friends, and you signed a new client, and I started my new job, and Madison is safe and sound and happy. Go home."

"*This* is my—"

"*Go home.*"

He stared at me for a moment, defeated, and then nodded. Before I could react, he'd stepped in, kissing my forehead and then the corner of my mouth, and then… he was gone.

At least that's what I assumed, because I was still frozen to the spot, not entirely sure of what had just happened, or what I should do.

Well… I did know one thing.

One more glass of wine.

Four

"This shit ain't working."

My assistant, Elliot, had already given me a heads up that one of the rookies – one of *my* rookies – was upset. When our inter-office IM pinged with the message, I hadn't thought much of it. The season hadn't started yet – hell, *training camp* hadn't even started yet, so there wasn't much he could be upset about.

Rutledge Amare's only real, work-related interaction with the team so far was the rookie mini-camp, and today was the last day of that. Of course I'd heard about his interaction with Coach Brooks on the first day, but things had been quiet since then, so I assumed they'd worked it out.

Apparently, I was wrong.

Rut sat across from me now, obviously frustrated by whatever had transpired today, declaring his refusal to work with Sloane. Only… this wasn't about to go like he expected it to.

"What happened?" I asked, genuinely interested in figuring out how to get forward momentum here. Ensuring his success was my job, but my reach only went so far.

"Man, that bit—*broad* is always on my ass about little shit that don't matter. *You're putting your arms out too early. Why you jumping for the ball? Quit the false steps. Don't catch the ball against your chest*," he complained, mocking her feminine tone. "I'm here to play football, not have her micromanaging every little thing I fuckin' do."

From my seat behind my desk, I shrugged. "Those all sound like solid tips for a pro-level wide receiver. You're coming to this team out of college – there's going to be a transition."

"I ain't stupid, I understand that. What I *don't* understand is why this… *female*… who don't get me or what we're even doing out there gets to nag me about dumb shit."

I scratched at my chin, then sat forward, propping my elbows on my desk. "You didn't read the welcome packet, did you?"

He frowned. "Welcome packet? I'on even know what you talking about man."

So the answer is no then.

"Last week, when we met, I *personally* put a welcome packet into your hands – a front office roster, a coaching staff roster, among other things. *Important* things."

"Oh. Yeah. You said there wasn't anything in there I needed to sign."

"That doesn't mean you weren't supposed to read it. If you *had*, you would've known that the team had a new position coach. *Your* position, wide receiver."

He sucked his teeth. ""Man, Divine threw that 'lil' mention in there when I met up with him a few weeks ago, but shit, I ain't catch it until she jumped in my face out there. I ain't wanna believe the *Kings* were on that feminist bullshit too."

"She wasn't hired because of an agenda, she was hired because she had the qualifications."

"A fat ass and nice lips?"

My jaw tightened as I mentally checked my anger over hearing him disrespect Sloane – this conversation wasn't personal, so I couldn't let my personal feelings guide my tongue.

"A winning record at BSU, a reputation for building excellent wide receivers, and experience on the field – with *phenomenal* personal stats."

Rut scoffed. "Experience on the field? On *what* field?"

"The football field. She played semi-pro, played in college, played in high school. She's been dominating in this game since before you were born."

Leaning back, Rut groaned. "I see you're on the same exaggerated facts she's on. Before I was born? Really nigga?"

"She's forty-three years old, so yes, before you were born. And there's no need for exaggeration here – the facts are what they are. Let me give you another one – Coach Brooks is *proven*. Her place around here is secure, unlike yours."

That made him sit up, a frown on his face. "The fuck does that mean?"

"It means that your position on this team is still probationary – contract or not. When we start training camp in less than two months, there's going to be more than eighty men vying for a position on a *fifty-two* man roster. Most of our vets are already guaranteed – we have *maybe* six positions to fill, between rookies, free agents, and those who simply didn't perform up to par last season," I explained, trying to make sure the urgency was clear to him. "Coach Brooks isn't going anywhere. But if at the end of training camp she declares you unfit for this team, you will *not* be wearing a *Kings* jersey come September."

Rut's scowl deepened as he sat forward. "You can't be serious, man. I thought you were supposed to be like my advocate or something?"

"Director of Player Success," I corrected. "And that's exactly what I'm trying to ensure here, but it requires your participation. The *Kings* already have two game-winning wide receivers – Terrance Grant and Jordan Johnson. The reality is that you're disposable. It's up to you to change that perception."

"So I'm supposed to go out there and kiss her ass? Bring flowers to the fuckin' field for her?"

I shook my head. "Nobody is asking you to do that. Go out there and give Coach Brooks the *same* respect you'd give her if she was a man. Listen to her, because she knows what she's talking about. And fucking *perform*. That's it. Your shitty ideas about women and their place and whatever else? Leave that shit in your car when you come onto *Kings* property, and any time you're representing this team. You're here to play football – conduct yourself accordingly. You've been seeing the therapist. Use that as a—"

"Don't!"

He stared at me for a second, mild betrayal in his eyes – a look I'd seen countless times, usually from other players around his age, those very young twenties. In their high school and hometowns, on the block, on their college campuses, they were the *man*. They were the ones people came out to see, they were local superstars. But then, they came face to face with the transition nobody warned them about amidst all the talk about the different rules on the field.

Wherever they came from, they were the shit.

Here in the pros though, sprinkled amongst seasoned veterans with blockbuster contracts and the stats to back it up… they weren't shit.

Yet.

Plenty of guys had excitement around them in the draft, they were hot commodities, wanted by every team. But then they hit the field in the pros and all that potential… fizzled.

Potential didn't win games, or endorsements, or the chance at a better contract.

Performance did.

And as long as *I* was responsible for easing them through that transition, I wasn't going to sugarcoat the shit. You worked, or you went home – and *stayed* home – bottom line.

"Man, what-the-fuck-ever," Rut grumbled, pushing himself out of his chair. He didn't bother looking back as he shoved his way out of my office door, and I didn't bother calling after him, because I'd already said what I needed to say.

The first offseason workout was coming up soon, in a little over a week. I'd find out from his coaches then if he needed further counsel.

Which means talking to Sloane.

She'd made it clear that our relationship was as good as done, as soon as she signed her official paperwork to become part of the *Kings* organization. I understood her position, and even – grudgingly – agreed with it, especially considering whatever this tension was between her and Rutledge. Navigating that could prove difficult, with my professional role as his advocate on the team, when the two of them were bumping heads.

I couldn't imagine it wouldn't lead to *us* bumping heads.

But even imagining that scenario didn't keep me from imagining others – or rather, reliving past interactions in my head. Sloane wasn't, on *any* level, a woman who was easy to forget. If she thought my desire for her was just a switch in my head, something I could easily turn off with a simple flip… she was wrong.

"Gimme a sec. I'll be right out – LA"

I glanced at my watch, and then the time on my phone, checking to make sure I hadn't gone crazy. Landon had sent that text nearly ten minutes ago at this point, and yet he was nowhere to be found.

The sultry sound of female laughter drew my attention away from my phone, up to where Landon was exiting the elevator with not one, but *two* tens, one of whom was draped over his arm, grinning at him like he'd been the one to hang the damn moon.

So… a typical day for him.

"Ladies meet Nathan Richardson, future heir to the Connecticut Kings," he joked, making me shake my head.

"Cut the bullshit please," I countered, extending a hand for our usual greeting.

"Unlike me," he said, returning his attention to the women, who looked too much alike to not be related. Same honey-toned skin, same big brown eyes, both dressed like they were on lunch breaks as well. "Nate is embarrassed by his family name."

"I bet that's not true at all, is it?" one of the women asked, stepping forward with her hand extended, for me to shake. "I'm Leya, and this is my little sister, Tyra. Since Landon doesn't have the manners for a proper introduction."

I couldn't help the little grin that crossed my lips as I accepted her hand, taking the opportunity to give her a closer look now that she was... well, closer.

Still a ten.

Her thick natural hair was pulled into a ball at the nape of her neck, leaving her pretty face fully exposed. She wore a pencil skirt that showed off fantasy-inducing curves, paired with a sleeveless blouse that offered a full view of her toned arms. And it certainly didn't hurt that when she moved, I caught a distinct whiff of brown sugar.

You could *never* go wrong with a woman who smelled edible.

"It's a pleasure to meet you, Leya," I told her, still holding her hand.

Her plum-painted lips curved into a seductive smile. "Likewise. Maybe we can double date next time, instead of me having to play third wheel," she added, with a pointed glance at Landon and Tyra, who were almost too consumed with each other to even notice.

"Yeah, maybe so," Tyra said, half-distracted by Landon's mouth on her neck, as if they weren't standing in the very public courtyard of the office park where he worked.

Leya groaned. "Girl come on. *We* have a real job to get back to," she said, throwing an obvious jab at Landon, which he simply laughed off. There was a quick exchange of goodbyes, and then Landon moved beside me to watch them walk away, neither of us saying anything until they reached their destination, which was just the next building.

"Life is *so* good," he declared, turning to face me. "Do you *see* her, bruh?"

"Do *you* see the time? Unlike you, I need to be back at my office at some point in the afternoon."

He frowned. "That's how you treat the man who lined up fine ass, professional ass, literal sisterly *ass* for us? You're so ungrateful, wow."

"And *you* are a piece of work. Come on and let's eat – unless you already…"

"Not in the literal *or* figurative sense," he answered, moving with me as I started toward our chosen lunch spot in his building. "I ran into them when I was coming down to meet you, so I took them upstairs for a tour of my office."

"You *just* met them? Today?"

Shaking his head, Landon grinned. "Nah. I bumped into Tyra out in the courtyard one day, and we've kicked it a few times. Today was the first time I met her sister… man, I really can't decide which one is finer."

"What a terrible predicament for you," I responded, my tone dry.

"And a come up for *you*. You heard Leya – double date. She's into it. Now the question is, are *you*?"

I didn't have a reason not to be, did I?

I was a single, educated, well-employed, good-looking man – attracting women wasn't an issue for me. What *was* an issue, however, was finding one on the same page as me – not looking for marriage, or babies, or moving in together and meeting families. It wasn't even that I was anti-monogamy. *That* part was fine. I just… wanted to have my life, on my terms, and sometimes meet in the middle with a woman who had her own shit going on, and wasn't secretly hoping that we would become something else.

It was a large part of my attraction to Sloane.

She wasn't… *pressed.*

But I was.

"I'm open to seeing what might happen," I conceded, once we'd settled at our table. "But the minute she drops a hint about a house and kids…"

Landon shook his head. "See, that's why I'm out here trying to help you – you have a "settle down" look about you."

"A settle down look?"

"Yeah – always all buttoned up, got your lil dark skin and facial hair pretty boy shit going on. Women see you and think – that man is gonna give me some nice chocolate babies. Women see *me* and think… fuckboy. They already know better."

I couldn't do anything but laugh at that, because, well… it was accurate. Landon Armstrong was absolutely affected by the trappings of *his* name – or rather, his more popular extended family, the Drakes. They were mostly centered in Vegas, but their money, power, and influence stretched far and wide- something I'd seen firsthand, having grown up in a world where Malcolm Armstrong – Landon's uncle – was good friends with my father.

Landon had been overly influenced by the antics of his older cousin, Braxton, and even though he was my homeboy… I couldn't pretend that it didn't show. During the day, he was a tech genius, the behind-the-scenes brains of countless startups. After hours? He partied and ran through women at a level equal to some of the players I worked with.

He always managed to stay on top of his business though, so… I let him rock.

"So you're telling me Tyra isn't thinking up baby names right now?" I asked, thanking our server as she dropped off the water we'd requested.

Landon sucked his teeth. "*Hell* no. She might be thinking up *daddy* names though," he joked, raising his hand out to the side with an obvious expectation that I would smack it in solidarity with him, but I shook my head.

"What *happened* to you, bruh?" He sat back, looking utterly disappointed. "You used to be in the trenches with me, bagging broads left and right. That mellow pussy fucked up your world, didn't it?"

I squinted. "*Mellow?*"

"Yeah," he nodded, sitting back. "Well-developed. Aged. Like a nice ass bourbon. A *fine* ass bourbon. Fine wine. You're probably not even hitting it right, are you?"

Sloane.

"I *never* should've told you that shit."

Wearing a goofy grin, Landon raised a hand in defense. "Your secret is safe with me bruh, no worries there. I'm jealous, honestly. I'm *right here* and she chose… *you?*"

"Man shut the fuck up," I laughed, shaking my head. "Not my fault she chose the winning team."

"Yeah, the *Kings*. And I already *know* Ms. Trinidad is *not* mixing business and pleasure, so you might as well just be honest."

"Ms. Trinidad? Really?"

"Fine ass older woman, I call it like I see it – and I *see* you keep dodging the question."

I shrugged. "Not dodging – it's really not your business, but… since you hyped me up to approach her in the first place…"

"*Finally, some fucking recognition around here.*"

"Nah. Ms. Trinidad is *not* mixing business and pleasure."

Landon flinched like he'd been physically wounded by my news, prompting me to laugh again as the server dropped off our food. If nothing else, he was always a good source of comic relief, and at his best… he was a good friend – the only reason I'd confided in him about Sloane in the first place.

After lunch, I headed back to my office, hoping I wouldn't end up having to put out any fires. Luckily for me, that really was the case – after hearing the Rutledge vs Sloane situation on a *Sunday*, I needed an uneventful start to the week.

No sooner than that thought crossed my mind, I got a reminder from Elliot about an afternoon meeting that had completely slipped my mind.

A meeting with Sloane.

To *mitigate* the Rutledge vs Sloane situation.

I spent the next fifteen minutes going over it in my head, then left my own office to head to the elevator, down to the first floor where the weights rooms, cafeteria, recovery rooms, and coaching offices were.

Past the head coach, and coordinators, straight to the smallest offices – the ones reserved for the position coaches. They were just big enough to fit a desk, bookshelf, and a few chairs for players, but when I stepped up to the one that was newly labeled *Coach Brooks*, Sloane seemed extremely pleased about it, if her humming a tune was any indication.

"I see you're getting settled in," I spoke up, calling her attention to my presence as I leaned into the doorway. She looked up with a warm smile that was like a double-shot, hitting me in the chest and groin at the same time.

Before she verbally responded, she finished placing the framed certificate in her hands – one of her many awards for coaching excellence – then dusted them off to approach me.

"Yes, I am. Been too immersed in game film, and field activity with the rookies to do it before now, but I figured I should get it done before workouts started. I assume you're here to talk about Amare?" she asked, crossing her arms, leaving the obvious implication that I'd *better* be there to talk business, and nothing else, unspoken.

"Yes," I nodded. "He came to speak with me yesterday. He has… concerns."

Sloane smiled. "Of course he does. Come in, please," she offered, motioning for me to close the door behind me when I did. Instead of taking the seat behind the desk, she leaned against the front of it, putting me right at eye level with the juncture of her thighs once I'd taken *my* seat.

I forced my gaze to her face.

"Let me guess," she started. "Amare thinks I'm a raging bitch who is picking on him and making up flaws because he is a perfect wide receiver already, who couldn't possibly need my help?"

Chuckling, I nodded. "Yes, that's about the gist of it."

"*Mmm.* So. Are you here to scold me, or…?"

"Not at all," I assured her. "Rutledge has the potential to be an elite wide receiver, and I believe you have what it takes to turn him into that. Don't take your foot off his neck – the pressure is doing him a favor."

Her eyebrows lifted. "*Oh?*"

"You didn't really think I was coming down here to fuss, did you?"

"I've never coached a pro offense before," she shrugged. "All these different titles and what not… I wasn't sure what to expect. But… if you *had* come down here to hassle me, I was ready to tell you exactly what I thought of your hassling, and where exactly you could shove it."

I smirked. "I wouldn't have expected anything else. But, as I said, I'm not here to fuss – just to make sure that there's not any… additional friction."

"Meaning?"

"I've heard about what he said to your face, and I've heard what he's said behind your back. I believe I've made it clear enough to him that he needs to make a change in his behavior, but part of his success is a productive relationship between him and his coaches. I need to know if you can work with him, or if he's pushed you too far?"

Sloane wrinkled her nose, and then laughed, waving me off. "I can assure you, he'd have to do much worse than a little coarse language to *push me too far*. I'm a big girl, Nate. I can handle these guys."

Unbidden, my eyes dropped to her bare thighs – on a work-appropriate level of display in standard khaki shorts – and on the way back up… it was hard as hell not to visualize what I *knew* was underneath.

"Yes… I know."

She shifted a little, biting down on her lip as she met my gaze for a moment before she looked away. "So how have you been?" she asked, pushing off the desk to go back to unpacking the box she'd been busy with before I showed up. "I assume we can move on from the Amare topic?"

"I believe we're on the same page, so why not?" I stood too, straightening my tie. "And to answer the other question… I've been fine. You?"

Placing a trophy on the shelf, she smiled. "I've got no complaints. Life is good."

"Glad to hear it."

For several moments, neither of us said anything, but then she let out a frustrated sigh.

"Do you *have* to look at me like that?" she asked.

I raised my shoulders. "Like *what*?"

"Like you want to put your nose in my pussy."

"Sounds like wishful thinking to me," I countered, running my tongue over my lips. "But it's fairly accurate."

My words brought the lust she'd been doing a masterful job of hiding right to the forefront, and she shook her head.

"See? Now you gotta go."

Her footsteps were swift across the small office, coming back in my direction to – presumably – open the door to show me out.

I wasn't letting her off that easy though.

I stepped in front of her, blocking her path as I met her eyes again. "Is that what you want, Sloane? For me to get down on my knees in this office, pull those corny ass shorts down, and your panties, and... put my nose in it? My fingers? My tongue?"

"Nate..." she warned, not offering any indication that she wanted to get around me.

"Just answer the question," I demanded, sending a *juuust* barely visible tremble up her spine.

"Yes."

"So say the word, Coach Brooks." As I delivered that little taunt, I ran a carefully positioned finger down the front of her shorts, giving it a little pressure when I reached a very specific spot. "You never did let me congratulate you on your new position."

Her eyes fluttered closed for a second, and then she shook her head. "Get out of my office."

As soon as those words were off her lips, I took my hand off her and stepped back. She'd already told me what the deal was between us, what it was going to be, so I knew I'd just tested my luck by even trying anything with her.

I was surprised she let me take it as far as I had.

"I'll be seeing you," I told her, offering a little salute as I moved to the door.

But then, she surprised the hell out of me, with words I didn't – not even a little – expect to hear.

"Yeah. My place. Madison is with her father this week, visiting his folks, but still… park in the garage. Nine o'clock."

She wasn't asking.

She was telling.

And I damn sure didn't mind.

Five

Loneliness was such a bitch.

It was the only reason Nate was in my house right now, after my "firm" resolution that my hiring for the coaching job would be the end of our fling.

If you could call having hot sex with someone for years a "fling".

In any case, with Madison gone for the week, off to California to see her father's people, the house already felt way too lonely, like just the *idea* of being by myself had ushered in those feelings.

It wasn't even like I was a stranger to solitude.

I had my *good* friends – Joan and Zora – but with one still happily married and raising her kids in New York, and the other thousands of miles away in Vegas, it wasn't like we were in each other's faces every day. With Garrett out of the house post-divorce, and Madison usually more interested in her teenage peers, when I wasn't working, I was alone, *often*.

But truthfully… it was time for myself that I appreciated.

So what the fuck was the problem today?

Maybe… this whole "loneliness" angle was an excuse I was forcing to happen.

So I wouldn't have to admit the truth – that I'd missed his young ass… beyond sex. And that was so, *so* problematic.

I leaned in the doorway of my bedroom, watching him try his best not to fall asleep. It was late – later than he should be here at all, but with the workout we'd had… I figured I could at least let the man get some sleep.

The glare from the TV cast a bluish glow across his dark copper skin, and reflected in his barely-open eyes. I tightened my silk robe around myself a little more as he took longer and longer to open his eyes again between "blinks". But then, something must have alerted him to my presence because he looked up, suddenly wide awake.

"I was starting to wonder what was taking you so long," he said, like he hadn't been on the verge of passing out thirty seconds ago.

I held up the bowl of fruit I'd gone down to the kitchen for as I approached the bed. "I told you what I was going to do. Grab us a midnight snack."

"Nice." He sat up to snatch me around the waist, and pull me on top of him. "Now, lay back and spread your legs, so I can serve myself properly."

I grinned, and plucked a strawberry from the bowl, feeding it to him. "What, like a pussy platter?"

"Exactly," he said, once he'd swallowed. "I have an idea – I'm gonna put on a blindfold. You're going to pick one of these," he said, pointing to the variety of fruit in the bowl, "And I'm going to eat it out of you."

"You are such a nasty motherfucker, and I *love* it," I purred, leaning in for a taste of the strawberry still on his lips. "But I have no interest in paying the copay for whatever happens in the wake of your… bobbing for pussy game."

He plucked another strawberry from the bowl. "You don't like my idea?"

"I like it a lot. My vaginal health might not though," I teased.

He looked like he wanted to say something else, but was distracted by a buzzing from his phone, on the bedside table. He picked it up, opening the notification, and I shamelessly read it too.

@Leyaness sent you a follow request

"You know her?" I asked, as I watched him hit the button to accept the request to his – now private – page.

"Vaguely," he said, looking up to meet my eyes. "My homeboy Landon is dating her sister. I met her briefly when I caught up with him for lunch today."

I smiled. "You must have made quite an impression, if she's up past midnight trying to stalk your page."

"Maybe," he shrugged, moving to put the phone back on the nightstand, but I quickly stopped him.

"Wait, no – I want to see what she looks like," I insisted. He raised an eyebrow, but brought the phone back in front of him, navigating back to the app, and then tapping her name. Her profile was private too, so he sent her a request that she accepted almost immediately, granting him access to her page.

"Oh Nate, she's *gorgeous*," I gushed, maybe overly influenced by the fact that she was a sista, with thick natural hair. "That beautiful skin, and those big brown eyes, and this *body*." I pointed to a picture of her lounged beside a pool with a woman who looked enough like her to be her sister, both in revealing bikinis. "Are you going to start seeing her?"

He tossed the phone back to the nightstand, then used that freedom to run his hands up the outside of my thighs, underneath my robe. "The only person I'm trying to *see* right now is in front of me."

I smiled as I stopped his hands. "I'm serious."

"So am I," he countered, bringing his mouth to my neck. "Very, *very* serious about... whatever round this is going to be."

My teeth sank into my lip, biting back a moan as his hot tongue swept over my skin. "You do realize that at some point, this *really* will have to stop?"

"Will it?"

His hands easily broke free from my hold, moving to my ass to clutch.

"*Yes.*" It was half answer, half encouragement as he nibbled his way to my collarbone. "How else will you ever *really* commit to whatever beautiful, age-appropriate woman –"

"Really, Sloane?" He pulled back, obvious frustration in his eyes. "You're back on this again?"

I nodded. "Yes, because I keep *hoping* that one day you'll heed what I'm saying."

"And *I* keep hoping that one day you'll understand that what you're pushing isn't what I *want*."

"What heterosexual man *doesn't* want what I'm pushing?"

"The one who wants *you*," he answered, making me laugh.

"You want *me* to have your babies? Cause uh…"

He waved me off. "Nobody said *shit* about any babies."

"Okay so then what?" I sat back a little in his lap, retrieving the nearly-forgotten bowl of fruit from beside us. "Tell me what Elijah Nathan Richardson is looking for in a woman."

"Damn, full government, huh?"

I popped a grape in my mouth. "Quit your stalling."

"I'm not stalling."

"Then answer the question."

He sat back against the pillows, arms crossed, contemplating. "I want… someone who is settled – established in their career, not interested in partying or any of that. She has to love football."

"*Obviously*," I agreed.

"Intelligent. Beautiful. Has enough business of her own that she doesn't have to constantly be in mine. Doesn't need my attention to always be on her. Great in bed. And she *must* be named Sloane Michelle Brooks."

I shook my head. "If you don't get outta here with that."

"What?"

"That last item on your list, fool. Except for that… why don't you look for all these things you want in a woman who is within five – hell, *ten* – years of you?"

He scoffed. "You think I haven't? Every woman who has held my interest past a night or two, they want what you think *I'm* supposed to want. The marriage, the babies, the dog, the house—"

"Because those are normal things to want, Nate. What the hell do you think *I* wanted when I was younger? The marriage, the babies, the dog, the house."

"And you got it, because you found somebody who wanted that too."

I laughed. "No, what *I* got was somebody who wanted it *all*. A wife who was intelligent, beautiful, great in bed, and would have his baby and keep his house, and stay out of his business while he fucked around."

"But you're past that. That's dead. What do you want now?"

I frowned for a moment, thinking about it, and then let out a sigh. "Certainty. And orgasms. That's all."

"Explain."

"Well, when sexual arousal reaches—"

"Sloane..."

I grinned. "Fine. Certainty. Meaning... confidence of my role, whatever that is. Never having to wonder if I'm enough. Being able to trust what's being said to me. Knowing that my needs will be met. Faith that my heart will be safe. Unshakeable sureness that honoring our commitment is at the forefront of every decision. *Certainty*." I sighed again, cupping a hand under Nate's chin. "Something that *you* cannot give me."

That hurt him.

I knew it as soon as the words left my mouth, that they'd pierced him like a knife to the gut, but... it was the truth.

"Wow," he whispered, his eyes not leaving mine. "That's what you feel?"

"That's what I *know*. You're *thirty years old*, love. What happened to wanting to be a sports manager, something beyond working for your father's team? Do you know what you want your life to look like at thirty-five? At forty? Nate, you want a woman who will watch the game with you and fuck you good at halftime and then what... leave you to sleep alone so you can put the temperature exactly how you want it? There's nothing wrong with that – it's *fine*. It makes sense. You are a single man, and you can do what you want, live how you *want.* Now that I'm divorced, I'm doing the same thing. I'm not prepared to give *anybody* a bigger role in my life than the one you have – have *had*, for years now. But when I *am* ready… guess what?"

His eyelids drooped, then came back up. "You need *certainty.*"

"Bingo."

He pushed out a painfully heavy sigh, sinking even further back into the pillows as he crossed his arm over his face. I gave him a moment, then moved the fruit bowl to the bedside table so I could drape myself over him, laying flush against his chest.

"Hey."

He moved his arm, wrapping it around my shoulder, heavy and warm. "Yeah?"

"This was supposed to be ending anyway, remember? The whole "inappropriate for me to be screwing the owner's son since I'm a coach now" thing?"

"So you say." He flattened his hand against my back, running it up and down.

"So *you* know," I replied. "In a lot of ways, you're a coach too. You're responsible for putting people - your players - on their best possible path. Look me in the face and tell me that you would *ever* recommend one of *them*, or anybody else, to risk their reputation and credibility for… *sex.*"

He was quiet – *thinking* – and then his fingers started moving again. "For sex? No. I wouldn't."

"Okay so then… why are you going all distant on me right now? Ten minutes ago you were talking about pussy platters."

"That was before you took a shotgun to my ego."

I grinned. "Not your ego, lover boy. This dick is good enough that all it took was a stroke of your finger and I was breaking all my little convictions to get you over here tonight. So your ego should be well intact. What *I* destroyed was any possible delusion that we'd ever be more than what we are *right now*. Not because of you, not because of me, but because we're just on two different orbits that happened to meet for a while."

"It doesn't have to be like that though."

Pulling myself up a little, I folded my arms across his chest, to rest on them. "So what… you're rethinking what you want?"

"Maybe."

"So in the space of this conversation, you're ready to change your whole trajectory? For what reason, Nate? A little more pussy? That, right there, is a mark of *immaturity*."

He rolled his eyes. "Ah, come the fuck on, Sloane. What is it that you want from me?"

"*Nothing*," I laughed, catching his face in my hands. "You're young, and still a little impulsive, and figuring everything out, and I *adore* that about you. Please understand that I hold you in the highest regard."

"Well shit, what kind of things do you say about people you *don't* like?"

"*Awww*." I lowered my lips to his, for the soft brush of a kiss. "Are you mad at me?"

Looking me right in the eyes, he shook his head. "No. Just… processing."

I nodded.

I didn't say it, because he didn't need me to, but *that* was why I thought so highly of him, while still recognizing the marks of youth. He was… *coachable*. He didn't get wrapped up in his hurt feelings, didn't get offended at the nerve of a woman critiquing him.

He was *listening*.

Adjusting.

And I remained confident that he would make some woman very happy someday.

Before I could mentally sign the mortgage on his house with a white picket fence, he shifted, flipping us so that he was on top. He didn't bother unbelting my robe, just pushed my legs apart and plunged in, taking full advantage of my consistent state of wetness whenever I was around him.

I sucked in a breath as he sank, swiftly, as deep as he could go, past the point of pain, with such force that his balls slapped against me. Instinctively, my hands went to his shoulders, fingernails digging in as he dropped his mouth to mine, swallowing any sound I could've made.

The sweet, *sweet* friction of him pulling back, then sliding into me again so, *so* worth it. His tongue swept over mine, still tinged with the fruit from earlier as he kissed me. Slow, careful swipes, tenderly measured bites, precise little sucks, all deliciously, *torturously* good paired with his deep, languid strokes.

He shifted us again, hooking my knee over his shoulder and pressing it all the way down to my chest as he kept his mouth bonded to mine. That gave him room to get comfortably deeper, perfectly deeper, *waiting-outside-his-office* deeper.

Something-to-prove deeper.

Only… he really didn't.

I was already very sure of who he was, and what he could do – he already had my admiration and honestly – adoration too.

But, without explicitly stating it, it was already understood that *this* would be our last time. This was where our paths diverged.

He was making sure I understood what I'd be missing.

Driving home what I already knew.

I was going to miss the hell out of him.

Hell, he was still here, still inside me, and I already did.

"*Fuccck,*" he groaned in my neck, unable to help letting me know it was good for him too.

I grinned as he pushed himself up onto his hands, still stroking, faster now, sweat dripping, looking like exactly what I saw in my head when I closed my eyes to pleasure myself when he wasn't around.

It was so, *so* good.

Too good.

But with him here, I couldn't close my eyes because he was staring right into them as he filled me up, over and over again. Pleasure coiled in me, rapidly, so fast that it caught me off guard, and before I knew it, an orgasm hit me so hard I couldn't feel my damn toes.

And Nate was still right there.

Still, stroking, still moving, still sweating and growling until he released, and collapsed onto me with a satisfied groan.

He was hot, and heavy, but I didn't have even the slightest desire to move.

Eventually though, he did, just enough to move beside me on the bed, giving me room for my lungs to expand fully. That was all the space he seemed inclined to give though – he hooked an arm around my waist, tight, keeping me close.

A few seconds later, his soft snores filled the room.

It was… nice.

Any other night, I'd be ready to fuss, and make a big deal about him leaving, or at *least* moving to one side of the king-sized bed. Tonight though… I let him be.

It was the least I could do, since this was our last.

That "one last night" with Nate caught up with me sooner than I expected – on the pavement, the very next morning. The lack of good rest the night before showed itself in the form of lethargic legs, horrible breath control, and that damn fruit seemed to be on the verge of making a reappearance, back up the same way it had come down. I was only a disappointingly slow half mile from home when I turned around and headed back.

Maybe I can get a nap in before I go to the office.

Right now, my load was still light. There was still a week before the first offseason workout, so the only thing on my agenda was hours and hours of film, watched in minute detail, with the purpose of tracking every single minor mistake. I needed to know my wide receivers' weaknesses, so I could work them out one by one, bringing them closer to the excellence I knew they were capable of.

Boring.

As I trudged back into my house, the first thing I heard was Nate's voice. I'd woken him on my way out before my run, giving my usual admonition to be gone when I got back. This time, he got a pass – I was home early.

I followed the sound to my kitchen, where I found him on his phone, frowning through what must not have been a pleasant conversation, presumably about a player. The glass of water beside him at the counter explained his presence in the kitchen, and I wordlessly motioned that my ears were closed, but I needed the same thing he'd come for.

Water.

Desperately.

For some reason, my presence made him frown deeper, and he met my eyes, mouthing, *"What's wrong with you?"* I was halfway ready to catch an attitude when he approached me, touching my forehead. "You're clammy," he said out loud, then immediately remembered he was on the phone. "No, not *you*," he explained to whoever he was speaking to. "Look, just… fix the shit, okay?" Without waiting for an answer, he hung up the phone, tossing it onto the counter before he returned to me, putting a hand against my back. "Are you not feeling well?"

I shook my head. "Just ti – just tire—oh *God*." Quickly, I moved away from him, to the sink, where last night's strawberries made good on the threat they'd been offering all morning. Nate was right behind me, flipping the water on and turning on the disposal for a quick clean up.

I felt too much like crap to be embarrassed.

"This isn't just *tired*," he muttered, grabbing a clean towel from the cabinet behind the sink. He wet it with cool water, and pressed it to my face for a moment before he wiped my mouth, and I let him. "You're not…"

"*Hell* no," I insisted, suddenly grateful for the firm strength of his body, to hold me up. "I'm just… I'm…"

"*Sloane.* Hey. Open your eyes for me. *Sloane!*"

"*What?*" I asked, flinching as sudden pain erupted in my jaw, quickly sweeping down my back and arms. I shook my head. "Nate. I don't… no, I don't feel good."

"Tell me what you're feeling," he demanded.

So fucking pushy.

"I… I'm *tired.* You kept me up all night, remember? And I can't… I can't catch my breath, from my run. I just need to lay down a second. Just… just a second."

"No, *no.* I need you to keep your eyes open for me, okay?" he asked, still propping me up as he reached for his phone on the counter.

"I just need a nap, that's all."

That was barely out of my mouth before the second wave of pain came, in my chest this time, spreading all the way to my shoulders and down my back, so suddenly, so severely that my knees buckled. If it wasn't for Nate's arm around me, I would have been on the ground.

"Yeah, I need an ambulance at…"

I could hear Nate speaking into the phone, but my eyes were closed, trying to block out the pain. I wanted to protest, wanted to tell him he was overreacting, but I couldn't seem to get that signal to my brain.

"Sloane. *Slo—"*

I heard my name.

I wanted to respond.

But then… there was nothing.

My arm hurts…

A scowl graced my face as I peeled my eyes open, searching for the source of the itchy, achiness in my arm. The lights were dim, and the incessant beeping did nothing to soothe the supreme agitation I felt.

That agitation spiked when I saw the IV catheter in my arm.

The assortment of wires attached to sticky pads stuck to my chest.

The nasal cannula across my face.

What the fuck is going on?

I flinched as a hand wrapped around mine, on the opposite side of where the IV was. My head rolled in that direction to find Nate seated beside the bed, the fatigue and concern evident in his eyes, even in the dim light.

"Welcome back, Coach Brooks," he murmured – words that did nothing to soothe my confused state.

I opened my mouth to speak, but it was so dry that it hurt. Nate was quick though, jumping up to wash his hands, and then coming back to my bedside to open a sealed package with a tiny spray bottle inside.

"Open."

I frowned, but did as he said, letting him spray what turned out to be cool, sterile water into my mouth.

"I know it's probably not the best, but they said I can't give you anything to eat or drink right now. Not while they're monitoring you."

"Monitoring me… why?"

Nate pushed out a sigh as he dropped back into the seat beside the bed. "I don't know the details – bribing only got me far enough to not have to leave you in here by yourself. The paramedics though… I was in the ambulance with you. Sloane… you had a heart attack."

"A *what?*" I asked, immediately pissed at the implication. Nate put his hands out, urging me to be calm, but there was no goddamn way. "I'm in my *early* forties. I run, every day. I eat well, I'm healthy, I did everything they say you're supposed to do."

"*I know,*" he agreed, in a soothing tone. "I know that, Sloane, I promise. You *must* calm down though. You're lucky to not have stitches right now, but if you stress yourself—"

"Stress *myself?* You're in my face talking about a fucking heart attack!"

"Sloane, *please*—"

"Is there a problem in here?" We both looked toward the door, where a pleasant-looking nurse was walking in. She, like Nate, went to the sink first, scrubbing her hands before she donned a pair of gloves and approached the bed.

"Yes," I told her, shooting a dirty look in Nate's direction before I gave my attention back to her. "What am I doing here, and why is he talking to me about a heart attack?"

She shot him a dirty look too, and he at least had the decency to look sheepish. "Well, you'll probably want to speak to your doctor when he gets back in a few hours. Until then—"

"Until then *nothing*," I snapped. "Tell me what the hell is wrong with me!"

She nodded. "Would you like him to step out of the room?"

"Just tell me, please."

"You had a heart attack, Ms. Brooks. He," she pointed at Nate, "Is one of the main reasons you're alive right now. The heart attack caused a brief cardiac arrest, and Mr. Richardson performed life-saving CPR until the ambulance he called arrived, to get you here, to us. Yesterday."

My eyes widened. "Yesterday? But I was supposed to go to work, I had film to watch, and— I… I need to get out of here."

"You don't need to do *shit*," Nate responded to that, shaking his head. "Except rest."

"I need to see if I still have a *job*. I need to see what people are – oh *God* once the media gets ahold of this…"

"They won't." Again, Nate shook his head. "Only me and the people here at the hospital know that you're here, and they aren't saying anything – by law. I called a private paramedic service, one that specializes in... discretion. And... I may or may not have lined a few pockets to make sure your privacy was maintained."

I blinked, hard. "I... thank you. Um... my family? Madison, and Garrett...?"

"Don't know anything yet," he assured me. "I... didn't have any details to give them even if I *had* reached out – the staff isn't telling me anything. And besides that, I assumed you would want to call them yourself since we... uh..."

"Are having a secret fling," the nurse spoke up as she moved to look at the constant output of the vital monitoring machines. "But don't worry, I won't tell anybody."

"*This isn't happening*," I muttered to myself, closing my eyes, only to have a soft laugh meet my ears.

"Sorry to report that it *is*, sweetie. You're going to be okay though. Dr. Sharpe will be back in a few hours to explain. And as for *you*," she spoke to Nate again. "You didn't want her to wake up alone – mission accomplished. Now it's time to go, so she can rest. This is still an ICU, remember?"

"How long do I have to be here?"

She turned back to me. "Just until you're stable, and then you'll be moved to coronary care."

"And how long do I have to stay *there*?"

"As long as it takes. Relax, Ms. Brooks. You'll be well taken care of." Her head swiveled to Nate. "Ten more minutes. Don't make me come get you."

Once she was gone, I sank back into the uncomfortable bed, struggling to process this new information. Somehow, it wasn't even my health that was at the forefront of my mind, even laying out in a bed, with oxygen being forced up my nose.

What would the Kings say?

"Your phone," Nate said, pointing to the plugged-in device on the bedside table. "Just so you know – and I already know I shouldn't have done this but still… - Coach Underwood sent a text, asking where you were, and I… responded."

"You did *what—*"

"I said, as you, that you weren't feeling well – that you thought you'd had some bad shrimp, might have a little stomach bug. So you wouldn't be in for a few days, so you wouldn't be getting anybody else sick before the first work out. And that you already had somebody to take care of you, so no need to check in."

The tension in my shoulders released.

"Um… thank you," I said, closing my eyes, fully understanding that he'd just been trying to – and honestly probably had – help. "That was quick thinking. *Good* thinking."

He tipped his head. "I just… thought it might give you a few days to… process. And *rest*. Without worrying about your place with the team."

"Did you tell your father?"

"Not my business to tell, Sloane. When and how you decide to tell the team is entirely up to you. And yes – you *should* tell the team."

I frowned. "What makes you say it like that?"

"The fact that I *know* you. More than you think I do."

"And what is it you think you know?"

"That as soon as you're released from this hospital you're going to be back on the field."

"What's wrong with that?"

"I'm not your doctor, so I don't know," he shrugged. "But I'm pretty sure he'll want you to take care of yourself, and part of that is almost certainly going to be knowing your limits."

I sucked my teeth. "I don't *have* limits."

"Correction – you *didn't*."

The truth of his words stunned me into silence. Of course I didn't know yet what had caused this, or what I'd be doing to protect my health moving forward. But, without question… something would be different.

Nate leaned down, pressing a kiss to my forehead before he straightened up. "I have to go for now, but I'll be back later… if that's okay?"

It took me a second to realize he was waiting for an answer, but then I nodded.

He gave me a little smile. "Just text me what you need – magazines, your computer, any of that, and I'll bring it for you. For now, try to get some rest."

With that, he turned to leave, but when he was almost at the door, I had to stop him.

"*Nate*!" I called, prompting him to turn back.

"Yeah?"

"Thank you."

That smile came back to his face, and he answered me with a simple nod. And then he was gone.

I closed my eyes, willing this to all be some fucked up dream, but the steady chime of the vital monitors kept me firmly tethered to what was, indeed, my reality.

My gaze fell on my phone, thinking about the almost certain deluge of missed calls and texts. Briefly, I considered checking it, or even just calling Garrett to let him know what was going on.

But I was so, *so* tired.

So instead of doing any of that, I took a deep, cleansing breath, and closed my eyes.

Of my own volition this time.

Six.

They always find a reason to blame the mother.

The wounded chorus of mothers everywhere when observing something that was, indeed, a mother's "fault". My own mother was *not* excluded from that number.

Hell, none of us were.

At some point, all of us wondered if our damage – whatever it was – was a direct result of the mistakes of our mothers, and every mother wondered how their mistakes would damage their children. How many decisions were *truly* our own, even when we tried to isolate, and make our mistakes in a bubble that affected no one else?

When I was released from the hospital, three days after I arrived, with a whole packet of instructions from my doctor and a verbal admonition to relax, I'd just nodded. I got in the car with Nate, who drove me home, and made me promise I would follow the doctor's instructions as carefully as I possibly could.

And yet… instead of doing that, I'd given myself over completely to pinpointing all the ways my mother had fucked me over, and all the ways that I, in turn, was fucking over Madison.

The Heart Health Edition.

As I sat on my own bed – supposedly recovering from a heart attack that was ultimately ruled "minor" whatever the fuck *that* meant – flipping through a photo album I hadn't looked at in far too long, I took notice of things that I'd long forgotten.

She always has a cigarette in her hand.

I distinctly remembered being seven or eight years old, begging her to put the Newports down. Back then, my push to get her to stop smoking had been all about what it was doing to her lungs. I showed her my printouts from school, with the healthy lung on one side and the smoker's lung on the other. I showed her the surgeon general's warning *right there* on the side of the package.

Cancer sticks.

That's what everybody focused on, it seemed.

Lung cancer and underweight babies.

That second part, she took seriously – she was always quick to tell me that she didn't smoke a *single* cigarette from the time she learned she was pregnant to the time she stopped breastfeeding me. Always presented as some grand *gift* she'd given me.

But when I showed her those warnings on the cartons and those school papers, she showed *me* something too.

Bills.

Constant, non-stop bills, whose arrival would have her searching for a working lighter and a fresh pack. According to her, the cigarettes staved off stress, and they staved off hunger while she made sure I ate, and they helped keep her skinny and fine.

And she was *that.*

Which, as the story went, was what attracted my stepfather to her. And he came in with his good job and cigars and he swept my mother off her feet. Clive was a good guy, honestly. The stress about the bills went away, and he was nice to me without being a creep, and he taught me to love football, and he *loved* my mother, dearly.

But now I just had *two* people I loved who I was sure would get cancer and leave me, because the cigarettes didn't go *anywhere*.

So imagine *my* surprise when, upon her sudden death, the day after her fifty-first birthday, it wasn't her lungs at all.

It was her heart that failed her – years of smoking had killed the lining of her arteries, and ultimately led to the massive heart attack that took her life.

Which was a wake-up call for me.

Smoking disgusted me, so that had never been a vice of mine. And I was already an athlete, so I lived healthily… but I decided I could do better.

I wanted to meet my grandkids – a chance my mother never got. I ate all my green leafy veggies and I started running and I took my vitamins and I juiced and I… *still* ended up with coronary heart disease.

My only "risk factor" was that my mother had developed it.

And now, I was consumed by the idea that, ten or twenty or thirty years from now, Madison's heart would one day decide to stop working.

Because *I* was her risk factor.

The sound of the doorbell pulled me out of my melodramatic mental wanderings, and I pulled myself up from the bed. My eyes went to the assortment of prescription bottles that now decorated my vanity. I already knew who was at the door, so I took a second to sweep all the bottles into the drawer below, out of my sight.

As if *that* made it any better.

I took my time getting to the door, even as the doorbell became more incessant. Once I was there, I flung it open, propping a hand at my hip to ask, "What the hell is your problem?"

"Nothing," Nate answered, sliding past me, uninvited, into the house. "The weather is beautiful, the market opened strong, and my dick was still where I left it when I woke up this morning. No complaints here."

I closed the door. "Right. The complaint is *here*," I said, pointing to myself. "Why are you at my door at six in the morning?"

"Because you wake up at 5:30 every morning, to go running."

I *had* been up since five, but that was beside the point. "Uh… you do remember that my heart failed on me three days ago, after a run?

"You *do* remember that I was here for that, right? CPR to keep your heart pumping, called the ambulance, all that jazz?"

I rolled my eyes. "Of course I remember. I have the bruised ribs to prove it – thank you for not breaking anything, by the way."

"You're welcome," he answered with a smirk. "Now why aren't you dressed?"

"Dressed for…?"

"Exercise." He motioned at himself, making me take notice for the first time of his running apparel.

My eyebrows shot up. "You are out of your mind if you think I'm about to go *running*."

"My mind must be nicely intact then, because no, that's not what I think. I *do* think I was right there in the room when you were cleared for exercise though, and Dr. Sharpe suggested that you start as soon as possible, within reason. So… get dressed. Let's go for a walk."

I shook my head. "I should probably give it a few weeks. My heart—"

"Needs you to not bullshit and make excuses. I saw the chart he gave you. You were already incredibly fit, and dropping to not doing anything isn't good for your heart. You need the exercise, and I'll be right there beside you if something happens again. Go put on some clothes."

"You are being *really* pushy right now," I snapped. "You are *not* the boss of me, *young man*. I am old enough to be your—"

"To be my *what*?" Nate interjected, clearly amused. "My big sister? Young aunt? Come on, say it. I gotta hear this shit."

"You *know* what I mean! But I don't have to have this conversation anyway. You can get the hell out of my house."

For some reason, he smirked, and then stepped right over to the couch, where he took a seat, stretching his arms across the back cushions. "I *can*… but I'm not. I'm not going anywhere until you take your fine ass upstairs, put on some of those little shorts, and come take a walk with me. A slow half mile. Twenty minutes. That's all."

"That's easy for you to say. You're not the one who went for a run, then woke up in the hospital."

"You're right. I'm not," he conceded. "But I *was* the one on his knees beside you, trying to keep your heart pumping. What you went through was *terrifying*. I know. But watching it was scary as fuck too, and I don't ever want to experience that again – something I'm sure you can relate to, right?"

I nodded. "Right."

"Okay. So… go upstairs. Get dressed. And let's go for a walk."

"I…" A million reasons *not* to cycled through my mind, seemingly all at once, all with the same root – *fear*. But then, conversely, fear brought a few other things to mind. Like the thought of this happening again while I was home alone, or while it was just me and Madison.

I couldn't decide which I thought was worse.

So I took my time up the stairs – with Nate jumping right up to help me - and put exercise clothes on.

Nate was right – it *was* beautiful weather. It wasn't quite summer yet, and the trail behind my house – which I didn't normally use because it was so wooded, and I didn't like being out there by myself – was even more scenic than my neighborhood route. The lush greenery, birds chirping, the sun on my skin… it was honestly nice, after three days in the sterile setting of the hospital. I wasn't about to admit it to him, but… I was glad he'd annoyed me into coming out.

"So what did your family say when you told them what happened?" Nate asked me, just a few minutes into our walk. I carefully kept my gaze focused anywhere except his vicinity, which must have been a dead giveaway, because he stopped moving.

"You haven't told them, have you?"

I kept walking, not answering his question until he'd easily caught up. "I don't want to worry them. And don't want *them* worried about me."

"And you don't think them knowing would be beneficial to your care?"

"I can take care of myself. I have timers set for all the medicines, I already eat well, I'm fit, and I… am willing to give up my beloved wine. I'm the only one who can do this for me. All they can do is get on my nerves – much like *you* are doing right now."

"Throw those jabs all you like – I'm not backing off."

I stopped at the little bridge that traversed one of the many brooks that fed into the lake nearby. "You know that this isn't going to get you back into my pussy, right?"

"Who said anything about that?" Nate chuckled. "You act like that's my only interest in you."

"Isn't it?"

"Not remotely," he answered, stepping closer. "Don't get me wrong – I am… *shamelessly* strung out on the glory between your thighs, but it is *far* from the only thing that has kept me coming back for… four years? I could've gotten a whole other degree by now."

I smirked. "Oh I have schooled you *plenty* over the years." My smile deepened as he put his hands at my waist, pulling me against him. "Don't you feel well-educated?"

"Absolutely. And I was looking forward to a lot of high quality continuing education until my teacher decided to—"

"Have a heart attack, and remind you that she was no spring chicken?"

He sighed, and stepped back. "See, there you go…"

"Yes, here I go. This only underlines what I was *already* saying to you. See how it happened the next morning? Prophetic."

"*Bullshit.*"

Instead of indulging my line of conversation, he moved on down the trail, forcing me to be the one catching up to him.

"Have you talked to Leya?"

He chuckled, shaking his head – over my question, not as an answer. "Yes, actually. I had lunch with her yesterday, and I brought you a salad back."

"Did she ask who it was for?"

"She did. I told her that my friend was in the hospital, and would probably appreciate some better food."

I nodded. "I did. That salad was good as hell. Thank you again."

"You're welcome again. Why are you asking me about Leya?"

I chewed at my lip for a second, stalling before I answered. "Because I… want you to be happy. I want you to find someone who changes your mind about wanting to be alone."

"What makes you think my mind can be changed – and didn't you call that a mark of immaturity a few days ago?"

"No," I corrected, laughing. "It was the *immediate* second-thinking that gave me pause. I think everybody can have their mind changed – through education, or experience, or deep emotions. I don't want you to decide to get married just because I say so. I want you to decide because you accidentally fall so intensely in love that you decide you can't live without… whatever lucky woman snags your attention… and drives you out of your mind."

"You consider yourself lucky then?"

I rolled my eyes at his quip, but couldn't keep the grin that developed off my face. I wiped it away quickly though, before he looked back to see the result of his words.

"You're not funny, Nate."

"Not trying to be, Sloane. When are you going back to the office?"

"Monday. So I can be prepared for workouts."

"You told Underwood yet? Coach Lou?"

Again, I looked away. Of *course* he wondered if I'd informed my two direct superiors that I'd had an emergency medical issue, but I felt like he *had* to already know the answer.

Or at least, he could correctly assume now.

"Seriously, Sloane? You're not gonna tell *anybody*?"

I shrugged. "*You* know. And my doctor knows. That's more than enough."

"Coaching in the NFL is a stressful job – do you know how many –"

"Coaches suffer from myriad health issues, especially the heart. Yeah, I do. Did *you* know that Mike Ditka had a heart attack, and was back on the field a week later? Dan Reeves – quadruple bypass – only out for *two* games, and the Falcons won the NFC Championship that year."

"I don't give a *fuck* what *they* did," Nate countered, stopping to look at me like I'd lost my mind. "And even if I did – they didn't do the shit in secret, and they were head coaches, with an entire coaching staff to pick up their load for them!"

I shook my head. "There's no *load* for anyone to pick up for me! The Kings have three wide receivers – I'm pretty sure I can handle them."

"Nobody is questioning your coaching ability. I am, however, questioning whether you're more concerned about looking like superwoman than you are about your health."

"Don't you *dare*," I hissed, jabbing my finger into his chest. "After all the sexist bullshit I've been through, the harassment – sexual and otherwise – I've endured getting this position, you are *goddamn* right, I want every motherfucker who thinks my dark brown skin or the existence of my pussy should've disqualified me, to look at me and see a *fucking badass*. It is *not* that I'm not concerned about my health – I will take the pills, and I won't even look at a bottle of wine, and everything else that I'm supposed to do. But the fact remains that the *last* thing I need is a reason to be labeled *weak*. I don't expect *you* to understand that though."

I turned to walk off, but he was right behind me, catching me at the elbow. "Hey." When I pulled away from his grasp, he simply stepped in front of me, blocking the path. "Hey. I'm *sorry*," he said, holding up his hands. "You're right – I'm not in your shoes. I *don't* understand. Nobody gives a fuck about the front office staff, nobody is digging into my business like that. I don't have people telling me to go back to the kitchen in comments under articles that are celebrating me. I don't know what that feels like, but… I can imagine. And I wouldn't want the people who were trying to drag me down to see me looking weak either."

Folding my arms across my aching chest, I let out a sigh. "Why do I feel like there's a *but* coming?"

"Because… there is," he admitted. "I'll keep it brief though – it's not weak to ask for help. And it's not weak to need it. Just… consider it, okay?"

"If I say yes, will you stop getting on my nerves?"

He grinned. "Absolutely."

"Then, yes. I'll consider it."

The walk back to the house was… less intense.

I teased him a little more about the Leya thing, and we talked about the players, and offered predictions for the team. Once we were back inside, he took me to the kitchen, declaring that he was making breakfast for us.

"Good luck with *that*," I told him, gladly taking a seat at the counter as I watched him pull a skillet from the rack. "I don't keep mu—where the hell did *that* come from?"

This was my first time back in my own kitchen since the heart attack, but I was quite sure of how I'd left it – in desperate need of a trip to the grocery store. Those strawberries we ate the night before had been the last thing in the fridge.

Now though, I took notice of the bowl full of apples on the counter, and the bunch of bananas beside it. When he opened my fridge, he pulled out fresh eggs, and avocados, and an armful of other veggies that *hadn't* been there before.

"The grocery store," he said. "I wanted you to have everything you needed when you came home. You… *do* know I know the code to the front door, right?"

Ugh.

I *did* know.

I'd given it to him about a year ago, after I'd twisted my ankle and didn't want to have to go all the way downstairs just to let him in.

"I never intended for you to use that beyond those few times," I scolded, and he nodded.

"And I haven't – but this seemed like a good enough reason to risk you being pissed at me for using it. And knowing now that you haven't told anyone else, I don't even feel guilty about it now. I never would've left you here by yourself last night."

"But I *told* you to go home."

"And I *said* what I *said*," he countered, tossing me a grin as he worked at the stove. "I was reading about whether or not the stairs were too much for you last night."

My face twisted. "Did you or did you not incessantly ring my doorbell to get me to come down this morning – when you *had the code to get in my front door*?!"

"I did. Because the stairs are good for you, if you take it slow. And I see now, you're not doing any exercise unless you feel like you have to, so if I have to create some urgency to get you moving…"

"What you're creating is a pain in my ass."

"Better than one in your chest."

"You did that already too, remember?"

"Yap, yap, yap. *Eat*," he insisted, sliding a plate in front of me. The omelet, sliced tomatoes and sliced avocado looked amazing, and smelled it too. I expected Nate to take a seat beside me, but instead I watched in fascination as he folded his omelet onto his fork and put the whole damn thing in his mouth at once, chewing while he cleaned up behind himself.

Which was a show of its own.

Garrett had *never* understood the concept.

"You gonna eat or not?" he asked me, when he glanced up and I still hadn't touched my plate.

"Oh! Yes, I am." I started – *damn this is good* – while he finished cleaning up, and then he turned and informed me that he was going to clean himself up, and change for work.

I really didn't have a choice except to nod.

He went out to his car to grab his bag, and then disappeared while I finished eating. I climbed the stairs myself – slowly – with a glass of water so I could take my proper medicines, and when I came back down, he was emerging from the guest bathroom looking good as hell.

But he *always* looked good as hell.

"I have to head out, but you can hit my cell if you need *anything*, okay?"

"I know."

"And there's two more of those salads in your fridge, in case you get hungry before I come back."

My eyebrow lifted. "Assuming I *let* you come back."

"Whatever you say, woman," he teased, as I followed him to the door. He leaned a little, but what I expected to be a kiss on the lips – his most frequent parting gift for me – ended up… on my forehead.

Despite my best immediate efforts… I felt a way about that.

A way that I *quickly* swallowed, because wasn't this exactly what I wanted? I enjoyed Nate as a friend, and prior to almost dying, had been trying my best to return him to that place.

I had zero room to feel salty about him taking me up on it.

I was about to make one last teasing remark as he opened the front door, but it died on my lips when I saw Garrett and Madison walking up my front steps three days sooner than they were due back from California.

Don't have another heart attack, Sloane. Just stay calm. Just stay calm.

"Thank you for being willing to discuss this with me so early, Coach Brooks," Nate said, cool as a cucumber, without so much as a hint of strain in his tone. "I appreciate your dedication to the team. We're lucky to have you."

And without even telling a lie.

Wow.

"Good morning!" he said, waving to Garrett and Madison as he passed them to get to his car, which he'd apparently already pulled out of the garage, and into the driveway.

"Is that Nathan Richardson? Eli Richardson's son?" Garrett asked as they approached the door. Nate pulled off, and I nodded to answer Garrett's question.

"Yes. He works for the Kings – *Director of Player Success.* Offense."

Garrett frowned. "So he was here to what, talk about the players or something? It's not even seven in the morning."

"It's called dedication. There was something to discuss, and we discussed it."

"That Amare kid?"

"I'm not really at liberty to talk about it. What are you doing here?" I asked, trying to change the subject as I extended my arms to Madison. I tried my best not to cringe as she squeezed me tight, then planted a kiss on my cheek."

"You had him in the house while you were dressed like this? And why did he have a bag?"

"His laptop bag?" I asked, knowing damn well it was a stretch.

"Why does he keep his laptop in a duffel?"

"You'd have to ask him that. *Why are you here?*"

"Oh." he waved me off as he passed me to get inside with Madison's bag. "Emergency situation with one of my clients, and Mads was missing you anyway. What's up with you?"

"Huh?"

"*What's up with you*? You look… tired."

I rolled my eyes, finally closing the door. "Thanks, that's exactly what I want to hear from you," I told him, dryly, then turned to Madison. "You have a good time out there with your cousins?"

"The *best*. Can I go call Langston?!"

"Go ahead," I agreed, knowing her father had probably been hating on her when it came to Langston the whole time they'd been gone.

In fact, I expected him to start up as soon as she disappeared up the stairs, but he was too distracted by my ass in my shorts.

"That lil' nigga didn't try anything with you, did he?"

I sighed. "Why would you even say that?"

"Because, he popped up on you all early in the morning, before you were dressed… that ain't dedication. That's creeping."

"I promise you, the *last* thing he was trying to do was get some ass. Okay?"

"Maybe not *overtly*, but—"

"Didn't you say you had an emergency you had to handle? Couldn't you be doing that, instead of questioning me?"

I asked that question just as his phone went off – probably Miles, calling to see where the hell he was.

"I'll talk to you later," he told me, rushing out the door as he pulled it from his pocket, *finally* leaving me alone.

Once I'd closed and locked it, I put my back to the door, letting out a sigh. I took a second to breathe, and then moved to start my trek back up the stairs, to my room, to lay down.

Heart attack or not… this was too much excitement for one morning.

Seven

I always knew my father had a way with women. From casual observation of his – and their – mannerisms, the things said about him in the media, and the stories he'd told me that I unquestionably believed, because Eli Richardson was the fucking *man*. I couldn't deflect a single accusation that I lionized my father, and didn't care to. He wasn't without his flaws, but all in all he was well-liked, well-respected by the public, and well-loved by people who knew him better.

Especially his wife.

There was – to my mind, at least – no other possible reasoning for her to agree to move back into the house where Cole and I had been raised.

Our *mother's* home.

Mel had to *really* love his ass.

There were other factors involved in the decision of course – Mel's pregnancy two years ago had sparked heightened interest in her and my father's relationship, and made the relatively easy media access to their Bridgeport townhouse less than desirable. Then there was Emma. Just like he'd done with me and Cole, he didn't want her growing up with cameras stuck in her face at every turn, and Mel was on board. They wanted space, and grass, and privacy for her, all of which were in abundance at the house he'd lived and loved with my mother before she passed away, which he'd kept with the intention of one of us – the twins – having it.

Now though, it was *their* place.

They could have bought a new house, that they chose together, but Mel had insisted it was unnecessary. I still thought she'd just been in a hurry to get out of the city so she could have some peace, but she didn't seem to be suffering in the home of her husband's previous wife.

In fact… she was thriving.

Hence, the party.

Every year, Eli hosted a "Welcome Back" party. This year, Cole and I had been referring to it as a kickback, since he'd decided on a house party.

Mel was a *great* hostess.

Emma was off with her grandmother – Mel's mother – and Mel was all over the place, socializing and making sure there was a drink in everyone's hand. The house was decorated in blue and gold streamers and balloons, just enough to not be gaudy. Staff wore red coats, Frankie Beverly and Maze pumped through the speakers, and the place was *packed.*

And damn near everybody had a glass of Mel's *Richardson Punch* in hand.

That woman knew how to make a damn drink, and that was just a small thing in the long list of reasons Mel was cool by me. Probably because age-wise, we were closer to peers than anything else.

Cole had always been a little resentful – to Mel *and* my father – over him marrying a woman that was only seven years older than his kids. The age difference between *them* was almost twenty years.

Which is why I didn't understand Sloane tripping over our *barely* thirteen.

It was nothing, as far as I was concerned.

"Hey Nate!"

I looked up from my current Mel-appointed task of lining up martini glasses in the busy kitchen. I wasn't quite sure how I'd gotten recruited – along with one of Mel's friends - into helping with the punch, so I wasn't surprised to see she'd rustled up new help, in the form of Parker, who was a mainstay in the Kings' front office.

She'd started with the team as a cheerleader – like Mel's story, only with not as desirable an ending. Parker had gotten wrapped up with James "The Boulder" Wright, another former player who was now in a near-vegetative state from a myriad of health issues. I wasn't sure how old she was, but knew she was close to my age – too young for Jimmy, who she was saddled with caring for when she wasn't even married to him. I was happy to use her as a temp for Elliot whenever he was out, knowing that the job in the front office gave her a break from that house.

Parker had just enough time for that short greeting before Mel put her to work beside her homegirl.

"Don't let her work you too much," I teased her as I lined up the last glass and then left the kitchen before Mel found *anything* else for me to do. I headed out to the main area, looking around. Damn near every face was familiar, and everybody had something to say, so it took a bit of time to travel through all the space available for the party, still looking.

It was a minute before I realized who I was doing all that *looking* for.

Sloane.

We'd spoken the day before, at the Kings' facilities, and she claimed to be coming. Her proximity to Rut, Terrance, and Jordan gave me just the excuse I needed to lay eyes on her at work, under the guise of checking on my players. They were in preseason workouts now, which didn't really require any physical exertion on her part. If anything, she was more of an observer, since there were trainers in the room.

There was another minicamp coming up though, in June. And then training camp after that. As a coach, Sloane had a very hands-on style – I'd seen film of her practices with the BSU wide receivers. She'd get out there and throw passes, run routes, do drills with them like it was nothing. As physically fit as she was... I didn't see her being ready to handle that.

But a week – almost *two* weeks later – she was still insistent on not telling anybody.

She was good and grown though – I knew I couldn't press too much there. What I *could* do though was stay all over her ass about the things her doctor had insisted on – a conversation she hadn't asked me to leave the room for there in the hospital.

Even if it was subconscious, she *wanted* the accountability.

Stay active, take your meds, lower your cholesterol, and minimize stress.

It was the driving force behind me showing up to make egg white omelets and take her on walks. She'd been good with her meds, and put up a minimal fuss about the adjustments to her already mostly-clean diet, and on the days she had her house to herself, our little walks had started to gradually get a little longer.

About that stress, though…

Once the season started… maybe even before… I didn't know *how* that would be managed. It was a stressful job by nature – dealing with big, rich, immature men and their egos. I thought about the bullshit she was bound to get from fans, the media, the other people on the field, and dreaded it in advance.

It could send even the healthiest person into stress-overload.

The bit of worry in the back of my mind dissipated all at once when I turned a corner and came upon a group set a little apart from the players and other staff – the coaches. The sound of Sloane's voice drew me a bit closer, and I grinned when I realized she was the center of attention, telling what was apparently a riveting story about an experience she'd had coaching semi-pro. The other coaches were fully engaged, laughing and joking with her, something I felt no need to interrupt, even just to say hello.

Because I was looking for it, I could see the little bit of fatigue that lined her face from working all week, but other than that, she looked… *happy*.

So I needed to mind my business.

It was the other corner of the room that held *my* crowd – the players. Even before I saw them, I could hear Jordan and Trent clowning – in a good way – and headed in that direction, knowing *that* was where the fun was.

I was almost there – had laid eyes on my sister and Jade, Trent's wife, whispering together about something – when I got interrupted by a hand on my shoulder.

Landon.

"What the hell are you even doing here bruh?" I asked, giving him a quick greeting before I turned my attention to the familiar faces that accompanied him. "Ladies," I greeted Tyra, and Leya, who immediately moved closer to me.

"Here for you, nigga," Landon said, glancing around. "Came to rescue you – you're around these same motherfuckers all the time. It's a Saturday night, I'm trying to find a *real* party."

I shrugged. "My old man already made his speeches and whatnot, so my presence isn't required and won't be missed. What do y'all have in mind?"

"Well," Leya purred, slipping her arm through mine. "I was telling them about the bar at *Veil* – you know the hotel in the city where *everybody* goes to have their illicit affairs?" she laughed at that, then continued. "*Well*, they make a *Macallan Rare Cask* Manhattan that is just…" she moaned a little, kissing her fingertips for effect. "You *have* to experience this."

"Damn, when you describe it like *that*, I feel like I *need* to," I laughed, with Landon joining in.

"Okay so then what's up?" Landon asked. "You need to say something to your people or what?"

I shook my head. "Nah, they're all occupied, and if I'm going, I need to get the fuck outta here before Mel tries to make me pass out more drinks or something. Which one of us is driving?"

"I'll drive!"

"*Hell no,*" me, Tyra, and Leya all chimed at once, immediately shooting down the idea of Landon playing chauffeur.

"I'll drive," Leya offered. "Since I *did* drive us here. Nate, you've got shotgun, since I already know Landon and Tyra will be all over each other in the back seat."

"You sure?"

She nodded. "I'm positive. Because that way, *I* don't have to worry about coming back out to the boonies to get my car back. Everybody has to find their own way home."

"Understandable," I laughed. "I'm sure my father will want to debrief tomorrow anyway, so it's not a big deal for me to come back for mine."

"Well," Tyra spoke up. "Sounds like it's settled. Let's go have Leya's bougie ass cocktail."

"So… neither of us is surprised by this, right?"

"Not remotely. I had a pretty strong hunch."

Ten minutes ago, Landon and Tyra had disappeared together, citing a trip to the "bathroom". We all knew what they were going to do, so the *"don't wait up"* style text I got from Landon – Tyra sent a similar one to her sister – hadn't been unexpected at all.

I'd already suspected that my night would end without either of them present.

"So… you haven't made any effort to see me since lunch at *Zoe's*," Leya said, grinning across the booth at me. All the tables in the bar were private, sectioned off by sheer veils that doubled down on the hotel's privacy schtick. "Is there some sort of hint I should take from that?"

"Only that I'm a busy man. Definitely nothing to be offended by."

She smirked a little as she brought her drink upward, sipping from her straw for a moment before she replied. "I didn't mean to imply any offense was taken – there wasn't. I just … how do I say this… I like to be very clear about where I stand with someone, no matter where on the roadmap of possibilities that is."

"That's fair," I agreed, taking a swig of my own.

She had *not* lied about the whiskey.

The shit was… *transcendent.*

Which is why we were both on our second one.

"So… where *do* I stand for you? Am I just a beautiful woman to provide the pleasant scenery and stimulating conversation while you enjoy a nice meal, or are we testing the waters for more?"

My eyes widened a little, surprised at how straightforward the question was. Most women, in my experience, were afraid to ask a question like that, because most men were afraid to give an upfront, honest answer. I did *not* share my brethren's leeriness of the truth, partially because I understood this situation for what it was.

Neither of us was desperate.

We were whole.

We didn't *need* this situation, and we were both willing to walk away – there was no urge to fit the square peg of what we wanted into the round hole of what was immediately available.

"It's complicated," I admitted, looking her right in the eyes. "You are… *incredibly* attractive. You're smart, you're successful, you seem mentally stable so far," I teased, making her laugh. "Any man would jump at the chance to be in my shoes."

She leaned in, propping her elbows on the table. "Wait, don't tell me yet. Let me guess what the *but* is… hmmm… with you… I think there's probably someone else. Someone who is just waiting for you to choose them – and *only* them – over all the other beautiful women in the world. But you're not ready to commit."

"You're halfway there," I chuckled. "Or maybe just a quarter. Hell, I don't even know. I told you it was complicated. She's doesn't want to commit to me either though."

"Oh so that's perfect then," Leya gushed. "Assuming she's fine with you dating other people?"

I scoffed. "She actively encourages it."

"Sounds like my kinda woman. And… my kinda complicated."

My eyebrows lifted. "What does that mean?"

"Sex pact," she said, so matter-of-factly that it almost sounded like a completely normal thing.

"Excuse me?"

She took another long drink, then nodded. "You heard me right, Nate. I'm twenty-nine years old – I have a pact with my best friend that if we're both single when we're thirty, we will, for one night, fuck each other's brains out. His ass is *fine*. I can't mess around and get too involved with someone and end up missing my chance."

"I'm sorry... *what*?"

"I mean... I guess there *is* the fact that I've secretly been in love with him since seventh grade. I'm hoping that if I blow his mind in bed, he'll start seeing me differently. And he'll fuck me again... and again... and then we'll get married. But in the meantime... mama has needs. Which is where *you* come in."

I frowned. "Are you... are you serious right now?"

"*Hell* no," Leya laughed, finally breaking from her serious expression to shake her head. "I really had you going there for a minute, didn't I?"

"Uh, yeah, I'd say so," I chuckled. "What the hell was that?"

"Not gonna lie – I'm a little tipsy right now, and I just felt like being silly, but dude – do you know how many times I've told a variation of that story, just to get someone off my back? *Why don't you settle down, Leya, get a husband! Don't you know you have limited time to have kids? Why don't you find something serious? I feel so bad, you have everything except a family? Don't you know life isn't complete without that?*" She waved a hand as if she was dismissing all of that, and finished her drink. "Don't you know you can *suck my dick*, how about that?!" Her eyes got big, and locked with mine. "Oh my God – I do *not* have an actual dick, and I'll even let you check. The dick I want to offer people who say such things to me is *only* metaphorical."

I laughed at that, clapping a hand to my chest as I sat back, shaking my head. "No worries – I have a twin sister with a similar mouth, and she works in the sports industry too. Trust me, I've heard her offer that nonexistent dick plenty of times."

"Okay so please tell her thank you on my behalf, for making me seem a little less… how did you *so* politely phrase it… mentally unstable. That was it."

"I will make sure to pass it along. But… yeah, people can get very… aggressive about the whole marriage and kids thing. It's right for some people, and I have much respect for it, but… I'm just not built for it, I don't think."

"Well I can drink to *that*," she concurred, raising a glass that was… empty. "Oh, shit – I *would* drink to that, if there was anything here."

"Would you like another?" I asked, but she'd already started shaking her head before the question was fully off my lips.

"No, two is my *firm* limit when I'm out alone with strange men."

I drew my head back. "Damn, I'm strange now?"

"Let me rephrase," she grinned. "My rule is that I do not partake in more than two alcoholic beverages when I am on dates with men who I am not intimately acquainted with yet, and that does *not* mean sex."

"So you're saying that there are men who you date romantically, but there's no sex… or there's just no sex *yet*?"

"Actually… the first. We simply enjoy each other's company – not as friends, because there is a definite attraction, and romantic interest, but… no sex. Is that what you'd like to pursue with me?"

"*Hell* no," I answered immediately, laughing at *that* shit. I wasn't at all opposed to female friends, by any means, but sexless dating was a fat ass no for *me*.

Leya ran her tongue over her lips as they spread into a sly smirk. "Yet another thing I'd drink to."

"Shouldn't have finished so fast."

"Funny, I've said those exact words before putting a man out of my bed. You've never heard those words before, have you? Because if so… we could probably save ourselves a little time."

I laughed. "No. Not at all. *Never* heard that complaint."

"Not even from your… complication?"

"*Never*. Sex was never an issue."

"Then why not commit?"

"Because it's not what I see for my life," I told her. "I thought we already established this part of the conversation?"

"We *have*, it's just… I actually *believe* you, when you say it," she mused, in disbelief. "Most men… they claim they're on the same page, claim they're okay with dating. But what they *really* mean is that they want to date me, and four other women – conservatively – but want *me* – and the other women – to only date *them*."

I nodded. "Yeah, sounds familiar. I used to *be* that guy, until I realized… the "ideal" that I imagine has to be approached from equal footing. Either I'm free to entertain people, and so are you. Or we're both only entertaining each other. And with the way I work, my social life, all that… hell, I may only want to see someone once every two weeks. But that doesn't work for everyone."

"Exactly. I have to sit here lonely for three weeks while you're away on business or whatever the hell? *Why?*"

I sat back, staring at her. "Goddamn, we really are on the same page."

"It's fate," she laughed. "If Landon and Ty had never started their doomed to fail affair, you and I may have never crossed paths."

"But here we are."

She grinned. "Yes. Here we are. Or… we could be upstairs. In a room. Getting better acquainted?" she said, eyebrow raised.

Of course I knew what she was saying, easily picked up on the innuendo, but…

Shit.

Barging in out of nowhere, thoughts of Sloane appeared.

Had she made it home safe?

Was she feeling okay after attending the party?

Did she eat?

Did she take her meds?

And that's why, when it came to Leya, I'd had to be transparent about the fact that shit was complicated – even when it seemed like she was perfectly on board with the same type of informal, unorthodox arrangement I wanted.

The same type Sloane insisted wasn't going to be enough.

"Actually," I spoke up, reaching for her hand. "I prefer to be better acquainted before we get *that* well acquainted. Just a personal preference."

A genuine smile reached all the way up to her eyes. "A preference I absolutely respect… and honestly admire." She scooted closer to me in the booth. "It honestly makes me like you more. I *love* it when a man isn't all easy, putting out on the first night like a *whore*," she teased, and I chuckled.

"That's right. Gotta work for *this* dick."

She bit down on her lip as she looked at me. "You are just… I'm going to enjoy this."

"I wouldn't have it any other way."

"Where were you this morning? I had to do my old lady shuffle all by myself. I should get a puppy, like the doctor suggested. – SB"

"Wait now, what is this? Are you admitting to enjoying my company in the mornings? Oh my God. Wow."

"Don't get ahead of yourself. I've grown accustomed. Not the same thing as "enjoying". – SB"

"Whatever you have to tell yourself. To answer your question – had a late night, which practically forced a late morning."

"A late night… with Leya? – SB"

For some reason, that text made me frown as I jogged up the steps to my childhood home, after spending an unreasonable fare to get all the way out here. Not because of Sloane's insistence on pushing her Leya agenda, but because of what that text was missing.

I waited a second before I approached the door, looking at my phone expecting a follow-up. I knew Sloane, knew how that big brain of hers worked, knew her humor and unfiltered mouth. *Oh, you must have been laid up in Leya's pussy all night, huh?* Or *Why are you texting me when there's new booty beside you?*

Those were the kind of responses I would expect, after the perfect lead-in I'd given her to tease me about it.

I shook my head.

She's probably just tired.

"Yes, we had drinks. Just drinks."

I didn't know why I felt the need to clarify that.

Well... I *did* know, but still.

Sloane had made her position clear, and I wasn't typically in the business of trying to change a woman's mind about *shit*. My concern for her – caring for her health, protecting her privacy, all of that... none of it was about getting an "in" with her, it was about a genuine desire to help a friend.

I wanted her though.

Wanted her *badly*.

And if seeing that I was more than just some spoiled playboy was going to be the thing that turned the situation in my favor, well... my father didn't raise a damn fool.

"Ah. Drinks. I only barely remember the taste of wine... - SB"

I chuckled at that, hearing it in her voice. Before I could respond though, the front door swung open and my father stepped out, with his bag of golf clubs on his shoulder.

"Just the man I need to talk to," he said, greeting me with a hug. "Walk with me, son." He motioned to his Bentley, already pulled into the driveway. "You coming to join me on the course today?"

I shook my head, following him down to the car. "No sir, not today. Just came to retrieve my car actually."

"That's right," he nodded. "You snuck out of here last night with Landon, and two beautiful young women." *Of course he knew.* "So tell me about her. Or was this just some one-night thing?"

I chuckled. "Definitely not that, but… also nothing to tell you about. It's not serious."

"Perhaps it *could* be though," he suggested. "You *do* know that one woman's company is good for more than a week at a time?"

Ah, fuck.

"Here we go with this again, huh?" I asked. "Yes, of course, women are valuable beyond what's between their legs. I'm aware."

My father chuckled, raising his hands. "Testy about the topic, are we?"

I blew out a sigh. "Sorry. But yes. Everybody is in my ear about settling down, wife, children, blah, blah, *blah.* I'm not interested. Maybe that will change, maybe it won't, but for now… can we talk about *anything* else?"

My father met my gaze for a moment, then nodded. "Sure – let's talk football. Sloane Brooks – I've heard a bit of feedback that she's been reserved as of late. She works with your players. Have you seen anything, heard anything?"

I think low energy is standard operating procedure after a goddamn heart attack.

"It's probably just because she's not out on the field – that's where she seems to thrive most. I mean… there's not a lot for her to do right now, is there? These couple of weeks, they're mostly working with the trainers, so maybe she's just bored?"

Of course I was omitting the whole *three days in the hospital* thing, but it wasn't my business to tell – especially when I found out Sloane had opted against the team health insurance when she signed her job contract, choosing to continue paying for it herself, like she had since the early, unstable days of her semi-pro career. The *Kings* weren't paying for it, so it wasn't the *Kings* business, as long as she was performing the job she was hired for – her words.

And… I couldn't disagree.

My father nodded. "Yes, possibly. We'll see how things look for minicamp in a few weeks. You sure that new rookie hasn't already worn her out?"

"Amare?" I asked, then shook my head when he confirmed. "Nah. I haven't gotten complaints from or about either of them, not since the first incident. They're settling in, both of them."

At that, my father snorted. "A little *too* well, on Mr. Amare's part. Speaking of who left the party with who, our rookie left with the *wrong* one."

My eyebrow lifted. "Who?"

"Parker."

"Seriously?" I asked, tipping my head. I had *not* expected that, but still… "What's the problem though? Parker and Rutledge are both adults, so…?"

His eyes narrowed. "The last thing she needs is… corrupting."

"You mean *further* corrupting?" I corrected. "She's a healthy, beautiful young woman, saddled to a dying man two decades older than her."

"I'm well aware." His nostrils flared. He never liked being reminded of the fucked-up situation his friend had placed Parker in. "Which is why I'm trying to make sure she's not going from one valley into another with this immature *kid.* You need to talk to him."

I shook my head. "All due respect, I'm not saying anything to him about who he takes home, as long as he's not out here making babies like it's a trend. They're *adults* – unless you tell me you're concerned he's smacking her around or something, it is *not* my business. I was hired for a job – ensuring player success. Managing another man's dick really isn't part of it."

My father let out a deep sigh. The mutual respect between us ran thick, but it wasn't going to influence me into unwarranted intervention in my player's personal life – *especially* not on behalf of fucking Jimmy Wright.

"You know... you're right, son. This is a personal matter, and I shouldn't ask you to get involved." He extended a hand to me, and I took it, easily, because there was no beef – would never *be* any beef – between me and my father, not over something that wasn't a family matter. Still gripping my hand, he pulled me in. "I still want you to settle down and start working on my grandchildren though."

"Come *on*, man!" I laughed, pulling back. "What's up with you, are you hassling me about grandkids because my mother isn't around to do it?"

He shrugged. "Somebody has to!"

We said our goodbyes and moved on, him to his Sunday afternoon golf, me to… nothing. I didn't have plans. But as I climbed into my car, I remembered the text I hadn't responded to yet, from Sloane.

I pulled my phone out, intending to go straight to it, but was sidetracked by a different text.

From Leya.

It had been nearly two in the morning before we left the bar at Veil, *separately*. I'd been serious about my desire to know her better before we jumped right into sex. Maybe I wasn't ready to "settle down" in the traditional sense, but my days of sleeping with women I barely knew were over.

I liked Leya though.

Well enough that her invitation to lunch was decidedly tempting.

But… as I'd told her, my own definition of my situation with Sloane was… complicated. Maybe she didn't think I was old enough, or mature enough, to fulfill what she was looking for, and again – I didn't have any sort of goal to change her mind. The fact was that I enjoyed her, and wanted to be around her, so until that desire faded, any time I had a choice…

I was *going* to choose Sloane.

But I wasn't a fool.

Before I declined Leya's invitation, I shot Sloane a text, offering to bring lunch to *her*. I was glad to get an almost immediate response that it was fine, since her daughter was expected to be out all day, with her friends.

After I hit Leya back, I pulled out of the driveway, chuckling to myself at how annoyed I'd been about where Sloane lived at first. A good twenty minutes out of the city, gated subdivision, and enough space between houses to fit two more houses.

I understood the value of that privacy now.

Four years of sneaking around had taught me well enough to appreciate *not* seeing neighbors when you were coming in and out. And the fact that she was the one with space for us to handle our business without any real fear of detection gave *me* the opportunity to see her relaxed, and comfortable – she was *home*.

Hell… I was comfortable there now too.

Maybe a little too comfortable.

I pushed all that aside though, focusing on the here and now. Even though I hated the circumstances, this was the most consistently I'd *ever* been able to spend time with Sloane, especially without sex even being involved.

I'd be damn if I'd waste these moments waiting for the other shoe to drop.

Eight

June 2018

"*Yes* Johnson! Looking *good*!" I raised my hands high, clapping for my star wide receiver as he easily switched direction at the last minute to catch a pass. "*Beautiful* footwork!"

I wasn't just gassing him up – there was a *reason* Jordan Johnson was the face of the franchise, and it certainly wasn't his good looks.

He could catch the hell out of a football.

Any football, apparently, and he was still moving with the same speed that had earned him his "*The Flash*" nickname. I grinned as he took off down the field – showing off, honestly, since it was the last day of mandatory minicamp. Everybody was relaxed, settling into the flow of being a team again coming from offseason.

I just hoped they wouldn't lose too much of this feeling before shit got *real*, in training camp.

With minicamp, it was mostly about figuring out the bare bones of what these guys could do. They were in jerseys and shorts, helmets. Knee and elbow pads if necessary. Other than that, all the padding and stuff was put away, since the mandatory minicamp held a no live contact restriction. We could run drills, just to get everybody reacquainted with the essentials, but the last thing we needed was a player getting hurt before we even made it to July.

Especially not Johnson.

As well as he was doing, I couldn't help noticing that he was favoring one side when he caught the ball. There was nothing particularly wrong with having a "good side", but he was putting in extra work to avoid catching on his left.

The same side he'd had a rotator cuff repair on a few years ago.

"Hey, let me talk to you a second," I called to him, stepping to the side so we could speak privately.

"What it do, Coach B?" he asked, showing off his dimples as he flashed his signature smile. "You want to know if I'll appear in the documentary they're gonna make about your life, right? You know I will. I'll even pose with you for the front cover."

I laughed. "Whatever, Johnson. Don't speak that type of evil over me."

He frowned. "First female coach for the Kings, and you don't want the fanfare?"

"I want to coach football," I told him, shaking my head. "That's my focus right now, a great season. If I get approached *after* that... I might be open."

"That's what I'm talking about," he said, extending a fist to bump mine. "You know the media is coming for you once the season starts though, right? Everybody has been all excited about the NBA finals, now they're all wrapped up in where Lebron is going. But *real* soon…"

I nodded. "Yes, I know," I told him, my tone much calmer than I felt about that situation. This was the "boring" time of year, but things were ramping up, and he was right – football was about to have all the attention. Increased scrutiny of my hiring was going to come with it.

But I'd assess that bridge when I came to it.

"For now, I want to understand why you're shying away from fully engaging your left side," I spoke, letting him know it was time to get serious. "There something you need to tell me?"

He looked away, avoiding my eyes as he shrugged. "Trainers, team doctors say I'm good to go. Ready to fuck up the field for another season."

I moved, getting back in front of his gaze. "I didn't ask you that. I don't care what they say. I care about how *you* feel. Is that shoulder giving you trouble?"

For a second, he didn't respond, then his eyes narrowed as they settled on something away from me. *Again.* "It's obvious like that?"

"To most people, no. You look great out there. To me… I'm going to take notice when my star is doing more than he needs to."

He shook his head. "It's just… a little bit of a twinge. A little more than I'm used to. Not bad. Not enough to bring up. I just…"

"Don't want to make it worse," I nodded. "I get it."

"It'll be fine by training camp," he said, confidently. Like he was trying to convince me. "I'm going to rest it."

"I'm sure you will."

"You writing this down? Telling Underwood?"

I raised an eyebrow. "Everything we talk about isn't Underwood's business. You stop performing? *Then* it's his business. You understand me?"

He gave me a little salute with two fingers. "Aye-aye, captain." He started to turn away, then looked back. "I appreciate it."

"I appreciate your honesty," I countered. "Go refuel." He turned again to leave, but once he was a few feet away, I stopped him. "Hey – *stay off that shoulder*. Let your wife do the work on the honeymoon, if you get my drift," I warned him, completely serious even if my tone said different.

He laughed at my warning, giving me a deep nod. "Can you write that on a note for me? *Jordan is excused from all activities except getting his dick ro—*"

"If you don't get the fuck outta here," I laughed, sending him off. Once I was done with him, I called out to Amare as he was heading inside. "You *killed* it this week Amare!" I shouted, prompting a shocked scowl at first, and then a nod of acknowledgment before he jogged off. That attitude still needed a lot of work, but as long as he took direction and performed – all I ever asked, and what he'd *done* this week – we'd get along just fine.

Or not.

Either way, we'd do our jobs.

As I headed in myself, Coach Underwood stopped me, pulling me aside similarly to what I'd done to Jordan.

"You feeling okay Brooks?" he asked, speaking quietly as the other players and coaches passed us, heading to the locker room and showers.

I nodded. "Yeah. Why, what's up? I do something wrong?"

"No, not at all. It's just that during the rookie minicamp, you were all over the place out there, running routes and showing everybody up with the footwork… you're kinda quiet now though. One of the guys say something, or…?"

"What? *No*," I frowned, shaking my head. "No, not at all. I… have just had a lot on my mind. Garrett and I are meeting this afternoon to buy Madison a car, and—"

Underwood whistled. "Say no more. I remember those days, and do not miss them at all. Godspeed and good luck to you," he chuckled, leaving me to speak to a couple of players who were waiting to talk to him.

My shoulders sank in relief at how easily he'd let me slide, especially since what I said wasn't even a real answer to what he'd asked about. But, I'd taken a tip from Nate's jar, saying something that wasn't exactly the truth at hand, but wasn't a lie either.

Obviously, his way worked.

While everyone was occupied, I slipped away to head to my office. I really *did* have plans to meet up with Garrett at a Volkswagen dealership today – the midpoint we'd come to after my absolute refusal to get on board with buying our sixteen-year-old a luxury car.

One of us had to be willing to keep her firmly tethered to the realm of regular people.

As I headed out of the office, my phone buzzed, notifying me of a new text received. I knew before even looking at it that it would be Nate, and that knowledge brought a smile to my face.

He was *really* committed to this.

That promise he'd made to look after me whether I liked it or not seemed to constantly be at the forefront of his mind. Initially, it had been a source of frustration, but almost three weeks after the heart attack… I'd gotten pretty used to his constant presence, even when it wasn't physical.

And I… didn't hate it.

I didn't hate it at all.

I actually… kinda liked it?

"You made it through minicamp… how do you feel? – NR."
"Relieved."

That was an understatement.

I'd been feeling a lot better since leaving the hospital, but still nowhere near 100% - which is why it hadn't gone beyond notice that there was something different about me.

There weren't any words to describe how glad I was that after this, the players were off for a month until training camp. That meant *I* wasn't expected to do any running, jumping, catching, anything like that myself, which gave me more time to recover.

I just wasn't sure another six weeks was enough to get me to a place where I was active enough to not arouse suspicion during training camp.

I hadn't mentioned *that* to my doctor yet.

I stowed my phone in my purse, and headed down the hall, deciding to skip the rowdy celebration that would be happening soon in the dining area. Underwood knew I had plans, and my players were too busy to notice if I wasn't there.

This downtime was my opportunity to enjoy my daughter, and rest, before the chaos of the season. It was imperative that I did it now, while I had the chance.

Jordan's shoulder wasn't the only thing I needed to be fine by the time we started training camp.

"Remember ours?"

Instead of verbally responding to Garrett's question, I simply smiled, keeping my eyes glued to the happy couple as they embarked on their first dance.

It was a *beautiful* night for a wedding. The heat of summer hadn't quite kicked in yet, so the air was crisp, but not cold – warm enough for bare arms and shoulders without breaking a sweat.

I'd raised an eyebrow at the *backyard wedding* descriptor on Jordan and Cole's quirky invitation – not out of judgment, but surprise. With Cole's personality, I'd expected a very formal, stuffy affair, with everything *just so.*

Well… everything was still *just so*, but there was nothing stuffy about the beautiful sheer canopies set up in Eli Richardson's expansive backyard, the lanterns and string lights creating a beautiful warm glow, the shouts of laughter coming from the dance floor, the

Earth, Wind, and Fire pumping from the speakers now that the "official" first dance was over.

I understood *exactly* why Garrett was feeling nostalgic.

"What exactly makes you think I'm interested in traveling down memory lane with you?" I quietly fussed, even though it was a direct contrast with how I felt.

He grinned as he leaned in. "Come on, Sloane. *It's a wedding.* You telling me it doesn't bring back good memories for you?"

"Of course it does," I admitted. "But those memories lead into memories of how we ended, and I get over my nostalgia pretty quickly."

Instead of being shamed by my words, he just grinned harder. "You keep bringing that up, and if I didn't know better I'd think you were trying to remind yourself you're not supposed to like me. Like you *really* want to be all about me, but then you have to catch yourself."

"Okay, no more liquor for you," I told him, pulling away his third *Mauve* and coke. "It's making you delirious."

He shook his head. "No, I think I see things quite clearly. You've been different lately. *Off.*"

"And you think it's because I'm… what, pining for you?"

Garrett laughed. "Okay. So maybe not that. Then what?"

"Then nothing. I started a stressful new job, we bought our teenager a car, and my ex-husband suddenly wants back in my panties – I have a lot going on."

He nodded, and remained quiet for a moment before he grabbed my hand. "What if I told you I was trying to get into more than your panties?"

"I would wonder what the hell was going on with you? Are you sick? Dying or something?" He laughed at that, but something about it was off enough that it made my eyebrows rise in alarm. "Do *not* play with me. Are you?"

"No, I'm not *dying*, woman," he laughed. "But… this Langston kid. His father. When I found out about that, it was… sobering. He's the same age as us!"

I frowned. "Who is *us*? Nigga you're knocking on fifty *by yourself*, okay?"

"Damn, that's how you do me?"

"*Mmmhmm* old man," I teased. "But in seriousness… I get it. Nothing like something to remind you that no matter how many miles you run to stay active, or cigars you turn down, or salads you eat… you're not invincible. This body is as temporary as everything else in the world."

"So you get me then."

I smiled, meeting his gaze. "Of course. *That* was never our problem."

"Then what the hell *is*?" he insisted, the mood suddenly shifting as he pulled my chair closer to his, then looked around. "You *know* how good we were together, Sloane. Why don't we stop these games?"

"This isn't a *game*. And it's *not* a conversation to be had in public, either," I warned, even though no one was paying any attention to us. "We're here to celebrate Jordan and Nicole – *not* for you to pitch yourself to me."

He held up his hands. "You're right. *You're right*." He sat back a bit, looking defeated. As much as I felt a little bad about blowing him off, I had to remind myself that this was all part of the Garrett charm, the reason I'd gotten my heart wrapped up in the first place.

He was right.

We *were* good together.

We were so, *so* good together, and that's why it had been such a hard to believe blow when I *first* found out he was cheating on me. I talked myself out of what I knew was the truth, in favor of having a "whole" family. Time after time I ignored it, and endured the embarrassment, and swallowed the hurt, until I just… I got *tired.*

Tired of always being the one to try to make it right, when *I* wasn't the one doing wrong.

Garrett hurt me.

Badly.

The only reason I was able to sit in his face now – hell, enjoy his company at all – was because we were so far removed from it now. Time and therapy had healed those wounds, and it would be silly of me to risk a repeat injury.

Another blow to the heart.

Maybe Garrett *was* a changed man, maybe he *was* sincere.

Maybe he shouldn't have fucked up a good thing when he had it.

"Dance with me," he said, more of a demand than a request, since he stood and offered his hand before I could answer. He whistled when I stood, like he hadn't already been doling out compliments left and right all night for the wine-colored cocktail dress I'd worn. I rolled my eyes, but accepted his hand to lead me to the dance floor, just as the DJ was calling for all the "couples".

"Happy accident," Garrett quipped when I frowned at his timing, knowing what our presence on the dance floor implied. I quickly got over any frustration when my eyes landed on a "couple" a few feet away from us.

Nate.

With Leya.

Damn, she's even finer in person.

She was a beautiful woman in those pictures I'd seen, but now, live and in color, I could see even more clearly what attracted Nate to her. As a couple, they were absolutely striking, and I... wanted to be happy about that.

I was *supposed* to be happy about that.

Instead, it made me feel a little sick to my stomach.

Before it could seem like I was staring, I turned my full attention back to Garrett, tuning in to whatever he was talking about as we danced.

Well... halfway tuning in.

In reality, I just nodded along, while I tried to sort through and figure out the baffling feeling I was experiencing.

"Excuse me? May I?"

The sound of Nate's voice snatched me from my thoughts, just in time to take note of the exchange taking place. Garrett didn't appear particularly *thrilled* about it, but he agreed to Nate's request of dancing with me as the DJ switched songs.

I was too busy trying to hide the fact that I was flustered to be annoyed by him asking Garrett's permission instead of mine. And by the time Nate's hands were settled onto my hips, it felt too much like right for me to be mad at all.

"What the hell are you doing?" I asked, keeping my voice low enough for the conversation to remain just between us. Dancing with someone at a wedding was an innocent-enough interaction, but the fact that I had to force myself to keep distance between us, fighting my body's natural gravitation to him, presented... a complication.

He grinned. "Dancing with the *Kings'* newest position coach. Is that a problem?"

"It might be for your date."

"Might be for *yours* too. He keeps looking over here like he wants me to meet him in the parking lot for a showdown."

I shook my head. I didn't even have to look to know it was true. "Don't mind him. He seems to have forgotten again that I'm his *ex*-wife."

"Is he trying to make you his *next* wife too?"

"Maybe. Are you trying to make Leya your first?"

Nate smirked about that. "Not remotely. *You* sure seem hell-bent on it though."

"No I'm not," I defended. "I'm just... I want you to be happy, Nate. That's all it's ever been."

"Then let's stop talking about Leya, and Garrett, and just enjoy our dance." He leaned in, just long enough to speak into my ear. "Just think... none of these people know how intimately familiar I am with the taste of your pussy. That's a little exciting, isn't it?"

Ugh.

He had no idea.

As of late, I'd been plagued with vivid dreams of Nate and me, doing filthy things in inappropriate places, not limited to my office, *his* office, the locker room, the bleachers, the fifty-yard line, and...

countless others. In all of them, I was jolted awake just before the point of orgasm, which left me more than a little frustrated.

Especially since I had no outlet *for* that frustration.

A psychologist would probably say that the dreams were based on my current, baseless fear that having an orgasm would make my heart explode – hence, the whole waking-up-before-it-happened thing. *I* would say that the psychologist wasn't the one taking the risk, so they could shut the fuck up.

Of course I missed sex, of course I missed orgasms, but neither of those things erased the fear. When I came, I came *hard*, and half the time, it *did* feel like my heart was stopping.

I was *not* trying to become a case study.

So, I squirmed a little in his arms, trying to *not* be affected by his warmth, and his smell, and his touch.

"Glad to know I've made such an impression on you," I told him, trying to maintain at least *some* power in this whole thing. I was past relieved when the song ended and I could step back, putting some real distance between us.

"Enjoy the wedding, Ms. Brooks."

I nodded. "You do the same."

I couldn't get away from Nate fast enough, and was in no hurry to get back to Garrett either. What was it about tonight that had these men getting under my skin?

When I got stopped by Wil Cunningham, postponing my return to Garrett's side, I could've kissed her – that's just how glad I was for the delay.

"I have been hoping to run into you," she gushed, pulling me into a hug. "Congratulations on the new job!"

I returned her warm smile with one of my own, and hugged her right back. I *loved* this young woman like she was my own – well, if I actually knew her personally – had rooted for her Olympic triumphs, watched her and Ramsey's sports show religiously, and cried like a baby over the mini-movie they'd released afterward from their own ultra-private wedding ceremony in Bali. *Especially* the fact that they'd been planning a bigger, later wedding, but then decided they didn't want to wait to call each other husband and wife.

It was *beautiful.*

"Thank you so much," I told her. "I'm excited to be part of the *Kings* organization."

"And they're lucky as hell to have you… which is what I wanted to speak to you about. Your hiring hasn't really hit the news cycle yet… how about you and I change that?"

Immediately, I shook my head. "Not before the season starts. Not before training camp," I said. "I don't need the circus around me any sooner than I absolutely *have* to."

"And I totally understand that," Wil assured me. "But this is… *monumental.* So many of these outlets are going to… drop the ball, honestly. Make it about how the *Kings* did you some favor, how BSU "took a chance" on you, and all that bullshit. You give *me* an exclusive interview for my show, and I'm going to tell the right story – how you're a fucking badass who makes every team you touch better than they were before you arrived. Not about how you manage to get things done despite being a woman, but about how you get shit done *because* you are a helluva woman."

"Damn, that sounds like an interview I want to watch," I laughed. "But seriously, you don't have to pitch me, Wil. I love your work, love what you do. I'd be honored to sit down for an exclusive with you. *After* training camp."

Her smile spread even wider. "*Excellent. I will be in touch to work out the details*," she assured, before we parted ways. I was lucky enough that after Wil moved on, I found a few other conversations to keep me occupied, among the coaches, players, and other people I knew there at the wedding – including Jordan and his new bride. On my way to finally stop avoiding Garrett, I ran across a sight that made me raise my eyebrows.

Rutledge Amare, with one of those media-hungry Erceg sisters – which one I couldn't tell – on his arm.

Damn.

Just when I was thinking maybe he *was* interested in more than the glitz and glam that came with the fame of being in the pro league.

"You ready to head out?"

I jumped a little as Garrett snaked his arm around my waist, approaching me from behind. Once I knew it was him though, I relaxed enough to nod.

"Yes, I am."

I was tired, honestly, and the reception was starting to wind down. I wasn't interested in the bouquet toss, and all the toasts had already been given, so there was nothing keeping me from making my way to my bed for some much-needed rest.

Alone.

Back at the house though, Garrett seemed to have other plans, stepping into the house with me once I had the door unlocked.

"What do you think you're doing?" I asked him, stopping in the entryway.

He shrugged. "Just making sure you got in safely before I said goodnight, that's all."

"Mmmhmmm."

"Don't *mmmhmm* me," he laughed. "Thank you for inviting me to come with you tonight."

"You're welcome. But don't read into it. I just didn't want to be there alone."

Garrett twisted his mouth. "I know you're not trying to tell me you don't have other men sniffing around. We've been divorced what… five years now? Your appetite is *too* big for you to have not indulged."

"I never said either of those things – that other men don't want me, *or* that I haven't indulged."

"Right, cause you made sure I knew I wasn't the best dick you'd ever had anymore."

I raised a finger. "Uh, in fairness, *you* walked yourself right into that one."

He laughed. "Yeah, I did. In seriousness though… you're not dating anybody?"

"Formally? No. Just enjoying being a single woman. Coming and going as I please. Especially now that Madison is older, spending the night with friends and all that now. I can have a big bowl of fruit and walk around naked for the rest of the night if I want to."

Garrett perked up. "I mean, you can go ahead and get that way right now if you want to."

"The *whole* point is to be by myself," I laughed. "No company. Including *you*."

He scoffed. "Yeah, well, you just make sure you put on a robe before you answer the door – especially since that lil' Nate nigga likes to "stop by" early as hell in the mornings to "check on his players". He's not fooling anybody."

"What are you talking about?" I asked, hoping my voice didn't relay the sudden panic I felt.

"I knew he looked familiar to me – beyond him and his sister being the liaisons for the some of the players I've managed before. He went to BSU, didn't he? I remember seeing him thirsting after you when you first started coaching there. And then a few years after that, he was all on social media calling you his *Woman Crush Wednesday* – and you were still my wife. Blatant violation. Disrespectful."

I laughed. "It is *beyond* rich for you to accuse *anyone* of disrespecting our marriage."

"I'm just *saying*. I saw how he looked at you tonight, saw where his hands were."

"Yes, on my *waist*," I defended, rolling my eyes. "Besides, did you not see the pretty young thing he had on his arm? That man is not messed up about me!"

Garrett chuckled. "I'm *telling* you, Sloane. I *know* men. He would've shoved that *pretty young thing* in front of a moving train to get to you."

"You're exaggerating. So he thinks I'm attractive? *And*? It doesn't mean he's going to pass up a woman fifteen years younger than me, whose breasts are still where they started."

"It's not even about that, though," he said. "Do you look the same as you did when you were twenty, or thirty? No, and there's nothing wrong with that. You still, *easily* can stand next to a woman like that and outshine, not because you can still compete, but because you don't *have* to. You've *been* fine, and you're *still* fine, and you're in a category by yourself. If you think that man isn't trying to get between your legs, you are *crazy*."

I sighed. "Then I guess it's a good thing the shop is currently closed. Good night, Garrett."

Laughing, he approached me again to wrap me in his arms. "Good night, Sloane," he responded, giving me his usual forehead kiss. But then… he didn't pull away. He kissed my temple, then my jaw, and even though I knew it was coming, and had plenty of time to stop it… I didn't.

Maybe it was the compliments, or the horniness I'd been fighting. Maybe it was the familiarity, the comfort of him being someone I'd known for *so* long.

Maybe it was seeing Nate with Leya.

Maybe it was the magic of the wedding.

Whatever it was, when Garrett's lips pressed against mine, I didn't fight it. When his tongue slipped into my mouth, I welcomed it. When his hands slid down, gripping my ass, pulling me closer, I moaned over how good it felt.

When I felt his dick pressed against my stomach, thick and heavy, it snapped me back to reality.

Sloane, what the hell are you doing?

"You have to leave," I told him, suddenly pulling back, so fast that I almost tripped over my own feet in my heels.

Garrett easily caught me, holding me against him until I was on steady ground, then letting me go. He didn't argue, didn't press his case. He just… nodded.

"Good night."

I didn't feel like I was breathing well again until he'd closed the door behind him, and I was there immediately to lock it. Literally and figuratively, the door between us *needed* to stay closed.

*I **know** that is not my goddamn doorbell.*

The only person I usually got up early for was Jesus, and I'd had every intention of taking a break from my bedside Baptist routine. It was Sunday – *perfect* – for sleeping in, especially after the long night before, with the wedding.

But whoever was at my door obviously didn't intend for that to happen.

I had a feeling of who it was, so I made him wait – for old time's sake. I went to the bathroom, washed my face, brushed my teeth, put on a robe, and *then* headed downstairs to find Nate sitting on my front porch, lounging, with a paper bag in his lap. When he saw me, he grinned and held up the bag.

"I brought breakfast."

My eyes narrowed. "Yeah, you'd *better* have brought a peace offering with you. It is eight in the morning, and I was sleeping. And *you* know the code to the keypad. You could have just come inside."

"Just in case you had company."

"I told you already, Madison spent the night with her bestie."

He nodded. "Yeah, but she *lives* here part-time, right? I said *company*."

"*Oh.* You mean of the male variety."

"I *mean* your ex-husband."

I rolled my eyes, motioning for him to get up from his seat. "I see you've lost your mind. Come inside before somebody sees you."

"From a half mile up the road?" he teased.

"Boy just *come*," I demanded, and he followed, even though he took his damn time. I was curious to see what was in that bag, and was excited to find it wasn't oatmeal – some bullshit he'd pulled on me before – and was, instead, healthy sweet potato waffles from a place he'd found for me near the *Kings'* facility. "Okay," I told him, greedily chewing a mouthful of goodness. "I forgive you for dropping by unannounced now. And for thinking I screwed my ex-husband last night."

He shook his head. "That's not *exactly* accurate. I felt like it was a possibility, based on him being all over you last night. Based on you being who you are. And looking like you look. And—"

"I get it, Nate. Everybody wants me, blah blah."

"Blah blah *nothing*," he chuckled.

"I see the prospect didn't stop you from popping by. What if Garrett had answered the door?"

"I was going to tell him I was here to have breakfast with you."

"You *wouldn't* have?"

"What the fuck else would I say?" he laughed. "Thinking about it now, this was probably pretty risky, huh?"

I nodded. "Ya think? But anyway… like I said. You're forgiven. But only because of these waffles. What happened, you had an early breakfast with Leya, thought about grabbing something for me after?"

"Not in the slightest. I dropped Leya off at home last night, then went to my own place, where I slept alone."

I stabbed another forkful of waffle. "So… you telling me you haven't sealed the deal with her yet?"

"There's no deal between she and I to seal. But if you're asking if we've had sex yet, the answer is no."

"*Why?*" I asked, before I could help myself.

Nate ran a hand over his head, letting out a sigh before he spoke again. "Honestly? Because it doesn't feel right. Leya is beautiful, and smart, and everything I said I wanted in a woman, but the shit doesn't feel right, because Leya is not *you*."

"Don't say that."

"Don't ask questions you can't handle the answers to."

My eyebrow shot up, and I put my fork down. "Can't handle? Excuse me?"

"Yes, Sloane, I said what I said." He dropped his own fork, turning to me. "For some reason, you *cannot* handle the fact that I want you. You always want to explain it away, brush it off, whatever. But there's no getting around it for me – yes, we're friends, absolutely. But I want you as more than that, and I want you as more than a lover too. You don't think I'm equipped to give you what you need, you're not ready to not be single, I *get* that. I accept it. And I'm not here trying to talk you out of it. Can you just… give me that same damn respect, of not trying to talk me out of what *I* want? You may be *a* coach, but you are not *mine*."

I swallowed hard, trying to give myself time to form a rebuttal that simply wouldn't materialize. Probably because he was right. Age difference aside, Nate was a grown man. I *shouldn't* be trying to tell him how to live his life.

I *wasn't* his coach.

I was his friend, and sometimes lover, and…

Fuck.

I'd had the nerve last night to feel a little jealous of a situation I'd pushed him into in the first place. Just like with Garrett, I didn't know what the hell I was doing, and the lines I'd carefully constructed over the years were getting a little *too* blurry for my tastes.

"I'm sorry," I admitted, giving him the respect of looking him in the eyes. "You're right. I shouldn't be trying to manage your life, or… *coach* you. You haven't asked for that, and more importantly… you don't like it. I should've listened."

He narrowed his eyes in surprise – he *obviously* hadn't expected me to say that. "Thank you. For listening."

"You're welcome. But…okay… if I'm giving up on trying to get you not to want me, or… whatever. Where does that leave us?"

He shrugged. "Not on the same page, honestly. But my thing is, that only becomes a problem when we start looking ahead, trying to fit things into a certain little box. When we aren't doing *that* – when we're just going with the flow – when I'm just meeting you for a walk in the morning, or bringing you breakfast, or you decide you want me to come through after work one night, or I hit you up to see if you want some company in the middle of the day… we're good. Why can't we just let it be good?"

"I… I guess we can. I guess you're right. But nothing you've said changes the fact that we work together, or our age difference, or what the media—"

"You're doing it again," he interrupted. "We've been doing this for *four* years. If we maybe need to be a little more discreet, a little more careful, that's fine. I'm not asking to hold your hand at the movies and share popcorn. I'm asking why what we've *been* doing needs to change? I mean I know the answer to that, I'm just—"

"I get what you're saying," I assured him. "And… I don't know where we'll go from here. But I enjoy your company. I enjoy… *you*. I do know *that*."

He grinned. "Even if we can't get on the same page anywhere else… *that* feeling is mutual."

When he leaned in, my mind briefly flashed to when Garrett had kissed me – and I kissed back – just the night before. A twinge of guilt hit me, but *all* feelings and thoughts were quickly overshadowed by the syrup-flavored kiss Nate drew me into.

Faintly, I registered the chime from the security alarm, indicating that the front door had opened, but it wasn't until Nate suddenly pulled back that it really hit the forefront of my mind that someone had come in.

Madison had come in.

She stood in the doorway, her face puffy and eyes red, obviously from crying. Her mouth was open in shock – probably at the sight of her mother in the kitchen, kissing a much younger man.

"I… am going to go," Nate said, his voice low. "So you can… you know."

I nodded. "Yes. Probably a good idea."

There was no overstating the awkwardness of the moment, so instead of trying to make it better, we simply didn't prolong it.

Nate got the hell out of there.

"So I guess you and dad are just… like really over?" she asked, finally speaking once I'd stood to approach her.

I swallowed a bit, then nodded. "Yes, baby. That ship has sailed. But it doesn't change how much either of us loves *you*. Okay?"

"I know *that*. It's just… I don't understand why people can't just… *stay together*."

After those words left her mouth, she dissolved into tears that were too bitter, too mournful, to be about me and Garrett. I wrapped my arms around her, giving her a few moments to cry it out before I led her into the living room, pulling her into a seat beside me on the couch.

"Baby… why are you crying? Did something happen?"

She nodded into my shoulder. "You know me and Isabella had the sleepover, right? Well, this morning we were hungry, and we'd promised her mom we wouldn't mess up the kitchen, so we decided to just go eat somewhere. Langston was there. With another girl. Some *twenty-year-old*, from his summer classes. He was all over her!"

My eyes went wide over the way she said *twenty*, like somebody's grandma had stolen her little boyfriend from her. I quickly tamped it down though, tightening my arm around her shoulder. "Oh *baby*. I'm so, *so* sorry. But honestly? It's his loss. If he did something like that, being all over another girl when you two are dating – *especially* to do it in public… he doesn't deserve you."

Sniffling, Madison looked up, meeting my eyes. "Is that why you don't want to get back together with daddy?"

I pushed out a little sigh, then nodded. "Yes. Garrett is great as your father, and I think he's a good person, but… he wasn't a good husband to me. There are some things that you give people second chances for – chances to fix. Betraying my trust the way he did – the way *Lang* did to you – I can't say that's something that's a simple mistake, or miscommunication. With some things, you just have to let that person go. It doesn't mean you hate them, or anything like that. Just that you won't allow yourself to be treated a certain way. You understand?"

She bobbed her head. "So… that guy… he's your boyfriend?"

Ah hell.

I'd been *very* adamant, all this time, about not exposing my daughter to Nate – or any man I wasn't serious about. For my privacy, and her safety, he was never here when she was, something that having informally shared custody with Garrett had easily facilitated. Her coming and going was managed by *us*, and we almost always announced ourselves with a phone call before we ever even climbed in the car.

That was changing now.

"Um… something like that," I told her, giving an honest answer. "Which means that… now that you have your car, and your license… even though you live here, and you are *always* welcome in this house, no matter what… You're going to have to start giving me a little warning. I don't want you walking in on what you saw today, which was just a kiss... or something worse."

"*Ewww*," she groaned. "Gross, mom."

"Exactly. Gross. You don't want to see that. So if you know I'm not expecting you here, you know I think you're at your dad's, or with a friend... just shoot me a text, call, something. Is that okay?"

She nodded. "Yeah."

"Are *you* okay?" I asked, shifting the conversation back to her. "That little boy had a funny shaped head anyway."

"*Mom!*"

"What?" I shrugged. "I'm just telling the truth. But anyway... hmm... this is your first breakup. We have to figure out your relationship mourning flavor?"

She frowned. "My what?"

"Sorry," I laughed. "We have to figure this out – are we binging ice cream and Netflix, or hot Cheetos and burning his pictures?"

"I don't have any physical pictures of him."

"Oh don't worry about that, we'll print them out," I assured, making her giggle. "*Or*... you know what? Maybe we can mind our waistlines, and our brains, and *not* destroy anything? Let's see if any animal shelters are open today. We should get a puppy."

Her eyes went *huge*. "*Really* mom?!" she gushed, and I nodded.

"Sure. Um... there's something else mommy needs to tell you... it's related to the reason for the puppy. But I don't want this, *or* the man, reaching your father. I'm not asking you to lie for me – *don't* lie for me, if you're outright asked. I want to tell him in my own time."

"What, mom? You're scaring me!"

I shook my head. "It's nothing to be scared about. But um… you know your grandmother, my mother, died of a heart attack, right?"

She nodded. "Yes."

"Well… it turns out that I have heart disease as well. But unlike her, I know about it, so it's being treated. And I'm okay, I'm mostly healthy. I just have medicines that I have to take every day, and I have to eat well, and exercise."

To my surprise, Madison nodded, not at all as freaked out as I thought she might be. "This group came and talked to us at school, about all of this. About keeping ourselves healthy, and looking out for our parents."

I smiled, reminded of the seminars I'd attended at her age – the dangers of sex and smoking. "That's good. So this isn't entirely new information."

"No. I knew how grandma died, before I was born, but you're an athlete, you're so healthy that I figured you didn't need any of that stuff. So I never said anything to you. It's not like you were gonna have a heart attack or something."

When I didn't say anything, her eyes got big again.

"…You've *had* a heart attack, haven't you?"

"Yes. It's how I found out about everything. And I didn't tell you, because I didn't want to worry you. I didn't want you to be scared, because your mommy is just fine… as long as she does what she's supposed to do. Okay?"

Madison nodded. "Okay. It's just… a lot to take in."

"I know. I *know*," I admitted. "And this is not how I imagined telling you, moments after your first heartbreak, but… I don't want to lie to you, Madison. My doctor recommended a dog because people with dogs tend to be more active, and dogs are good exercise companions. And if you get them trained, they can even help *if* – biiig, big if! – an emergency happens. But I think having something to take care of will help you right now too."

"I get it. And I'm glad you told me. I'd noticed you didn't seem like yourself, and I told Lang, and he said *his* mom got like that before they told him that his Dad had cancer. This is actually a lot less scary than what I had in my head."

"Oh, *baby*. I'm *so* sorry," I told her, pulling her into my arms again.

"It's okay, mom," she insisted. "I'm just happy to know what's going on."

"Okay. Okay," I nodded, pushing myself up. "Well, let's go then."

Madison took on a crazy expression as she looked at me, and when I glanced down, I couldn't do anything but laugh.

I was still in my robe, still in my headscarf, and my knees were reminiscent of powder.

"Okay, *I* am going to go get dressed," I told her, laughing. "And *then*… we're going to adopt a puppy!"

Nine

July 2018

Who the fuck decided to host training camp in the middle of nowhere?

I sat back in the chair at the desk, tossing my useless phone across it. Of course I understood, logically, *why* we had training camp at a mostly-empty campus in the Connecticut woods, instead of our own perfectly capable practice facility.

Minimal distractions, peaceful setting… and apparently, extremely shoddy internet access.

It was that last one that had me so annoyed.

I *needed* to see what was being said about me on the internet.

Training camp had started out just fine. Everybody was present, and focused, and doing their best – even my rookie, who hadn't given me a single problem. Things were *good.*

And then more people started to catch on.

Changing locations hadn't changed the fact that training camp was open for the public to observe, and the Kings fans were out in full force. I didn't mind the crowd – I had *plenty* of experience with tuning outside noise off. I would have been completely content to act like no one was there at all, if it weren't for the text from Madison late last night, that I hadn't seen until this morning.

Mom, everybody's talking about you.

Between the spotty service and inconsistent internet, I hadn't been able to get much more out of Mads and even less from social media, since I couldn't keep a strong enough signal for anything to load.

Shit.

Maybe it was for the best anyway.

We had to finish these last few days strong, and this was a distraction I could do without. So instead of wasting further time, I headed to breakfast to start another long ass day.

At six in the morning.

It was breakfast, then morning walkthrough and practice, and interviews, then lunch, then afternoon practice, then smiling and shaking hands with whichever corporate sponsor or VIP was observing that day, and scrimmaging, and losing a player to an injury, and then the end of practice, and then dinner.

Every damn day.

Of the players we'd brought to camp, eleven were wide receivers. Only six would be lucky enough to be recognized as a *King* once the season started. Some would be cut, some relegated to the practice squad, and it was a decision that was widely up to me.

As if I needed more pressure.

Stepping into the coach's dining hall, I acknowledged those who acknowledged me. No one had given me any direct grief – yet – but I'd be flat out stupid to think *every* man employed by this team appreciated a woman – a vocal Black one, at that – infiltrating a club they considered to be *boys only, no girls allowed.*

Luckily for me, I didn't give a fuck.

"Morning, Brooks," Underwood spoke as I joined him and a couple of coaching assistants at one of the tables. "Looks like you have a lot on your mind."

"Always," I told him, accepting a cup of decaf from one of the wait staff. "Only a few days left to give my recommendations for the team."

He nodded, chomping down on a thick slice of bacon. "Understandable. Who are you thinking?"

"Well," I sighed. "Johnson and Grant, obviously. And Amare. The kid is a star in the making."

"Okay, so who are the other three?"

"Uh... Hart. Kittredge. Sanchez. Filmore. Gage."

Underwood frowned. "That's five."

"So you understand my dilemma."

Laughing, he sat back in his chair. "Yes, I do. But hey – think about it like this – three more days for them to prove themselves, not for you to decide. The performance makes the decision, not you."

I nodded. "That's true. A great way to think about it."

"Besides – the bean counters might override you anyway. Could come down to who we can afford to keep."

"Which is bullshit politics."

"No, it's professional football," he teased. "Don't just drink that coffee – eat something. I want you working on some drills with those guys today. Sponsors want to see some catches."

I fought the urge to roll my eyes, and instead, simply nodded. He was right – *this* was football, even the bureaucratic bullshit that went on behind the scenes.

I just had to survive it.

"Somebody chasing you with a chainsaw, Grant?" I called out, frustrated as hell, but trying not to cuss his ass out too early.

So far, his antics had me barreling toward failing that mission.

Conventional wisdom suggested that it was wrong to have a favorite child, and even worse to just flat out not like one. Despite all that, if Terrence Grant were to have a sudden bout of amnesia, rendering all knowledge of his position and this team completely useless, but maintaining all other physical and mental capabilities… I wouldn't be mad at that.

At all.

He got on my *goddamn nerves.*

"What's the problem Coach B?" he asked, shuffling toward me with a wide grin – the kind that worked for the Jordan Johnsons of the world, but just looked irritatingly goofy on him.

"Did you forget what we're doing? The scenario we discussed ahead of time?"

He shrugged. "What's the problem, I caught the ball?"

Jesus, help keep my hands off his neck please.

"Too soon, Grant," I reminded him. "The other positions are off working on *their* scenarios, so I understand that might be throwing you off, but listen up… *again.* What we're working on right now is the fake-out. Making the defender guess what you're doing next. We don't want them looking at *you*, and instantly knowing our play because you're heading top speed in a certain direction, and you're moving too fast to switch without hurting yourself. You want to slow down, or you want a broken ankle?"

The look on his face told me he thought I was being dramatic, but I didn't care. "You want me to do it again?" he asked.

"I want you to do it *right*."

He blew out a sigh, mumbling something under his breath as he ambled away to get back in position for the drill.

And *still* fucked it up.

How the hell does he manage in a professional game?

Seeing Grant in action made me feel for the coach who'd retired, which had opened my place on the team. He was no Jordan Johnson, but numbers didn't lie – Grant's stats could hold their own with most professional receivers, but he was hell to coach – the problem I'd *expected* to have with Amare.

Amare was keeping his head down and doing his work though.

Grant was too busy trying to look good for the fans who were watching.

"Hard to catch a ball when you're too far in front of it," I insisted, not liking that I had to harp on him about the same damn thing – his speed. Yes, speed was important, but if you couldn't modulate, there was no point to it. Full-on sprinting didn't work for *every. Damn. Thing.*

"Since you know so damn much, why don't you show me," Grant challenged – obviously, he was as tired of being nagged as I was of nagging. He probably, like most, had no idea of my history beyond coaching at BSU, thought this was just something I'd learned from observing. Too bad he hadn't been there at the rookie minicamp, to see what happened last time a player tried to challenge my knowledge and experience.

Amare did that so Grant wouldn't have to go through it.

But alas, here we were.

I'd demonstrated things here and there throughout training camp, but had managed to mostly stay low key. Now though, in front of all the receivers, a group of fans in the stands who were observing, and Underwood who'd ambled over with several assistants… I couldn't back away from this challenge.

Which scared the hell out of me.

"Of course," I quipped, my voice sounding about a million times more confident than I felt. "I can run through it for you. Pay close attention."

I gave a few directions to set up the play, hoping no one noticed how badly my hands were shaking. One of the assistants blew the whistle, and I started off, going in the opposite direction of where in a game, my quarterback would be looking for me. Then, suddenly, I pivoted, using a burst of speed to get where I needed to be, just in time to spring upward, snatching the ball into the safety of my arms.

As I came down, I slipped a little, but kept the ball secure as my knee hit the turf. Knowing I couldn't just leave it at that – in college football, that knee hitting the ground would've been the end of the play. I needed the incoming rookies to see the difference - I pushed up, taking off again because the ball was still live.

I didn't go far, just enough to make my point as the female fans in the stands went crazy, yelling out several cheers, including one

"Bitch you better show them how it's done!" that made me look up and wave as I jogged back to where my players were standing.

"*That's* what I mean," I told Terrence, tossing the ball to one of the assistants. "Take over for a minute for me," I told Coach Underwood, a little under my breath. "I've been holding it, but I *really* need to pee."

Underwood laughed, patting me on the shoulder. "Go ahead, morning drills are almost over anyway. Take your time, while we discuss your nickname. I'm thinking *Bullet Train*."

I chuckled, then headed off to the sideline, exchanging words with a few people as I went. My footsteps got more and more urgent as I went, rushing to the fieldhouse and heading straight past the bathrooms to find somewhere, *anywhere* private.

I found my solace in an empty stairwell at the back of the building, where I put my back to the wall, sliding to the floor with my hands pressed over my left breast, trying to calm the rapid-fire pounding of my heart, trying to convince myself that *wasn't* an ache in my chest.

Trying to convince myself I wasn't dying.

Just breathe, Sloane.

Just breathe.

Breathe.

Breathe.

It wasn't working.

None of it.

The calming or convincing or breathing.

I swallowed hard as I fished my cell phone from my pocket, praying it would have enough of a signal to get a call out. The two little bars my screen showed only seemed to make my heart rate spike higher as I navigated to the number I'd practically begged for before the team piled on buses to get here.

"Dr. Sharpe," I gushed, relieved when he actually *answered* the number he'd assured me was his personal cell.

"Ms. Brooks? What happened?" he asked, already knowing there had to be an issue for me to have used the number. I'd *promised* that an issue would be the only reason I utilized it.

"I… I did something stupid. And I'm really scared," I admitted, trying my best to choke back tears. "I ran a play, and I… my chest hurts, and I'm having trouble breathing, and I—"

"Ms. Brooks. *Sloane*," he said, in that soothing ass voice that I appreciated more than he knew. "Calm down. I know it's hard, but I just need you to stop for a second, and just breathe. Nothing else right now, just focus on breathing."

Did I not just tell this man I was dying?

"*Breathe*," he insisted, like he knew I was still too busy bugging out to listen. I closed my eyes, trying my best to do what he'd said, and after a few moments, I *was* able to fall into a natural pattern and catch my breath, when I hadn't before.

"You still with me?"

I nodded, as if he could see me, eyes still closed. "Yes."

"Still hurting?"

"No."

"Okay, let's give it a minute or two. Where are you? Can somebody help get you to the team doctor?"

Instantly, my heart rate spiked up again. "I *cannot* go to the team doctor," I snapped as my eyes popped open.

"Then can you get back here, to me?"

"*No*," I said quietly, shaking my head. "Not for… another three days."

Dr. Sharpe sighed. "Ms. Brooks, if you're feeling chest pains, you *need* to see somebody. Are you still hurting now? Has the pain come back?"

"No. No, it hasn't. And I can breathe. I'm just freaked out."

"And that's probably all this is – anxiety-induced angina. It doesn't feel good, but it's not a heart attack. This is probably the most you've gotten your heart rate up since your cardiac event, and it frightened you. That on top of the stress of your job, on top of your fear of another heart attack… did you ever get that puppy we talked about?"

I pushed out a sigh of my own. "No. My daughter didn't see one that "spoke" to her, so we put it off until after training camp. I did consider it though."

"Good. Pets are excellent companions for managing stress and anxiety. I also want you to consider starting a yoga program."

"I don't have time for that," I immediately shot back.

"Then *make* it. Listen… I want you to see your team doctor, today, just to be safe. But I can't make you, and I know you're probably not going anyway. I want you to promise me though, that if you feel chest pains again – persistent ones that don't go away when your heart rate comes down, or when you lay down, or anything like you felt the first time it happened… get your behind to the team doctor."

"I promise. I do," I swore, and really meant it. I believed what he said about me having just scared the shit out of myself – *this time.*

But if this happened again, especially unprovoked, I was going straight to the team doctor, weakness be damned.

After I wrapped up the call with Dr. Sharpe, I took a few more minutes to myself before I eased back into the mix of the day, enduring my teasing about needing to do more than pee with good humor. Getting joked on was leaps and bounds better than the truth coming out right now, as far as I was concerned.

The remainder of the day was uneventful for the most part, and as soon as I could, I got myself back to the privacy of my room. My concerns about my heart may have been a false alarm, but the fatigue was real.

I took a much-needed shower after being in the sun all day, thankful once again that the coaches had been placed in faculty housing, which meant my bathroom was private. I *needed* to just stand under the hot spray, letting it soak over me for as long as I wanted, without any worries about who might walk in.

Once I was out, a quick glance at the time told me it wasn't even nine at night yet. Some of the other coaches were probably out in the common areas, socializing, but they'd have to miss this face tonight.

I was taking my ass to bed, to get up and do this all over again the next morning.

Or so I thought.

I'd just gotten comfortable underneath the covers when my phone rang.

"*Hello?*" I said, answering when I saw Nate's initials pop up on the screen. The text messages had been ongoing since I left for camp, but this was the first time he'd *called* me.

"Coach Brooks," he replied, good-natured as usual, even though the line was staticky. "I see you're making quite the splash at training camp. You are a very popular search term on Google right now. How are things going?"

I flipped onto my back, with the phone pressed to my ear. "Things are going well. The team is looking great. Well... the offense is looking great."

Nate chuckled. "Yeah, that's what I hear too. Cole isn't very happy with the defense, but... we're a team in transition, you know. We have to be willing to accept the growing pains that come along with it."

"Definitely. I know one thing though..."

"What's that?"

"Our receivers? I'm expecting record stats out of them."

I could practically feel Nate's eyebrows go up. "Seriously?"

"*Seriously*. None of them are without their flaws, but you damn sure aren't going to see last year's mistakes. I have Johnson spending thirty minutes a day doing basketball drills, working on his vertical. Grant... if he listens, I can keep him from looking goofy out there, running pell-mell at *everything*. Amare... I can't say enough about that kid's potential. You know he hasn't talked back, not once, this whole camp? You give him an instruction, he's listening, absorbing and then just... delivering." After I said that, I pushed out a sigh that Nate immediately latched on to.

"Wait, why don't you sound that happy about that?"

"It's not that I'm not happy about it, it's just... unlike him. Don't get me wrong, I don't miss the attitude, but he's been a little lifeless out here. You may want to drop him a line."

"Thank you, I will. And the other receivers?"

I shrugged. "A mixed bag. But we definitely have what we need for a strong squad."

"Excellent. *Excellent.* This is the kind of report I like to hear. And now… what about their coach? How is she?"

"*Great*," I said immediately. It wasn't even fully off my lips before I registered how unconvincing it sounded. Too quickly delivered, too falsely excited.

And of course – *of fucking course* – Nate was already on top of it.

"What happened? Don't lie."

I frowned. "Wow, you say that as if I'm just *known* for lying!"

"You're right, let me rephrase – don't *omit.*"

Shit.

He kinda had me there.

"Why don't you tell me what you already know? Because I'm sure you know something."

He chuckled. "I know plenty, about plenty, but *you* my dear, can be quite the mystery. But… I know you ran a route today – full speed, full power, impressive as usual. And you're talking to me right now, so I know it didn't kill you. You want to fill in what happened in-between?"

"Not particularly. You have all the pertinent information."

"I don't have how you feel. You've been fearful of even a short jog, and yet you managed a full sprint… are you happy? Proud of yourself? Are you less paranoid about getting your heart rate up now?"

I scoffed. "Yeah, I'm going to go with none of the above. And also um… I'm tired, and it's late, so…"

For several seconds, he said nothing, just let the staticky line fill with his disappointment.

"Okay Sloane. Good night."

"Good night."

I snatched the phone away from my ear, hurriedly pushing the button to end the call before I let it drop onto the floor beside me. That hadn't exactly been the smoothest way to get off the phone, but it had been quick. Either way, mission accomplished.

How the *hell* was I supposed to explain that my fear of my rising heart rate had *increased* instead of decreased now? At least before I hadn't known how it felt – now I just never wanted it to happen again. Who the hell wanted to stop, assess, and self-diagnose every time their heart rate lifted?

Hell no I wasn't proud of myself – doing it had been stupid, and had everything to do with ego. Not teaching. If it had been about teaching, I could've asked Amare to run the route again, since he'd already executed it perfectly.

But *noooo.*

I just had to show Terrence Grant that football wasn't just some shit I taught and talked about it. I'd *done* this.

And I could have killed my dumb ass, trying to prove a point.

So no.

I wasn't happy.

I was scared, and angry at myself, and confused as to what my life could or would look like moving forward from this. I'd been so confident in my ability to not just *do* this job, but to excel at it. Now that my body had betrayed me, *so* deeply… I wasn't so sure anymore.

Which was a really, *really* shitty feeling.

But instead of dwelling on it, I went to sleep.

Tomorrow was a fresh day.

Ten

"Coach Brooks?"

I looked up from the huge TV screen where the players were, as some type of soldiers were destroying a colony of fearsome-looking aliens. It was one of the last few days of camp, and instead of being holed up in the faculty dorm, all the coaches were mingling with the players. Talking shit, playing cards, pool, on the video game. In theory, it was a good team-building activity – having fun together that had nothing to do with football.

That did *not* change the fact that I would've rather been in my bed.

But that wasn't something to take out on the nervous-looking intern who'd approached me, probably choosing me because I was the only other woman in this room.

"Yes, how can I help you?" I asked, having to yell a little over the noise.

Her gaze bounced to her left as a loud string of curses erupted from the men playing the game, and then came back to me. "Uh… Nate Richardson is here. He wants to see Rutledge Amare, but I can't find him. Everybody is supposed to be in one of the common areas, but I've been over both, twice."

"You checked his room?"

She nodded. "No answer."

"Okay. Um…" I thought about how, throughout camp, Amare had been all about following instructions. I doubted that today was any different, so he was probably out here… *somewhere*. "I'll find him."

"Great!" She immediately brightened. "He's waiting in conference 4C!"

Before I could object, she'd taken off, leaving me to, apparently, not just *find* Amare, but get him there too.

Ugh.

Because I was familiar with him, it didn't take long for me to spot the man, tucked off in a corner to himself, with a towel hanging over his face. I nudged his knee, prompting him to take his sweet time removing the towel to see who it was and what they wanted. When his eyebrows lifted to question my presence, I answered.

"Someone wants to see you. Come on."

I started moving, not questioning for a second that he would get up and follow. The conference rooms were in the next building over, down some halls and through some doorways. Once we made it, I fought the urge to peek inside myself – I just showed him where he was supposed to be, and then moved on about my business.

The business of sneaking away from this forced socialization so I could get more familiar with my bed.

The quickest way back to faculty housing was through the players' dorm, which I'd left through the back to escort Amare to Nate. Now, I exited through the front entrance, and was surprised to find Jordan Johnson sitting alone out on the front steps, instead of upstairs clowning with his teammates.

"You look like a man with the weight of the world on his shoulders," I said, stopping beside him, but not sitting down. "You good?"

"Always," he shot back, with much less confidence than I was used to from him.

"That doesn't sound very convincing." I took several steps down, moving so that I was closer to eye level with him, but still not sitting down. "What's going on?"

He shook his head. "Just gotta get out of my own head. Focus. Stop being a pussy."

"Ahhh," I sang, propping my hands on my hips. "This is about your shoulder?"

Jordan's head pulled back as he frowned, apparently stunned that I'd so easily hit that mark. "How the *hell* did you…?"

"I *know* you Johnson… remember? Don't forget who turned you into a first-round draft pick now," I teased, making him grin.

"Never that. Why you think I volunteered to be featured in your documentary? BSU to the *Kings*. A fucking success story."

I nodded. "For both of us. And now… your shoulder has you concerned. You're afraid to use it. Afraid it's going to fail you. *Again.*"

"Coach Brooks, you know you're one of my favorite people, right?"

I tipped my head. "Sure."

"So don't take it personally when I tell you I'm not really trying to hear any platitudes or shit right now. It doesn't help."

"Oh I wasn't about to encourage, I was about to commiserate. When some vital part gives out on you, it's fucking scary, and I can't blame you for being paranoid. I *get* it. More than you know."

His eyes narrowed. "What does that mean?"

I pushed out a sigh, glancing around to make sure we were alone before I stepped a little closer. "Can you keep a secret?"

He shrugged. "You've kept mine. Say what you need to say."

"Well… a little over two months ago… I had a heart attack."

Jordan immediately frowned. "*What? You?*"

"Yeah," I nodded. "Me. And since then… I've been afraid to do almost anything. Afraid a blood clot is going to cause another attack, or that I'm going to overwork it, or worse… that I'll go into cardiac arrest again. And that this time, there won't be anyone around."

"That's… scary."

"Damn right it is. My doctors say that if I take my meds and eat right and all that, I'll be fine. I can go back to normal activity as soon as I feel ready. I can jump, and run, and do all these things, just as soon as I… I don't feel ready. I don't know when I'll feel ready, *if* I'll ever feel ready."

He shook his head. "But you *ate* that route yesterday like it was nothing."

"Only because I felt like I *had* to. And then I went and had a fucking panic attack. Because I didn't feel ready, and I still don't."

"But that's the lesson right there, isn't it?"

I shrugged. "I didn't say *shit* about a lesson, did I? I'm trying to tell your ass *I'm* scared too!"

"That's *still* the lesson though," he laughed. "Whether you admit to it or not. You were scared, and you did it anyway, because you had to. And you killed it. When we hit that field for pre-season –"

"You're out of your mind if you think we're putting you on the field in pre-season for some newbie lineman to try to take you down for clout. No sir."

"But you get my point though? That even if I'm scared, it doesn't change what I have to do. I can't be ruled by fear."

I smiled, and nodded. "Yeah, Jordan. I get it."

He extended a fist toward me, and I tapped it with mine, using that gesture as a goodbye before I headed off. I hated that his words resonated in my head, sticking with me through the short walk to the faculty dorms. I didn't *want* to think about how self-defeating it was to allow fear to dictate my moves. It was so much easier to just be scared.

The building was empty with almost everyone still hanging out with the players, which meant I didn't have anyone stopping me for small talk. I went straight to my room and sat down, toying with the idea of styling my freshly washed hair into the twists I'd put off after my shower earlier, in favor of making it to the joint dinner and activities with the players on time.

I decided to take another shower just because it was so hot, and lay out on the bed, wondering what the hell Nate was doing here instead.

It wasn't as if training camp was just up the road from our normal practice facilities – out here, we were *hours* away. Nate hadn't even hinted that he was coming up to check on his players today, and if it hadn't been for the intern looking for Amare, I wouldn't have even known he was here.

I… didn't like that.

I didn't like it at all.

In the weeks since Nate had shown up at my door the night after the Johnson wedding, not much between us had changed. He was still showing up for walks, still with the late-night texts, still checking to make sure I was taking care of myself. The difference, I guess, was… *me.* Instead of tolerating, or even expecting, I'd started looking forward to his presence.

Or rather… *allowing myself* to look forward to it.

Even though I knew it was a dangerous thing.

Sure, I may have opened my mind to seeing Nate differently – seeing him *seriously.* But that didn't even remotely address the fact that there were still major barriers to us having a relationship of *any* type.

At least having it *publicly.*

The conflict of interest with our jobs, the age difference, and as much as I hated to admit it… it mattered to me what the public would have to say. It wasn't just about my feelings, either. I had to consider my daughter, and the things she might hear or see. High school was a fragile time for teenagers, no matter how mature. Garrett and I had been lucky with Madison so far, but that only made me worry that the hellish years everyone had warned us about were right around the corner. I did *not* want my love life to be the trigger for any of my daughter's pain.

And then, of course… there was Garrett.

I shook my head, telling myself that none of it mattered, not right now at least. It wasn't like Nate and I were in a place to even put a name to what we were doing. We were just… *living.*

Anything beyond that could, as Nate said, wait until later.

As if I'd thought him up, a knock sounded at my door.

I wasn't sure how I knew it was him before I left my bed, but I did, which made me move quickly, not wanting anyone to see him at my door. He slipped inside as soon as I opened it, looking *impossibly* good in a white *Kings* tee shirt, a royal blue hat, and blue and gold shorts – the standard uniform for staff, but on him, it just looked…

Shit.

"Hey."

I sucked in a little breath. "Hey back at you. What are you doing here, Nate? It's a four-hour drive, and training camp is almost over. What emergency couldn't wait two more days?"

"What emergency do you *think* couldn't wait two more days, Sloane?"

I shrugged, backing up when he took a step toward me. "I don't know. Did someone tell you I was on the verge of clotheslining Grant next time he takes off faster than he should?"

Chuckling, Nate took another step. "Nah. But that's good to know."

"Amare, then? My report about his demeanor concerned you?"

"His report about *your* demeanor concerns me."

"Excuse me?" I asked, backing up until I couldn't unless I planned to climb the wall. "You met with him to talk about me?"

Nate shook his head. "Nope. But he was concerned enough to bring it up. Referred to you as… *motherly.*"

I frowned. "Seriously? Oh *God.* And it doesn't help that I'm old enough to be his mother. I must be being too nice to them."

"I *definitely* don't think it's that," Nate assured me, laughing. "But I'm more interested in hearing why you've been off… supposedly. Talk to me. Tell me what's going on."

"There's nothing to tell."

"Don't do that."

"Don't do what?"

"Shut me out," he said, placing his hands at my waist. "I'm here because I didn't like how you sounded on the phone. I only talked to my players so that if anybody saw me, there would be a logical explanation for my presence. The emergency that couldn't wait… is *you*."

"Oh," I nodded. "You came to hear in person how I did something completely stupid and scared myself into a panic attack because I was trying to prove a point that didn't need to be proved?"

"I came to see with my own two eyes that you were okay. I don't know anything about this other shit you're talking about."

I sucked my teeth. "So you're just gonna *always* have the right thing to say? *Ugh*. Move!" I shoved him off so I could move toward the bed, and he followed me, laughing.

"Never before have I experienced a woman getting pissed because I said the *right* thing," he teased, dropping to a seat on the bed beside me. "This is new."

"Won't be the first *or* last thing I teach you, youngin'."

He smirked as he leaned back onto his elbows, his wide shoulders taking up a good amount of space on the bed. "Why I gotta be all that?"

"Because you are," I told him, turning to put my back against the headboard and stretching my legs across his lap. Immediately, he shifted his position and his hands went to my bare feet, squeezing with just the right amount of pressure. I closed my eyes for a few seconds, moaning as he worked away weeks of stress in what felt like just a few minutes.

"You keep moaning like that, I'm gonna have to remind you what this *youngin'* can do."

I cracked my eyes open, grinning. "How much pussy have you foot massaged your way into?" I asked him. "On campus, at that? Does this little scenario bring up good memories for you?"

"As a matter of fact, it does," he quipped. "Memories of being a young, horny sophomore, imagining myself doing the *filthiest* of things to the fine ass football coach. And now… I don't even have to imagine. Because I'm a man of action."

"*Mmmm.* That you most certainly *are*," I purred, my back arching as my toes disappeared into Nate's mouth. I moaned again, feeling it between my legs, all the way up to my nipples as his tongue dipped between each digit, warm and wonderful and… *familiar.* His lips pressed to the arch of my foot, and then the heel, then on up my ankle and calf, and thigh, and then he bypassed everything to get to my collarbone, then my neck, then my ear.

"Coach Brooks," he groaned – yet another thing I felt between my legs. "Exactly how much action are you willing to get into?"

"Not *too* much… unless you're trying to kill me," I told him, keeping my tone playful even though I was completely serious.

He laughed in my ear. "Well, you've *definitely* asked if that's what I was trying to do before. Usually a sign I was doing something very, *very* right."

I sucked in a breath as his hand slipped into the waistband of my sleep shorts and between my legs, touching me where I'd been reticent to even touch *myself* for months. That lack of stimulation was probably the culprit behind my hyper-sensitivity now – just the brush of his fingers had me throbbing.

I called on every piece of willpower I had to circle my hand around his wrist, stopping. "Nate… no."

I *felt* that word register to him – first the surprise and confusion, then the removal of his mouth from my neck and his hands from my shorts.

"You're serious?" he asked, shifting up to look me in the face.

"Yeah," I nodded. I watched, feeling helpless and stupid and a little hurt as he maneuvered himself out of bed, and headed for the door. "I'm afraid to have an orgasm!" I shouted after him, feeling like I needed to explain myself. "I know my doctor and the internet say it's okay, but I… this is terrifying, okay? Not knowing if the things that used to be like second nature to you might make your heart stop working! This isn't easy for me!"

When I finally stop speaking long enough to focus on Nate again, I found him frozen by the door, halfway through the act of taking off his shoes. His expression was a mixture of sympathy and bafflement, but that started to melt away when *we* realized my mistake.

"You thought I was leaving?" he asked, and as my gaze dropped to my hands, all I could do was nod.

To Nate's credit, he didn't laugh. He just went on about what he was doing before – taking off his shoes to leave by the door, and stripping down to his boxers to join me in that itty-bitty college standard twin bed.

He took the spot against the wall, laying on his side so he could poke at me until I stretched out too, staring up at the ceiling instead of looking at him.

"Don't tell me you're trying to fake like you're embarrassed," he teased.

"Fake?" I sucked my teeth. "No, the embarrassment is real."

"For *what*?" he asked. "Daring to tell me how you really felt? *The horror.*"

"Don't do that." I finally shifted to look at him. "It's not funny."

"I'm not laughing. I'm serious, Sloane. I appreciate that you opened up to me."

My eyebrow lifted. "Because I so rarely do?"

"Were you *not* trying to get me to fuck another woman last month, even though it wasn't what you really wanted?"

I sat up on my elbow, turning to him. "Correction - I didn't want you to just fuck her, I wanted you to make her your girlfriend. And I didn't *know* it wasn't what I wanted until there was a real possibility of it happening, so that doesn't even really count."

"So you're really about to try to just speak some sense into your actions?"

"Emotions aren't about making sense," I argued. "Which is what makes them so dangerous. *Feelings* will have you in some bullshit every time, and you will just merrily wallow, because your stupid ass "heart" said so."

Nate chuckled. "Is that what we're doing right now, you think? Merrily wallowing?"

I smiled, reaching out to run a hand over the soft, low-groomed hair on his chin. "Right now, you and I are downright filthy."

He caught my hand, pulling my fingers to his lips. "I don't know… I kinda like the sound of that."

"Feelings. It's all their fault."

He used his grip on my hand to pull me closer, right up against his chest. We were squeezed together tight on that little bed, but it didn't feel remotely uncomfortable. It was… *cozy.* Cozy and comfortable, and so absolutely *right* that I couldn't help melting into him a little more.

"You're not falling asleep on me, are you?" I asked, feeling the subtle shift in his breathing after neither of us had said anything for a while.

"Hell yes," he mumbled into the top of my head. "Why not?"

I pulled back so I could look up. "Well, there's the whole, *somebody might see you sneaking out of here in the morning* angle to think about…"

"Nah." he shook his head. "I have a room in the building. I showered and all that before I came to your door. I'll slip out while everybody is at breakfast to go back upstairs."

Oh.

He'd thought it all the way through.

"And you're sure you wouldn't rather have one of these itty-bitty beds all to yourself? This can't be very comfortable for you."

Nate ran his tongue over his lips, pinning me with sleepy eyes. "Sloane… I am *exactly* where I want to be."

I couldn't help the smile those words brought to my face before I leaned in, pressing my lips to his. I knew better – was too old *not* to know better – than to be swayed so easily by words. I'd spent a good chunk of my life married to a man who always knew exactly what to say to keep me.

Looking back now, I could see the manipulation. Back then, it hadn't been quite so clear.

Am I making the same mistake again?

The soft press of Nate's lips was so, *so* persuasive, and the warmth of his tongue was even more convincing. His hands on my ass were especially influential, making it easy to forget my little nagging fears. And the fact that he seemed content to stay just like this, making out and grabbing ass, but taking it no further… well… for me that just sealed the deal.

"Is there a such thing as like… just a *light* orgasm?"

Nate laughed, rolling onto his back to press a hand to his chest. "A *light* orgasm? What does that even mean?"

Replaying it in my head, I laughed too. "I'm *serious*. I know it sounds a little silly, but all orgasms aren't built the same, right?"

"Right," he agreed.

"Okay. So… maybe if we take it easy…"

"I get what you're saying, Sloane. I'm just messing with you. You sure you want to do that though? If you're concerned, then—"

"I'm sure. *Very* sure."

Nate chuckled at my sudden enthusiasm, then nodded. "Well, in that case… one *light* orgasm coming right up."

"Do you *have* to say it like that?" I asked, giggling as her brought his mouth to my neck.

"Just repeating *your* term."

I wanted to quip back, but with his tongue behind my ear and his hand between my legs again, I only got as far as opening my mouth. It stayed like that, bottom lip just hanging in the air as his fingers strummed and stroked, very easily creating that familiar pull of pleasure, deep in the pit of my stomach.

"Is that okay?" he asked, and all I could manage was a nod, because *hell yes* it was. His fingers kept working as he moved, lowering his mouth to my breasts, covered only by the thin fabric of my tank top. With one hand, he yanked it up, giving my breasts *exactly* the kind of awe-filled stare they deserved before he pounced, licking and sucking and nibbling until I was squirming underneath him. And then he asked again, "Is that okay?"

My answer was the same – a *hell yes* communicated with just an emphatic nod.

His fingers left my pussy so he could use both hands to grip my waist as he kissed his way down to my belly button. I pushed myself up on my elbows, wanting a better vantage point as he grabbed the waistband of my shorts and panties at the same time, pulling them down, and off, and tossing them across the room.

My heart rate spiked as he pushed my legs open, situating himself between my legs. He wasn't even touching me yet – he was just *looking* at it, staring between my legs with a hunger that had my heart thumping so hard I could damn near hear it.

But I wasn't about to say *shit*.

We were too far now.

He picked my leg up, trailing his tongue up my thigh, right to the sweet spot in the middle. Twin appreciative moans came from both of our throats as he closed his mouth over my swollen clit and sucked me there.

Hard.

"Oh, *God*," I exclaimed, backing away as my whole body seemed to contract with pleasure. But Nate was right there, locking an arm around my thigh to keep us connected, and with the other hand, threading his fingers through mine as he slurped me up. I bit down on my lip as it got harder to breathe, harder to relax, harder to just... let go and enjoy. Nate must have felt it too, because he squeezed my hand, his non-verbal plea for me to calm down.

But how the hell was I supposed to *calm down* with his face buried between my legs, tickling me with his hair and soothing me with his lips and nibbling with his teeth and doing some shit with his tongue that I couldn't even describe but seemed capable of making me turn myself inside out.

"Nate, *please*. I... I *can't*."

The long, slow swipe of his tongue was like a sudden calm in the storm, the tame nature of it giving me a break from the onslaught of pleasure. He did it again, and then his eyes came up to meet mine.

"Do you want to stop?"

"I don't know. No. I... I don't know."

He pressed his lips to the inside of the thigh his arm was still wrapped around. "Hey... I know you're a little scared, but... I'm *not* going to let anything to happen to you. Okay?"

I nodded. "Okay."

I believed him.

Even though it was an impossible sort of promise to make, even though there was legitimately *no* way that he could guarantee that… I wholeheartedly believed him.

You've got it so, so bad.

I shoved my inner thoughts away as he kissed me again, a little higher on the thigh this time. And then again, and again, and again, until he was back at my clit, kissing me there as he looked me right in the eyes. I couldn't hold his gaze though. His mouth on me was so good that I *had* to close my eyes, and just lay back. Had to stop trying to see and focus on just… *feeling.*

No doubts, no fears, no worries, just the pleasure of his mouth and the security of his grip and the reassurance of his fingers threaded through mine, and then…. *Sweet, sweet* release.

Not in the soft, lapping wave I thought I wanted, but the abrupt crash I needed, wracking my entire body. My chest *did* clinch, and it *did* seem like my heart stopped, but instead of being scary, the deep familiarity of it was comforting. I relaxed back into the sheets, intensely, unexpectedly relieved.

Like I'd successfully reunited with an old friend.

I must have looked a little goofy, because Nate chuckled to himself once he'd kissed his way back up my body to reach my face. I didn't ask though, just greedily accepted the sex-flavored kiss he offered. I moaned over the warm caress of his tongue against mine, getting familiar all over again with the taste of myself on Nate's lips.

"You happy?" he asked, when we finally came up for air.

I nodded, running my hands over the broad expanse of his back before I dropped them to the band of his boxers, tugging down. "But you could make me even happier…"

"You don't think we might be pushing it?" he asked, but made no moves to stop me from pulling him out of his boxers.

"I don't care. I need you inside of me. *Now*."

A little smirk crossed his lips, and he adjusted to just the right position between my legs, then plunged into me.

"When have I ever denied you anything you claimed to need?"

Never.

That was the answer to his question, but I didn't say it out loud. I was too busy – *we* were too busy – enjoying the second overdue reunion of the night. In the four years we'd been at it, these last few months were one of the longest periods we'd gone without indulging each other. I whimpered and moaned as my body adjusted to him all over again, welcoming him home.

Home.

This time, that was what it felt like. Nate and I were incredibly well-versed in the intricacies of each other's bodies, which was one of the major things that made the sex so incredible. But this… wasn't that. Not that his long, deep, carefully measured strokes weren't as good as always, it was just that… something had shifted.

Something had changed.

And somehow… this was even better.

He was kissing me deeper, holding me tighter, intuitively adjusting his stroke, his depth, his pace, before the thought could even fully cross my mind. There was nothing fancy, no acrobatics, no feet on the headboard, nothing *extra*. Just me and him. Face to face, nothing between us, and it was… *perfection.*

I opened my legs a little more, hooking them around his waist so that he could sink even deeper. He growled his appreciation in my ear as I dug my nails into his shoulders, not caring if I left a mark.

As far as I was concerned… he was mine now, and I was his.

Complications be damned.

Eleven

Aug 2018

"Old King Cole," I greeted my sister as I breezed through the door of her office uninvited – since apparently, her assistant had decided to take a break, leaving the desk empty. I knew Cole was in though, because of the light illuminating her closed blinds.

My twin did *not* seem happy to see me though.

"Nate! Get the *fuck* outta here!" she screamed at me, scrambling to get up and come around her desk. "Why would you burst in here unannounced?!"

Confused as hell by her reaction, I stood my ground as she yanked at my arm, trying in vain to get me toward the door.

"Damn," I said, pulling away from her. "What the fuck did I do to you?"

She took a breath, obviously realizing how crazy she was acting. She stepped away, holding up her hands. "Nothing. It's just… really rude to burst in here like that. What do you want?" she snapped, her eyes bouncing toward the desk before they came back to me.

What the hell is she so damn nervous about?

"Ramsey Bishop. While you were out, on your honeymoon, he came to me wanting to set up some free movie screenings for kids in Bridgeport." I held up the flash drive I'd brought in with me. "My email is acting stupid, so I put all the info here – the theatres, address, amenities, budget, all of that. Everybody hadn't gotten back to me yet, so I was waiting until they did to put it back in your hands. *You're welcome.*"

She took the drive. "Thank you. Now can you *go?*" she insisted, again glancing toward her desk.

My eyes narrowed, and before she could realize I was on to her, I sprinted to her desk, ignoring her frustrated scream as my eyes landed on her computer screen.

I froze.

She froze.

And then we spoke at the same time.

"You *can't* tell anybody!"

"You're... *pregnant?*"

Cole pushed out a sigh, covering her face with her hands as my eyes went back to the screen.

Your baby at six weeks.

Holy shit.

"Nicki..." I spoke, and she looked up, tears in her eyes. I rounded the desk again to approach her. "Are you happy about it?"

She ran her tongue over her lips, shaking her head. "I... I don't know yet, Nate. You know what six weeks ago was, right?"

I squinted a little as I backtracked in my mind. "Ohhh... *Oh, shit!*"

"Right," she nodded. "I got pregnant on my honeymoon, and… I *love* Jordan. You know that."

"I do."

"And I *want* to have his babies. I want to have *this* baby. I just…"

"You feel like it's too soon?"

The tears she'd been trying to hold back finally dripped down her cheeks, and I took the last step I needed to pull her into a hug.

"Come here," I told her, after giving her a few moments to cry, pulling her toward the little love seat against the wall. I sat down, and she took the seat right beside me, head resting on my shoulder. For another few moments, neither of us said anything, and then…

"I was just… getting my body ready, you know?"

"And *here* is where I tap out of this conversation."

"No!" Cole insisted, pulling me back down beside her. "I'm just… explaining. I stopped my birth control because I knew we'd want to… *try*. In like a year or something. I didn't want the hormones in my body, I've been juicing, and started prenatals, and I've been exercising, so that when we *did* decide we were ready, we'd *really* be ready. I wasn't even supposed to be fertile yet."

"And yet, you *were*."

She sucked her teeth. "If you're going to be an asshole…"

"I'm not being an asshole," I insisted. "You didn't let me finish. I'm saying, this may not be the situation you meant to be in, but… *here we are*. You probably wanted to enjoy being married before you became a parent – that's understandable. Kids change your whole life. But the fact is – that baby is growing inside you, ready or not. You're married to someone who loves the hell outta you, and if I remember correctly, has been politicking to put a bun in your oven since before he even showed you that ring. You're healthy. You've got friends and family who would go to any length to make sure you're *good*. What the hell is there to be down about?"

She nodded. "You're right. You're *right*," she repeated, nodding her head.

"So?" I held up my hands. "Same question – are you happy about it?"

Cole stared at me for a moment, and then a slow grin spread over her face. "Yes. I am."

"In *that* case… congratulations baby sister."

She put out a stiff arm, holding me back from hugging her. "Hold up – *first* of all, baby sister? Nigga, stop it. *Second* – what would your response have been if I wasn't happy?!"

"Do you need me to drive to the clinic, and do you need me to pay?"

Cole's eyes got big, and watered all over again. "*Wow*. You really do love me, huh?"

"Stop playing," I laughed, putting an arm around her neck to pull her into a hug. "Big head ass. I *know* you're having a c-section, between you and Jordan. Baby gonna have a watermelon."

Instead of getting offended, she sucked in a bit of air and shook her head. "Dude – googling *how to keep my baby from having a big ass head* was like, the first thing I wanted to do when I looked at that test!"

"We're gonna pray. Call mama's people, I think some of them still have a direct line to the man upstairs."

She nodded. "Yeah. You think daddy can get a prayer through too? I should ask Jade to talk to Ezra. We gotta start going to church. Like yesterday."

I laughed. "How does Jordan feel about it?"

Our little back and forth stopped as Cole shook her head. "I haven't had a chance to tell him yet. I *just* found out. Read my test results maybe ten minutes before you walked through that door."

"So… I'm the first person to know?"

She smiled, then gave me a nod. "Yeah. Only makes sense though… Ramsey's movie theatre thing didn't bring you through my office door. It was *twintuition*."

I pulled her in again, kissing her forehead. "Yeah, maybe so. How are you feeling? You sick or anything? What made you take the test?"

"Cycle was missing in action. No other symptoms yet though. Or hell, maybe I was just in denial. Now that I know, we'll see. I hope it stays like this though, because the *last* thing I need is another reason for people to think I can't do my job."

Sounds familiar.

"Everybody knows you kill this shit, Cole," I assured her. "And I'll be there to pick up any slack. Don't worry about that."

"I know you would, Nate. But… *still.* Pre-season just started. Don't tell anybody. Not even Daddy. I want to tell him in my own time. When *I'm* ready. Not before. Okay?"

Yep. Familiar.

I nodded.

"You've got my word. My lips are closed."

"… expected a little more out of those Kings' wide receivers tonight. Sure, it's only preseason, but the new wide receiver coach was the talk of training camp. Maybe she's not living up to the hype."

"Well that's not a fair assessment to make after two preseason games, is it? We haven't seen Johnson on the field yet, or even Grant. Hell, we haven't even seen their controversial rookie. She's giving the other receivers a chance to get some miles on them, without putting her proven receivers at risk. That's good coaching in itself."

"Nah, that's scared coaching if you ask me. Which… I expected."

"Why, because she's a woman?"

"Because she's coming to the pros from college football – it's a different world here."

"And in **that** world, she was damn good at her job. I see no reason – **yet** – to expect any different."

"I beg to differ. Coach Brooks can impress me with a swimsuit spread any day, but her coaching leaves a lot to be desired based on these last two games, preseason or not. I read one of her interviews, where she talked about **excellence, excellence, excellence,** it was every tenth word out of her mouth. Where is it out on that field though?"

"I thought we agreed to turn this *off*?" I asked, pulling the remote from Sloane's hand to shut off the nightly sportscast on the TV. Not that I thought she was incapable of having her performance critiqued, but she was getting a little overzealous with the constant consumption of it – especially when there was a big deal being made about nothing.

Nobody *actually* gave a shit about a pre-season loss, they were just there to give people something to talk about. At least, that's about as far as *I* cared.

To Sloane though, the imperfect performance of our *backup* receivers was a scathing indictment on her abilities as a coach, and there didn't seem to be anything I could say to keep her from internalizing it like that.

I could, however, keep her from binging on it while I was around.

"I am going to *murder* them on the field next practice. They're going to run those routes until their legs fall off – but their legs will know the routes so well that their bodies aren't even necessary. They'll just be legs, running the *proper fucking routes*," was her response to my questioning how the TV had gotten back on. I'd been downstairs not even a whole three minutes, fixing her a glass of water so she could take her meds.

She was *supposed* to be relaxing.

"I've been too nice," she declared, taking the glass from my hand to walk to her vanity, where the pills were already out. "That's the problem. If they thought I might rip their *useless* arms out of socket for missing a wide-open pass, they'd run the fucking routes! I'm too nice!"

"*Why* do you think that? *Nobody* thinks that," I informed her, shaking my head. Everything I'd heard was that Sloane was fair, and honestly easy to get along with, but she was tough. Relentless. Swift with precision critique, but equally quick to offer praise.

Nice was not a word ever used.

At all.

"Well I guess I need to drive it home a little more," she snapped, swallowing her pills in one gulp that she chased with a long drink of water.

"What you *need* is to… *relax*. You haven't gotten the puppy, you haven't started the yoga."

"I've been *busy*, and I've been--"

"Stressed the fuck out? Yeah, I've noticed."

It wasn't exactly surprising that now that wins and losses were at stake – even just pre-season – Sloane's stress level had been through the roof. It didn't help that there was an undue focus on her performance – position coaches being talked about on the newscast wasn't really a *thing*, at least not as long as I'd been watching, which was… a long ass time.

But apparently it was a thing *now*.

Everybody had something to say.

I'd never been more grateful that she lived in a gated community than I was now, because I had little doubt she'd be getting harassed. As it was, home was still a much-needed safe haven.

At least for now.

"I don't know how you expect me to react to this. This is what I do – I hear the critique, I analyze it, and I adjust myself accordingly."

I raised an eyebrow. "Oh *that's* what you do? You hear a critique, and you analyze it, and adjust accordingly?"

"Why do I feel like you're about to make me curse you out?"

"Cause I probably am," I smirked. "You want to take in the negative critique? Cool. But take this one too – *you need to fucking relax.* Adjust accordingly."

She huffed. "If *only* it were so easy."

"It *can* be. Listen... I know you're into the little fancy bubble baths and stuff. I'll fix it for you. You go pour yourself a glass of wine."

"My *one* itty-bitty carefully measured glass per day?" she scoffed. "What am I supposed to do with that?"

"Last I heard, you were supposed to drink it, but who knows these days?"

"You really do enjoy being an asshole, don't you?"

I smacked her on the ass, then stepped into the bathroom. "Go pour the damn wine!"

She said something back that I couldn't make out, but the fading volume told me she said it while she was moving to do what I'd said. In the bathroom, I shuffled through a few tins and bottles before I settled on something that claimed it was calming, moisturizing, and pussy-safe – my own words. I followed the instructions to add it to the oversized bathtub that I'd already started filling, and by the time Sloane came to the bathroom, wine glass in hand, the candles were lit too, just waiting for her to step in.

Sloane leaned against the counter, pushing out a little sigh before she raised the glass to her lips for a tiny sip.

"What's wrong?" I asked, and she rightfully raised an eyebrow at me.

"A *long* list. But… you're right. I'm focusing on it too much. Thank you for urging me to step back."

I shrugged. "It's no big deal."

"It… kinda is, though. I mean… you don't have to be here on a Friday night, managing my feelings while your friends are probably out getting lap dances." She tipped the wine glass in my direction. "You're thirty years old. No kids. Fridays should be for fun, not… dumping your cougar into a lavender bath so she doesn't have a widow-maker."

"Here I was, thinking we were past this age shit, but—"

"It's not even the age difference," she interrupted. "We could be the *same* age, and I'd still feel like… thirty is too young to have to take care of somebody. I don't feel like this is fair to you."

"Why are you acting as if you're some heavy burden?" I asked her, confused. "Listen, it is a *rare* occasion in my personal life to do a goddamn thing I don't want to do. I care about you, more than I've cared about… *any* woman."

She shook her head. "Even though I've done nothing but hold you at arm's length, and called you immature, and acted as if you were a nuisance to me?"

I leaned into the counter beside her, crossing my arms as I thought about it. Then, I nodded. "Yeah, actually."

"*Why*?" she asked. "I mean… when I look at us, and how our relationship has changed since that conversation we had the night before my heart attack… it's clear to me what *I* get from this. That "certainty" that I claimed you weren't capable of… you have made a *complete* liar out of me. But I don't understand what *you* get, other than the fulfillment of your teenaged fantasies."

"That's because you're still – mistakenly – only looking at it through *your* lens," I told her, moving to turn off the water for the tub. "You're a woman – a divorced mother. At this point in your life, you want certain things, and you made that clear to me. The same goes for me – I'm at a point where *I* want certain things, that on the surface look like opposite goals. But the more I've thought about, I'm not sure it is."

Sloane narrowed her eyes. "Um… you're gonna have to explain this to me."

"Not a problem," I grinned. "So, my wants in a woman are, superficially – beautiful, takes care of herself, great in bed. You easily knock all of that out of the park. A little deeper – smart, successful, funny. You have all of those too. Then, the specifics – someone who challenges me. Someone who won't be pressed about how I spend my time. Doesn't want to have babies, and blah, blah, blah… you check all the boxes. You see now that I check all yours."

Shaking her head, she pushed out a sigh. "You don't see how impersonal that sounds?"

"You asked an impersonal ass question," I countered. "A question I *hate*, by the way, no matter who has to answer it, because yeah, I can list off all the ways you check my boxes, because you want something… quantifiable, I guess. But anybody could check off the boxes – *Leya* checked off all the fucking boxes, but guess what, Leya isn't you. I can list off the qualities I like about you, the things you do for me, the things you do for other people, and I guess all that would be cool, but the real, *for real* answer is that I like you because I just *do*.

I care about you because I *do*. Why do I have to justify it with some made up shit that I'm only saying because the *why* is... something I can't even really put into words?"

When I stopped speaking, she didn't say anything. She just looked at me, and after a moment, I shrugged. "My bad. That was..."

"Really sweet," she interrupted, lifting a hand to my face as she graced me with a smile. "And... hell, you might be right. Garrett and I... we tried marriage counseling. And that "*why?*" question got asked. Something that I noticed was, if you mentioned things they did for you, it meant you were selfish. If you listed qualities you liked, it was superficial. If you mentioned how they treated others, it was like... well maybe you like the *idea* of them, or something like that. It was exactly like you said – you wind up feeling like you have to justify why you love someone when really... it kinda is selfish, and superficial, and liking the idea of them, and a whole slew of other shit all mixed up, some things you can verbalize and some you just... *can't*. I get it."

My eyebrows went up. "Well hell, I'm glad *you* do, cause I confused my damn self, and I'm not even sure how we got here."

Sloane laughed. "Well, I see it like this – After being a wife, and still being a mother, I'm at a place that's a little selfish, so I've been placing a high value on the things you've been doing for me. You're in a different place, so your appreciation for me is based more on who I am, and how I fit it into your life."

"Right," I agreed, finally feeling like we'd gotten back to common ground. "I just need you to be you, nothing else."

She nodded. "And if those needs change... I'll be sure to adjust accordingly."

"That was never in question to me," I told her, putting my arms around her waist. "Now… enough of this sappy ass conversation. Take your bath. Drink your wine. I'm going to head out."

"Okay. I got a text from Mads while I was downstairs, she's on her way home."

"Girls night?"

Sloane sighed. "Probably not. She's still kinda sad about her breakup, especially since her bestie got a boyfriend, so she's been having to split time. So Madison has been holed up in her room a lot. School starts in a few weeks, so I'm hoping that can take her mind off it enough that she can get over him."

"Yeah, those high school breakups are tough," I laughed.

"They are *so* emotional! And… not gonna lie, I don't think I could handle it tonight, so I'm not even going to bug her about it. Just going to let her listen to whatever artsy whisper-singing black girl is putting out the current heartbreak music in peace."

"Probably a good plan."

After she laughed, Sloane let out a deep sigh before lifting a hand to my face. "Thank you," she murmured, then pushed up on her toes a little to press a quick kiss to my lips. "For everything."

"You are very welcome."

I left Sloane in the bathroom, closing the door behind me before I crossed her bedroom to leave. I was getting ready to step out when Madison rushed up, her face showing low-level panic.

"Oh!" she yelped, obviously not expecting my presence. She stopped short, clutching a laptop in her hands as she looked up at me. "I was um… looking for my mother."

"She's here," I answered, quickly. "Just in the bathroom – in the bath*tub*, actually."

I wouldn't have thought it was possible, but Madison's deep golden skin flushed red. "Um… oh. I am sorry for interrupting."

"Wait, *nooo,*" I denied, holding up my hands as I realized what she thought I was saying. "*Nah*, not like that. She had a rough day, so she's relaxing. *I* was leaving."

She nodded, seeming relieved by my explanation. It was fleeting though, because her expression shifted to disappointment as she blew out a sigh.

"Is… something wrong?"

Even though Sloane and I had been involved for years, that involvement had never extended to her daughter – it had no reason to. That day in the kitchen, after Cole's wedding, was the first time I'd ever even seen her outside of pictures. As such, Madison and I hadn't exchanged enough words to form any kind of connection. Our communications were limited to the steadily increasing – thanks to the shift in my relationship with Sloane – times that we crossed paths coming or going.

But I wasn't about to ignore her when she was clearly having a problem.

For a moment, she hesitated, then sighed again. "It's just… there's this program through my school, where you can apply to take classes at a local university, so you're basically earning college credits while you're still in high school."

I nodded. "Right. It's smart, especially if you can get your gen-eds knocked out early."

"Yeah. But… tonight is the deadline. I wanted my mother to help me, but… it's fine."

"I can help you."

The offer was out there before I really thought it through, but I couldn't take it back. Especially once this hopeful look spread over her face.

"*Really*?" she asked, like she barely believed it, but I nodded.

"Yeah, it's no big deal. What is it, an online application? A couple of short paragraph answers?"

Her eyes got a little wider. "Uh… yeah, actually. How do you know that?"

"I've helped a few players with college-related things, and I mean… I *did* go to college myself. Even worked through a program like what you're talking when I was in high school. I doubt much has changed. We can sit in the kitchen at the counter with it. Come on."

Downstairs, she sat down at the counter and I took the space across from her, with the computer turned so we could both see it. Once she had the application page pulled up, it prompted me to ask something that probably wasn't my business, but that didn't stop me from wanting an answer.

"Hey… why did you wait until today to fill this out? Your mother talks about you often, and I'd gotten the impression you were a pretty type-A kinda girl. This last-minute application doesn't really mesh with that."

Whatever her reason was, she must have been embarrassed about it, because her gaze dropped to her hands. "It's stupid," she mumbled, prompting me to shake my head.

"You know – it doesn't even matter though, right?" I glanced at my watch. "Midnight isn't until hours from now, and as long as it's in, it's in. Let's do this."

That seemed to bring the smile back to her face, and she nodded, moving her fingers to the keys. She'd typed her basic information – name, address, all of that – enough times that the browser window auto-filled it, so it only took a few minutes to get to the meat of the application.

I didn't say anything about it, but was quietly impressed by what I read as she typed in her grades, clubs, sports, community involvement, and other extracurricular activity. With parents like hers, it wasn't surprising that she'd been pushed to excellence, but that didn't change the fact that she'd had to work hard.

"You already know what you're going to major in?" I asked, when she came to a part asking about her post-graduation college plans.

She nodded. "Biology. But the specifics will depend on which particular school."

"Wow. *Biology?*"

"Yep," she grinned. "Everybody says your major doesn't really matter for medical school, as long as you have the grades to get in. But I just think it makes the most sense. I want to complete as much of my general coursework as I can before I even get to college, that way I can jump right into my courses for my major."

"That sounds like a very solid plan – especially at sixteen. You already know where you're going?"

She sighed. "I *did*, but then…"

"Then what?"

"It's stupid."

I *knew* better than to press this issue, especially with a teenager, *especially* with a teenaged girl, but this was the second time she'd dismissed something as "stupid". Usually, it wouldn't have even registered to me, but because this directly involved her college plans…

Shit.

My conscience wouldn't allow me to just let it ride.

"What school was it?" I asked, trying to ease into it.

"BSU. Blakewood," she clarified, unnecessarily.

"That's my alma mater. Blakewood is a great school, with a *great* pre-med program, medical school, University Hospital, all of that. Why would you have second thoughts about *them*?"

She tipped her head back, staring up at the ceiling for a bit. "Because… by the time I get there, Langston will be there too."

My eyebrow lifted. "And Langston is…?"

"My ex-boyfriend."

Ah, hell.

"You're kidding, right?" I asked, before I could catch myself. "You're going to make a major decision based around some knuckle-head ass little boy?"

Any ground I'd gained with her disappeared as her face settled into a scowl. "Of course *you* don't understand. You're… old."

The fuck??

She adjusted the laptop more towards herself, effectively dismissing me as she tapped away with renewed vigor – or maybe anger. Instead of saying anything, I slipped my cell phone out of my pocket and typed out a message to the one person who could probably help me.

"Hey… what do I say to a sixteen-year-old girl thinking about passing up BSU because her ex-boyfriend is going to be there?"

"*Nigga… where are you, first of all. – OKC*"

"**Cole, focus. Time crunch.**"

"*I'm just making sure you aren't on any Pied Piper shit. I mean I don't think you would be, but these days you gotta ask straight up. – OKC*"

"**IT'S MY FRIEND'S DAUGHTER.**"

"*I SAID I WAS JUST MAKING SURE. – OKC*"

I stifled a groan over Cole's derailment of the conversation, and was getting ready to let her know when another text came through."

"*Tell her… I dunno. Books before boys. Degrees before her little fee-fees. Catch footballs, not feelings? Nooo, catch frat, not feelings! – OKC*"

"**Can you be serious?**"

"*Fiiiine. Remind her that no man – or boy, or whatever – is worth sacrificing her best chances for her future. Are there other schools? Sure. But she doesn't want to be thirty years old wondering if she made a mistake based on a boy that she – trust me – is not even going to be thinking about in two years. Especially once she gets to the BSU campus. Fine ass higher educated buffet of boys… that she shouldn't be concerned with. Book before boys. – OKC*"

I let out a quiet chuckle over the content of Cole's text, then looked up to find Madison glaring at me, probably because I was making noise.

"Hey," I told her, attempting to break the ice. "My bad for responding the way I did. I probably could've been more tactful, but… the sentiment remains, Madison. I know your feelings are probably still hurt over this Langston dude, but we're talking about your *future* here." Her glare melted a bit, and that warmth gave me a little more confidence to just say what was on my mind. "You'll probably start applying for pre-acceptance around what… October? By then you won't even be thinking about him, you'll be on to new booty!"

Her eyes went wide, and she shook her head. "I… there's *no* booty. I'm a virgin!"

What the fuck did I just walk into??

"*My bad,*" I insisted, shaking my head. "I'm… used to talking this motivational stuff to pro football players, which you are not, because you're sixteen. You're right – there's no booty and shouldn't be any booty… I think? Good job?"

"Can we stop talking about booty?"

I answered her with a vigorous nod. "*Please.*"

The amused giggle she let out made my shoulders sink with relief as she turned the computer back so that I could see it too. "You don't have to tell me any of this anyway. I *led* with the fact that it was stupid, didn't I?"

My gaze followed where she pointed, to see that she'd listed BSU as her first choice. I nodded lifting my fist to bump hers as a grin spread over her face.

"Hey – since we're cool now," I started, as she moved on to answer the next question. "You want to tell me why you waited last minute on this application?"

She glanced up, nose wrinkled, but didn't say anything.

"Ah, hell. Because of him?"

"I *said it was stupid!*" she defended herself. "But with this, we're not talking about two years from now – we're talking about seeing him on campus with his girlfriend *next month*. I don't know if I'm ready to handle that, but Isabella got her acceptance email today, so I… I don't know. I wasn't going to do it, but I can't let him derail me."

I nodded. "Yeah. Exactly that. You know what, show me this dude."

She looked surprised by my question, but pulled out her cell phone, navigating to the Instagram page of some little wack ass little boy. I took the phone from her.

"Come on, Madison – *him*? What is this hairline? Why is his head shaped like this? And this little mustache… did he fill it with eyeliner or something?"

"I *told* him that was a bad idea," Madison sighed. For a few seconds, neither of us said anything, and then we both busted out laughing. "He was *really* nice," Madison defended herself, because that Instagram feed was indefensible.

"Looking like that, he *had* to be."

We shared a few more laughs at Langston's expense, then went back to her application, breezing through the essay questions and finishing it in much less time than expected. She'd just hit submit when her phone rang, and I gathered from her side of the conversation that it was the friend she'd mentioned earlier, Isabella. They went back and forth for a few minutes, excitedly giggling about the finished application before Madison hung up.

"Thank you," she told me, wearing a big smile as she held up her fist to tap mine again. "I'm going to Isabella's. I'll text my mom. Bye!"

If I was babysitting, I would've gotten fired, because she was gone before I could even register that she'd *told* me where she was going, instead of asking. And how the hell did I know if she was going to text her mother?!

"Don't panic," I heard from behind me, and turned to see Sloane standing in the other exit to the kitchen, partially hidden by the fridge. It was only because she'd said something that I even knew she was there. "Her permission to go to Isabella's is constant. During the summer, she doesn't have to ask."

My shoulders relaxed. "How did you know what I was thinking, and what are you doing out of the bath?"

"I could see the anxiety in your body language, and I've been out of the bath since I overheard you offering to help my teenage daughter. Not that I don't trust you, but… she's my daughter. I had to make sure everything was on the up and up."

I nodded. "I understand that. So… did I pass?"

"With flying colors," she purred, finally approaching and pressing her body to mine. She'd at least undressed for the bath, and I could clearly feel that there was nothing underneath the robe she wore now. "It was pretty sexy, actually. And funny. You were trying so hard."

"Well," I groaned, as her hands slipped into the waist of my shorts and boxers. "Just for transparency, I *did* reach out to Cole for a little help."

She squeezed me. "Mmm – a man who isn't afraid to ask for assistance when he needs it. I'm a fan."

"How much of a fan?" I asked her, dropping my hands to grip her ass, pulling her closer.

She drew away from me, wearing a sexy smirk as she unbelted her robe.

"Come upstairs and find out."

Twelve

Sept 2018

"I. Am. *Exhausted.*"

I pushed out a deep sigh, then accepted the margarita Joan was holding out. The time that I'd be able to enjoy my little backyard oasis was winding down, so with my drink in hand, I sank into the cushions of my chaise, closing my eyes.

"But you're an exhausted *winner*," Zora hummed, and I opened my eyes to find her accepting a drink too before Joan took a seat with her own margarita. "So, cheers to you."

I grinned, and joined them in raising my glass to toast Thursday's win – the first game of the official season. I'd been occupied with the season kick-off barbecue on Saturday, which had been even *more* of an event since the *Kings* won. That meant my much-needed get together with my homegirls had been pushed to Sunday, which was fine, as long as it happened.

It had been *way* too long.

Joan had always been the best mixologist in our little group, so my taste buds were excited about her fresh pineapple margarita. I raised the glass to my lips, nearly bouncing in my seat over the vibrant flavors until I quickly realized…

"Wait… bitch is this a damn *virgin* margarita?!"

Zora and Joan burst out laughing, and Joan nodded. "Uh, yeah. You had a shot with us when Zora first got here, so you're at your limit. You can't drink yourself into a heart attack around me sweetie – I can't keep your ass alive!"

"We'll just call Nate – I'm sure he's close by, since we can't ever get ahold of this bitch cause she's laid up somewhere with her young tender."

My mouth dropped open. "*Wow*, this is the first time all three of us make it to get together in like a year, and *this* is how you're going to do me?"

"Sure is," Joan laughed. "It took you four months to tell us about your lil heart attack, and three months to tell us about your lil man, so yeah… you're going to have to just take these jokes, ma'am."

"But you *knew* about Nate!"

"*Not* that you were catching feelings for him!" Zora argued. "For the last…however long you'd been fucking him, I *admired* the masterful way you kept him at a distance and kept everybody from finding your business out—"

"That wasn't that hard, when nobody would've expected it anyway, and it's not like we were around each other all the time. I was at BSU months at a time, coaching, while he was up here!"

Joan smirked. "Yeah, and he had his ass at *every* alumni event to uh… make donations."

"He was… Very passionate about his alma mater," I argued, barely able to keep a straight face as I did.

"What he was passionate about was *Coach Brooks*." Zora shook her head. "And to think, your ass wasn't even going to "go there" with him. You ought to thank me, honestly."

I rolled my eyes. "*Thank you*, Zoraya Whitfield, for encouraging me to corrupt that young man. I wouldn't be where I am today without you."

"Literally," Joan chimed. "Since he saved your ass."

Zora gasped. "That's *right*, isn't it?! Girl you *owe* me," she teased, sipping her – definitely *not* virgin – margarita. "You want to know something though… I think I'm *more* offended by you not telling us you were getting serious with him than I am about the heart attack. The heart attack, I get. I mean… you see what I did when you *did* tell me."

"Hopped your ass *right* on the family jet," I answered, nodding.

She was right – I *had* known exactly what she was going to do, which is why I'd kept it to myself. I loved my friends, and didn't want to keep anything from them – especially when these were two women I trusted with my life. Still though, after not telling them *immediately* afterward, it never felt like the right time. I didn't want them uprooting their lives to help manage mine, which I knew they would do because I'd do the same. Somehow, it became much easier to just *not* tell them.

So I hadn't.

Until it occurred to me that I couldn't keep counting on Nate to bear the burden of knowing alone.

He said it was no load for him, and I believed that, but that didn't make it fair. He used so much energy checking on and caring for me because he knew he was the only one doing so, as it related to my health. And not just that – he *worried* for me, because keeping secrets took a toll. Once I told Madison, it was a such a relief that I knew I wouldn't be holding on to it much longer.

After my daughter, the *obvious* choice of who to tell next was my friends. If this had happened to either of them, I would want to know. And they *had* wanted to know. It had been a conversation of tears and cursing me out, as I unloaded that burden the night before the *Kings* first game.

In the process, I kinda *had* to tell them about Nate too.

Which, as Zora said, they'd found more offensive.

Joan shook her head. "I still can't believe your ass was out here with a whole boyfriend and hadn't said *nothing*. Taking advantage of the fact that Miles trapped me with those two youngest kids I've had to entertain all summer!"

"While I'm over in Vegas *clueless*," Zora chimed in. "This man done saved your heart, made sure it was healed, then took it. Wow. A real man."

I laughed at her delivery, but couldn't deny it, and I couldn't deny their accusations either. I *had* taken advantage of their busyness and proximity, choosing to stay in my stressful little bubble. And now that I was out, I just felt… *lighter.*

"Guys, I… I don't know what I'm doing here."

Joan lifted an eyebrow. "With regard to…?"

"*Nate.* I mean… our role in each other's lives was clear, and we were firm in what we wanted – we knew that beyond our little affair, we didn't mesh. But then it all just changed, and it is confusing, and scary, and… wonderful. And I don't even know what that is."

"Sounds to me like you're in love," Zora answered, shrugging. "You're not surprised, are you?"

I bit down on my lip. "Yes and no?"

"Because of the age thing?" Joan asked, and I shook my head.

"Nah. I mean, it was a sticking point when we were just sleeping together, and my mind would wander. *Everybody's gonna call me a cougar*, and blah, blah, blah. But now that we're… whatever we are… I don't even think about it now. I don't feel like I'm a forty-three-year-old with a thirty-year-old, I just feel like… a woman with a man. *He* just makes me feel like that."

Zora leaned in. "So then what?"

"I just… didn't expect it. He was talking about not even wanting to be tied down, which was fine by me, because I wasn't looking for that from him. Now am I really sitting here falling in love with him? I mean, I know people can change their minds, they grow, and evolve, but… I was married to a man who didn't *really* want to be tied down. Garrett talked a great game about being together forever, and me being the only woman he wanted, and I believed him, because I loved him. Trusted him because I loved him."

"But Nate isn't Garrett. You can't hold another man's mistakes against him," Joan urged.

Zora shook her head. "She shouldn't ignore her experience either though. We see it all the time, right? Woman gets screwed over by a "good man", then gets called bitter or indecisive or whatever when the next "good" one comes along, as if they don't all look the same until they show their true nature." She pointed to the scar that ran up the side of her face to prove her point. "Done to me by what looked like, to me and everybody else, a "good" man. I'm not saying I think Nate is like that, or even that I think he's just pretending to be good. I *am* saying that there isn't a damn thing wrong with you questioning whether this is what you want, and not rushing to figure it out."

"So it's fair for her to hold this man who has been at her side since her heart attack, been nothing but kind, and caring, and supportive at arm's length while she waffles over what she wants?" Joan countered.

"Is it fair that women are expected to be goddamn clairvoyants when it comes to these manipulative, gaslighting ass men?" Zora shot back, her face pulled into a scowl. "If she dives in headfirst and he fucks her over, guess who gets the blame? Her. She should've known better. If she takes her time figuring out "what he is to her" and where they stand and what their future might be, all the shit we're not supposed to ask *them*, and he decides not to wait anymore, who gets the blame? Her. Shouldn't have taken so long. She's damned if she does, damned if she doesn't, so might as well work at *her* pace. If it's meant to be it's going to be, one way or another, but I'm damn sure not going to expect the woman who got screwed over by a man she was married to for seventeen years to *not* be a little skittish about giving another man her heart."

Joan held up her hands. "Whoa, it seems like you are taking this really personal."

"Because I *am*," Zora admitted, sipping from her drink before she laughed. "I'm just saying – I get where Sloane is coming from. Just because it walks, talks, and even *acts* like a good man doesn't mean he *is*. And when you've been burned before, it's scary trying to figure out the difference. *Take your time*," she said to me, with a nod. "If Nate is who he's portraying, he's not going anywhere, and he'll give you space to figure it out."

"Thank you," I nodded. "*Both* of you. I don't want to make him wait, but I also don't want to go all in, only to have him change his mind again, and decide he *doesn't* want to be with one woman. Or maybe he does, and that woman just… isn't me. Like I said, it's scary, but… I do trust him. I mean, I couldn't even tell you the last time we used protection, even before this shift happened, so…"

"Yeah, that's trust for that ass," Zora laughed. "But I knew that boy didn't want *any* pussy but yours when you told me he flew to goddamn *Texas* just to meet you in a hotel during a long layover."

"I don't believe this whole thing has been a real shift for him," Joan spoke up. "I think he was already in love with you. Or something close to it."

Zora's eyes went big. "You're probably *right!*"

"Oh, come on guys, don't do that," I shook my head. "Yes, he had a crush, but in love with me? No. And he's definitely slept with other women, and I've slept with other men."

"In the last year?" Zora challenged.

I sighed. "No."

"Well then what's your point?!"

"You *know* I don't have one!"

Zora laughed. "Yeah, just making sure *you* knew it too!"

"Okay so, we've established that you're… let's call it *falling* in love. Are you okay with it?"

I thought about it for a second, then shrugged. "I… don't have a solid reason to *not* be okay with it. As for whether I *am* okay with it… I'm coming around to it. Fears or not, Nate is…"

"A walking, talking, life-saving wet dream?" Joan supplied, and I nodded.

"Yeah, that's a pretty accurate summary," I laughed.

"Right. And… Madison knows about him. And she approves?"

I smiled. "And told her little friend, who, in a very giggly manner, told me she thinks Nate is *"dreamy"* and swore herself to secrecy."

"You know what question is coming next, don't you?" Zora asked, exchanging a look with Joan.

"Of course," I agreed. "*When am I going to tell Garrett?*"

Joan sucked in a slow breath between her teeth as she shook her head. "He is going to… blow a gasket. You know he still thinks he has a chance with you?"

I groaned. "I really don't know why. I mean… yes, we kissed, back in June, after the Johnson wedding. That was my bad, because I'm *sure* it gave him a little hope. But he has to understand, while I can be friendly with him – hell, be *friends* with him – and raise our daughter, I am not interested in going back to a lying, cheating man.

Maybe he's changed, and that is totally fine, but I… can't go backward."

"Completely understandable. And if *Mads* is even team Nate, after campaigning for you and Garrett to get back together… Sorry G," Joan said.

"Mads was probably influenced by her breakup. Didn't you say she caught that little boy with another girl?" Zora asked.

I nodded. "Mmm*hmm*. She still loves her father, but I think experiencing it herself put a little depth to her understanding of why mommy isn't trying to kick it with daddy like that again. And besides *all* that… she says Garrett has a new lady friend anyway."

"He *does*." Joan rolled her eyes. "A twenty-two-year-old yoga instructor – I heard him and Miles talking about her, and I was *dying* to ask him, so… *why exactly* are you all up Sloane's ass about getting back together if *this* is what you really want? But I didn't, because I wasn't supposed to have my ear to the office door, so…"

Laughing, I shook my head. "I'll tell you exactly why – Garrett is seeking comfort as he ages. He's still fine enough, fly enough, to get those young ass girls, so he does, I guess to prove to himself that he's still the man. But when the doors to the house close, and it's not about his ego or his dick, he wants a full-bodied *woman*, who he can talk to, who makes him think. Somebody to make his house a home. He can't seem to get it through his head though, that the woman who could give him what he needs, isn't going to play those disrespectful ass games with him. All these men in this industry, their old asses see Eli and Mel Richardson, and think, "Yeah, that's gonna be me." Eli scooped Mel up when she was maybe twenty-five, and he was in his forties. Everybody wanted to congratulate him, and everybody wants to replicate it, but everybody isn't treating their woman like *he* treats *her*."

Joan whistled. "Whew, cause that man *loves* him some Mel, and even with all the gossip and stuff, you *never* hear whispers of him straying. Treats that woman like a queen. *Happily*."

"And there's the key word right there," Zora sang. "It makes him happy to make *her* happy, and a lot of these men aren't about that life. You want a trophy, you better be prepared to keep her polished."

"Baby Mel stays *glistening*, okay?" I laughed. "It's easy to see why he loves her though, she's so damn sunny. And that *baby*, oh my goodness. She's like a doll."

Zora smirked. "Speaking of babies…"

"Oh don't you fucking do it." I shook my head, vigorously. "Madison is almost off to college, and I already got my tits fixed, okay? Are you *trying* to induce another heart attack?"

Both laughed, but they knew I was dead serious. None of us were interested in more kids, and in Zora's case, she wasn't interested in *any*. These baby factories were *closed.*

"Hey," I started, looking right at Zora. "Enough about me – let's talk about you and Trei Norwood, since that's a thing that happened. You've been riding *that* young dick since Valentine's Day. What's the scoop?"

Having effectively shifted the attention off my life onto hers, I settled back in the chaise to keep sipping my virgin drink as Zora launched into her tale. The smile that crept across my face had little to do with what she was saying, and everything to do with the deep comfort and joy of having my friends around me.

I'd needed it more than I knew.

"*Yoga?* Brooks, you gotta be shitting me."

I grinned across the desk at Kyle Underwood before I stabbed another forkful of my salad. "Not at all – I've been researching this, and I think it would be great for my receivers."

He picked up his napkin, finishing a mouthful of his messy, onion-laden chili dog before he spoke again. "So come on. Explain it to me then. And I'm counting on you to make this *good.*"

I laughed around my own mouthful of food and sat back, settling into the comfort of my chair. We were in my office having lunch – probably the last little bit of peace before the preparations for our next game, which we'd be traveling for.

Honestly, the only reason I'd investigated the possibility of yoga as a team was because Dr. Sharpe was insisting on it for *me,* since that whole puppy thing had never happened. Kyle didn't need to know that though.

What *mattered* was that, in my quest to figure out how to work yoga into my schedule, I discovered that it could potentially help my players.

Which meant I wasn't really asking permission. More like, I was running it by him.

"Strength. Flexibility. Increased rotation. I'm talking about making them better at catching balls, faster, more agile, and making them *less* prone to injury while I do it. Getting rid of that dreaded tightness in the hips that effects *everything.* They're going to be able to stretch out longer for the ball. Their bodies are going to handle impact better. And – *and* – there are indisputable mental health benefits to yoga."

Underwood rolled his eyes. "Ah, come on Brooks. You almost had me, and then you had to go there with it!"

"I'm *serious*!" I defended. "What do these guys get out there and do? They're taunting, they're talking shit, they're trying to get into each other's heads. But tell me this – Jordan Johnson, in… what was that, 2016? He gets in an on-field scuffle with Bobby Samuels, because Bobby said something slick about his baby sister. Remember that?"

"Hell yes I remember that."

"Okay, so how does that situation look different if we have a Jordan Johnson who is centered, has been on his yoga shit, can take a deep breath and recognize that this is just to rile him up? He looks at Bobby and says, "Fuck you very much, you be blessed", and walks *away!* Our receivers aren't worried about yo-mama jokes on the field because they left the bullshit on the yoga mat, and they can focus!"

He shook his head. "You really believe this bullshit, don't you?"

"I *do*," I nodded. "And watch – you're going to see a difference, I swear."

"I will believe it when I see it. That's all I can say," he chuckled, then frowned, putting a hand to his chest.

I stopped, fork halfway to my mouth, watching as he winced. "Hey… you good?" I asked, suddenly on high alert.

He was slow to respond, holding up his other hand in a gesture for me to give him a second, but his lack of speech – and the look of deep discomfort on his face – made *giving him a second* an impossibility for me.

As fast as I could, I was out of my seat, rounding my desk to grip his shoulder. "Kyle, are you okay? Tell me what's wrong! Do I need to call 911?!"

"*What*?!" he croaked, turning his frown up to me. "Brooks, relax – I just ate a big ass chili dog. I need an antacid tablet, that's all."

I narrowed my eyes. "Seriously? I could go upside your head for that right now."

He laughed as I stalked back to my seat, dropping into it with my arms crossed. "You telling me you've never seen heartburn before?"

"I'm telling you it didn't look like heartburn from here. And besides that, you're too damn old to be eating this stuff."

"You sound like my wife," he grumbled, gathering his empty dishes.

"She's *right*," I countered. "We're getting older, Kyle. We have to take care of ourselves."

"Isn't the average age for a heart attack somewhere in the mid-sixties? I have a good ten to fifteen years."

I scoffed. "Yeah, that's what I thought too."

He stopped what he was doing and frowned. "Wait a minute… what?"

"Yeah," I nodded. "It… happened to me. And it was scary as hell. I don't want it to happen to you and Sheila."

Kyle shook his head. "Sloane, when the *hell* did you have a heart attack? Garrett never said anything about—"

"That's because Garrett doesn't know," I interrupted, before he could get too far with that. "Because… *nobody* knows."

"When the hell was this? When you were at BSU?"

I sighed. "No. It was this past May."

There was complete silence as my words fully registered, and his expression shifted from confusion to… something else.

"As in… a month after you got hired? As in two months before training camp?! Four months before this season started, and you're *just now* saying something?!"

"It had *no* bearing on my job, and it hasn't affected my performance!"

"Of *course* you don't think so! What the *hell* Sloane?!"

"Kyle, it is my *private* medical information! The *only* reason I said something to you about it just now is because we've known each other a long time – long enough to call you a friend. I'm trying to keep your ass alive – the heart attack isn't the team's business!"

"And what if you keel over on the field? Is it their business then?!"

"You already know the answer to that, and you know I *damn well* wouldn't be the first or last. It's practically the nature of this industry."

He shook his head. "Deflect all you want to, but you *know* you shouldn't have kept this to yourself!"

"Why the fuck *not*?" I asked, seriously. "I *hope* you don't think I'm oblivious to the fact that not everybody wants me here. And those are the very people just *waiting* for me to fail, so they can say "*I told you so. I told you a woman wasn't cut out for this job.*" What the hell do you think would've happened if I'd come and run my mouth to the team?"

"I would've supported you, that's what! So would Lou, so would Eli, so would the receivers. We would've been on your side."

I nodded. "I absolutely believe that, Kyle. I *absolutely* believe that you all would've supported me, and been very vocal about it in your interviews. That I watched. From home. Because you know *goddamn* well I would've been released. It would've been a nice little feel-good story, how the *Kings* attempted to buck the status quo by hiring a Black woman… too bad she wasn't up to the task. And then everything would go right back to the same… except for me. I'd be branded as the woman who just couldn't cut it, and fucked it up for every Black woman behind me. You look me in the face and tell me I'm lying."

His eyes came straight up to mine, blazing and defiant as he opened his mouth. But then, his shoulders deflated, and he let out a deep sigh.

Because he knew I was right.

"You could've come to *me*," he finally spoke, quietly. "Everything you're saying… I get it. But Sloane we go back. I still play golf with G!"

"I didn't want to burden you with this, Kyle. Asking you, before I'd proven myself at all, to keep this secret for me – before we'd even been through minicamp?" I shook my head. "Not saying anything has given me a chance that saying something wouldn't have. These receivers are dropping fewer passes, getting more receptions, getting more yards per catch than this team has seen in *years*. I come to work, I do my job incredibly well, and if we want to keep it a buck, if we're talking about the health of the coaches on this team – on *any* team – I can outmatch probably ninety percent of the men you put next to me."

Kyle grunted. "Do you *really* not see the problem here?"

"Oh no, I definitely see what you *think* is a problem. I'm explaining to you why it's not. If I wasn't doing the work, if I was phoning it in, I would get it. But that's just not the case. It has not slowed me down. It has not stopped me from doing my job. The *Kings* have not lost anything – *only* benefitted. So, you know what, no. I *don't* see the problem. You tell *me* what the problem is."

Shaking his head, he chuckled. "You know… no one could ever accuse you of being stupid – *or* not being able to talk your way out of some shit. You really have me sitting here considering that you might have a point."

"Because I *do*," I insisted. "You can't fault me for not giving this team a chance to discriminate against me because of a medical condition I was *born* with, and couldn't help. I have fulfilled every duty, haven't missed a single practice, a single game –"

"You don't have to convince me anymore, Sloane," he said, holding up his hands. "You *are* right. You've done your job. Exceeded the person who was in the position before you, and you're even adding new ideas. Which is why – *after* you show me something from your doctor clearing you to be out of the bed, let alone in this facility – I'm going to let this slide."

I bit the inside of my lip to keep from popping off, reminding him that I'd done *nothing* wrong for him to "let slide". I wasn't about to talk myself out of a situation that was turning in my favor.

"I'll have Dr. Sharpe write something up. No problem," I told him. "So… this stays between you and me?"

He blew out a sigh. "Yes. If you're performing the duties of your job, there's no reason to report it to anyone. But Sloane… you know this can't stay under wraps forever, right?"

"Of course I do. Like I said, I only told you because I was trying to scare your ass out of those awful foods, but I didn't forget who you were. You're my superior on this team. But… still my friend too, I hope?"

"Take more than defending your right to be here to get rid of me," he said, grinning as he stood, taking his trash with him. "I want to see that note from your doctor *before* we get on this plane though."

I nodded. "Consider it done. But hey… while you're not bringing this up to anyone else… make sure "anyone" includes Garrett. Please?"

He narrowed his eyes. "Seriously?"

"*Seriously*. I don't want or need him all over my back about this. And neither do you, or anyone else, because you already know how he's going to get!"

Kyle pushed out a sigh.

Again, he knew I was right.

"Fine. But you're giving Sheila the recipe for your sweet potato pie."

My mouth dropped open. The *last* thing I wanted to do was put my mama's pie recipe in the hands of his non-cooking ass wife. But if that's what it took…

"You have yourself a deal."

Once he was gone, I reclined my chair as far back as I could, putting my hand to my own chest. The last few weeks had been full of reveals, and they didn't seem to be getting any less stressful. Keeping secrets was hard, anxiety-ridden work.

But as it turned out… *telling* them was no walk in the park either.

Thirteen

"You're preparing to do *what?*"

The tension in my father's voice cut through the pleasant vibe we'd carried all through dinner, bringing the conversation to a halt. Everyone – Cole, Jordan, and Mel – looked to my father, obviously stricken by his tone. Everyone except for my baby sister, Emma, who was in my lap, happily eating off my plate since she'd already finished hers.

Clearing my throat, I looked my father right in his eyes, *mostly* unfazed by the deep scowl on his face. In my peripheral, I could see Mel shifting in her seat, uncomfortable and probably feeling a little guilty, since she was the one who'd asked the question to which I'd given an – apparently – offensive answer.

What do you think you'll do once you move on from the DPS role?

Moving on from the position was no secret – between Cole and me, it had been talked about a lot. We'd grown up in this organization, both had law degrees and minors in sports management. Any internships we'd had were in the *Kings* building, and our first "real" jobs had been the *lite* version of where we were now. As far as the organization went, they were low on the totem pole, with much room for growth.

It was expected that we'd do just that.

Though it wasn't a conversation to be had over dinner, it was my own fault that we'd come to this. It was a big deal around here that the *Kings* were in transition – revamping coaching staff and recruiting risky players this year, new chefs, new diet plans, etc. It was rumored, but not confirmed, that front office shake-ups were coming next.

A rumor I found relieving.

"I said that I was preparing for my licensure to become a sports agent," I repeated, taking care that there wasn't even a hint of wavering in my tone. I loved my father, and he was typically a fair man, but when it came to his children, - me, more than Cole – he had these ideas about how our lives would go. And somewhere along the way, I'd given him the mistaken impression that I had even the *slightest* intentions of adhering to them.

I did not.

After a few more seconds of silence, Eli laughed, even though every adult at the table knew damn well there wasn't anything funny. "Why on earth would you need to do that, son?"

"I don't," I told him. "I *want* to get the license. I *want* to open my own sports agency."

No one else caught the narrowing of Cole's eyes, but I did. She'd just have to eat the annoyance of calling what were *our* plans, my own, unless she wanted to go at it with our father too. But the thing was – she still hadn't told him she was pregnant yet, so she'd probably want to tackle the bombshells one at a time.

This time, I had it covered.

Eli put his fork down, glaring at me across the table. "I thought we'd squashed this years ago? I'm grooming you to own this team one day, not babysit athletes for the rest of your life!"

"But I'm so *good* at it," I told him, grinning, knowing it would get under his skin. "Sorry though – no, *we* didn't squash anything. You didn't want to hear about it, so you haven't heard about it. Now you are."

"*Eli…*," Mel warned, but I already knew it would fall on deaf ears because my father just couldn't help himself.

"You have a path laid at your feet," Eli growled. "I would think you'd be grateful for that!"

I shook my head, nowhere near backing down from this. "I'm grateful for a lot of things you've afforded me – a great childhood, financial stability, an education, experience in this industry. As far as I'm concerned, that's quite enough – I'll pass on the keys to the kingdom."

"This team isn't good enough for you now?!" was *exactly* the response I expected, knowing that Eli's interest in *understanding* what I was saying was low.

"That's not even remotely what came out of my mouth. I'm not insulting you, not trying to appear ungrateful, nothing like that. I'm just saying I want to build something of my own. Which you *should* understand. You didn't build your empire on football alone."

It wasn't talked about much, because most people didn't really care – the Richardson name was synonymous with football. The

Richardson *money*, however, was built on tech investment. Before any of the big tech and internet giants became what they were now – hell, before I was born – smart people had urged my father to invest in them. Big risks back then had paid off in a *massive* way, enabling him to secure the *owner* title he wielded so proudly.

Deservedly.

But it had come from hard work and patience and smart investment and taking risks – *not* – from having shit handed to him.

Those were the footsteps I wanted to follow in.

"I built it so my kids would not *have* to," he argued, making me shake my head.

"Sorry, old man. But you raised the wrong kind of kids if that's what you're expecting from us, to just fall in line and follow instructions." I pointed to Cole, then back at myself. "Neither of us is built that way, and I'm baffled as to why you're expecting me to be content with what… working my way up to a couple hundred thousand a year and biding my time until you hand over the reins?"

Eli huffed. "So you want a raise? Is that what this is about?"

"It's not about the *money*," I barked, louder than intended, but… *shit*. It's like he was committed to misunderstanding me. "It's about not being satisfied to simply live the stress-free life you planned out for me. I want *more* than that."

"Well if my business isn't good enough for you, my food shouldn't be either. You can leave my table."

My face wrinkled up *immediately* over that shit, but hey – I didn't have to be told twice.

I kissed an oblivious Emma on her cheek, making her giggle as she polished off my pasta. When I stood, amid protests from Cole and Mel, I sat her down in my chair, pushing her up to the table.

"Nate, you do *not* have to leave," Mel insisted. "I made a cheesecake, and I—"

"Save me a slice, okay?" I kissed her cheek too, then moved to my sister and Jordan, offering both a quick goodbye before I waved to my father, who simply grunted.

That whole *asshole* thing I used to be pegged with often?

I got it honest.

I wasn't too bothered or offended by my father asking me to leave – I was no fan of being where I wasn't wanted, I was ready to go anyway, and I wasn't about to argue with another man over his space.

What got under my skin was his complete disregard for the fact that I was a grown ass man, more than capable of executing a successful plan for my life. The fact he thought I wanted or needed *more* of his influence, after he'd already gotten me this far.

That was the offensive part.

As I peeled out of his driveway, I called Sloane, hoping she'd pick up. When she did, I tried not to sound too relieved at the sound of her voice.

"You think you could meet me at my place?" I asked, once we'd passed the usual pleasantries.

"*Your* place?"

The surprise in her voice was warranted – she'd never even been to the condo I lived in now, since her place had always been the one that granted us real, nearly guaranteed privacy.

"Yeah. I'm headed back up from my father's house, and I—"

"Don't want to be in the car for over an hour," she finished for me. "I get it, it's just…yeah. Yes, I can meet you."

"You sure?"

She laughed, but it was soothing. "You kinda sound like you *need* me to, rather than *want* me to, so… yeah. I'm assuming your building has codes to get inside?"

I gave her what she needed and we ended the call, giving me the chance to turn up something loud and ignorant on the radio. The longer I drove, the more upset about that conversation I realized I was, which only made me *more* annoyed.

It wasn't like my father's disdain for my career goals had come out of the blue. The shit had just been lying dormant until I even *mentioned* taking the next step of making it real.

I wasn't surprised that I beat Sloane to my place, even though she was closer to it than I was when I'd called. The team had the next day off, before they began practice for the next game, so I was banking on her taking the time to pack a bag, and stay the night.

She showed up at the door in a baggy hoodie and sweats, half her face hidden by sunglasses, and her hair tucked away under a hat. She was barely inside before she started the transformation, stripping all that extra shit off until she was down to a tee shirt and shorts, her hair wild around her shoulders, and that pretty ass smile.

"Okay," she sighed, climbing into my lap once we'd put her things away and settled on the couch. Her words broke the veil of silence. "Tell me what's going on. Did something happen?"

I looked into her pretty brown orbs, finding genuine concern as her hand came up to stroke the short hair on my chin.

"This week, I'm going to start my league certification process."

Immediately, her mouth broke into a huge grin, and she grabbed both sides of my face. "*Really?*" she gushed. "You're finally going for it?"

"Yeah," I nodded. "I am."

I couldn't even describe how relieving it was that she just… *immediately* knew exactly what I was talking about, even though we hadn't talked about it in a while. It was ever-present in the back of *my* mind, but the last three years had been devoted to my position with the *Kings*. A position I felt had given me a great experience to take with me on my next step.

The sports agency thing was something I'd shared with Sloane long ago – something she had specific, valuable insight on because of her ex-husband. She'd never minimized it, never asked me about remaining under my father's thumb. As different as our relationship had been back then, she'd never been anything but supportive when it came to my personal development.

I was glad to see that wasn't changing now.

"Okay, so… tell me everything," she insisted, still wearing that big smile. "Are you just doing NFL certification for now, or are you doing them all? What firm are you looking to start with, or you're still thinking about starting your own? Is Cole coming with you? When did you decide to go for it?"

I laughed, grabbing her face to pull her in for a kiss. "Woman, do you really expect me to answer all those questions at one time?"

"Sorry," she chuckled. "I may have gotten a teensy bit carried away, but I'm just *really* excited for you. You told me about this… what, the *first* year we met? You'd just finished that law degree."

I nodded. "Yep. I just *knew* you'd be impressed."

"Because you didn't realize I was feeling very *anti*-agent because of Garrett," she laughed. "Almost ruined your chances. You're lucky I'm so nice."

"You *did* give me some great advice," I told her, burying my fingers in the hair at the nape of her neck. "I almost didn't even take that Assistant Director of Player Success job, but *you* told me the experience would be valuable. And that being able to say I worked the front office would be a draw for future clients."

She furrowed her brow. "Are you *really* about to sit here and try to convince me you didn't take that job just so your sister wouldn't have a one-up on you?"

"There was that too," I laughed. "But to answer one of your *many* questions… yeah, I think she's coming with me. Maybe. We'll see."

Altering her position to settle against my shoulder, legs draped across my lap, she shook her head. "It's exciting either way, and I know you'll thrive, but the two of you together? I can just imagine the energy. You two competing over who can sign the biggest clients, get the best endorsements – you know what you should do? Get Wil Cunningham's crew to follow you around, make a whole show of it. You and your twin competing against each other, talking shit, but then ultimately celebrating your shared success? TV *gold*."

"You know… I wish I hated that idea, but I don't," I admitted. "I actually agree with you."

She rolled her eyes. "*Duh*, because it's a great idea. But um… why do I get the feeling there's more to this? You didn't ask me to come to you just so you could tell me you were getting your… MLB license?"

"NFL first," I clarified. "Go with what I know first, and then yeah, we'll go for the others. But you're right… it's not just that."

A sad sort of smile crossed her lips – this was a situation where there was no pleasure in being right. "Something happened with your father?" she correctly guessed, making me narrow my eyes.

"How the hell did you know that?"

"Well, I've known you for four years, Nate. That's the *only* thing I've ever seen just really get under your skin. So… what was it this time?"

I blew out a sigh, closing my eyes as I sank back into the couch cushions. She didn't push when it took me a moment to verbalize my issue, just waited.

"I'm just struggling with the amount of influence he wants to have over my life, you know? I mean, it's always been kinda frustrating, but lately it's to a point where I have to wonder if he realizes that I'm a *grown man*."

Sloane smirked, but didn't say anything until I prompted. "Well… you sure you want *my* input? Because you *know*, I'm going to give it to you real, no water to wash it down."

"Please do," I insisted. "I want to hear your position on this."

Her eyebrow lifted, but she nodded. "Okay. I think… Eli is having a little trouble swallowing the idea that you're a *grown ass man*, because *you* have only recently swallowed it yourself."

I frowned. "Explain."

"Okay – think about it. Your father raised you, right? You were in his house, until you went off to his alma mater, on his dime. Well… I'm sure you had scholarships too, but you get my point."

I tipped my head in agreement. "Of course."

"So," she continued. "You get your business degree, minor in sports management, move on to law school – he paid for that. You finish school, yay, and then… you move right into a job on *his* team. Before that, you *interned* on his team. Everything you've done followed a very specific narrative and has always been under the careful direction or control of your father. But… I've watched you during that time. When you and I met, you were very content with your life, but as you approached thirty, you started feeling the discontent. And then the birthday hit, and you… I don't know. A switch flipped. Not like your biological clock exactly, or… I don't know, maybe it is. Only for you, it wasn't about a rush to get married, or have children… it was about being your own man. Be patient with your father. It's an adjustment."

Instead of immediately responding, I took a moment to digest the truth of her words. But after the moment had passed, I still shook my head.

"I get what you're saying, I really do. But… I don't believe I'm the only one who's changed. Something with *him* is different. He's getting more and more aggressive about it."

She nodded. "Oh it's *absolutely* not just you. Eli is getting older – he's probably trying to make sure everything is lined up for y'all, before he's not here to. And now with Emmanuelle, it likely feels *urgent*. Is that when you noticed him ramp it up? When she was born?"

"Now that you mention… *yes*. That *is* when he started getting super territorial, started *really* pushing kids. I guess he hasn't thought about his grandkids being the same age as their aunt Emma. This is some talk show shit."

Sloane laughed. "*Stop!*"

"I'm *serious*," I chuckled. "Madison is already old enough to babysit her step-aunt."

Her eyebrows shot up. "Oh so you're considering yourself her stepfather now?" she asked, grinning because she knew I was playing with her… *mostly.*

"Madison is my homie, aiight?"

"Mmmhmm, keep that energy when her *father* finds out about you. Which is… inevitable. Now that she knows, and Joan knows - which means it's only a matter of time before she slips and tells Miles - I'm expecting a confrontation at any moment."

I frowned. "So why not just tell him?"

"Because I'm afraid of what he'll do."

"To you?!"

She shook her head. "No. To *you.*"

"Man," I sucked my teeth. "Ain't nobody scared of Garrett's big ass."

"It's not about that. I don't want *any* drama, but we're past the point of that, so now I'm just… avoiding it as long as I can."

I grinned. "I appreciate your honesty."

"Good. So that means you'll give your father a break?"

My eyes went wide. "What the hell does he need a break from *me* for? He's the one acting like it's a slap in the face that I want to work for myself, *just* like he does!"

"Your father is a Black man who, against all the odds, has managed to amass enough wealth to afford his children a life where they don't *have* to work. Where they don't have to want for anything. He wants you to appreciate it."

"I *do*," I argued. "But the problem with that is, he didn't raise us not to work. He raised us to get our own. Now when I want to go do that, he's mad at it?!"

Sloane laughed. "Parenting is complicated, Nate! Yes, it's wildly contradictory, and he's going to realize that, and accept you, and support you, and be proud of you. He might just be mad and swear you're an ungrateful child first. Just try not to take it personally. It's not about you. It's about *him*."

"This is crazy."

"This is parenting. If you're going to be a stepfather… honey you better figure it out," she laughed. "Now… tell me more about how you're going to make this sports agent thing happen."

I was more than happy to shift the subject back to my plans, rather than dwelling on the baffling situation with my father. I didn't doubt that Sloane was right, but honestly… I preferred hearing her gush about how great she thought I was going to be overhearing her urge patience with my father.

I didn't want to be patient.

I wanted space to make my own damn decisions.

And I had every intention of taking it.

"Coach Brooks is here to see you."

"Send her in. Then you're good to go for the day," I told Elliot, using the intercom system at the desk. I pushed out a heavy sigh as I waited for her to breach my doorway, knowing that for once, this *might* turn out to be a not-so-pleasant visit.

She breezed through the doorway, doing a good job of appearing unbothered, but I knew her better than that.

Terrence Grant had gotten under her skin.

Because of that, she'd gotten in his ass.

Problem was... she'd taken it a little too far this time.

"To what do I owe the pleasure of this visit to the principal's office?" she asked, crossing her arms over her chest. Her expression was hard, but in her *Kings* v-neck and bright gold jersey shorts, and her hair pulled up in a puff, she looked *just* as soft as I knew she was.

Shit was distracting.

"Terrence Grant."

Her jaw tightened, and she shifted her stance, but didn't say a word.

"Really, Sloane?" I asked, and all she did was twist her lips to the side, casting her gaze somewhere out the window.

"He's going to be fine – since you seem to be *dying* to know."

She sucked her teeth. "*Duh.* Everybody except Terrence Grant knew he was going to be fine. And the only reason he didn't is because he's a little bi—"

"*Sloane!*"

"I am *fucking sick of him,* Nate!"

My lips parted, a little surprised by her outburst. Terrence was... a cornball, honestly. He never knew when to shut the fuck up, never knew when to leave a situation alone, was *constantly* inserting himself where he didn't belong, and he had a problem following instructions on the field. He grated the nerves of everyone on the team, from my father's office to the training room to the locker room to the damn field.

He had the power to get under damn near anybody's skin, I *knew* that. If it had been pretty much anybody else, any other coach, I wouldn't have even blinked about.

But *Sloane*?

"You made him run laps until he *passed out*."

"I bet he won't question my authority again."

"He might file a formal complaint though."

"And I'll make his ass run laps for *that* shit too," Sloane shot right back, obviously not interested in the whole *being the bigger person* thing, at least not this time around. "He will *not* get a single fucking yard Sunday, and when he wants to know why, somebody can let him know that there are precious few people on that field who can question my authority, and *none* of those motherfuckers are named *Terrence*."

She stared me right in the face as she said all of that, practically daring me to dispute it. But there was nothing to dispute. She was right – Terrence *did* need to respect her authority, just like all the other receivers, who had a great relationship with her. Even Amare, who everyone had expected to be the problem child. I wasn't sure what was going on with him this season – he'd always had an attitude problem, but it seemed especially potent this season.

Still though – she'd made him run until he passed out.

Not like he was a little tired, claimed he couldn't go any further, but more like *"get a medic out here, he can't open his eyes"*.

He wasn't the first to get such a punishment, and wouldn't be the last – Sloane wasn't even in any actual trouble, and the other coaches thought it was hilarious.

But *my* job was a player advocate.

Terrence asked me to talk to her, so that's what I was doing.

"Listen," I started, standing to approach her, since she'd ignored my nonverbal invitation to sit down. "I understand that Grant is… challenging. I've wanted to crack his head more than once myself. But this shit… it's not a good look outside the organization – and it's not Terrence that'll be the one getting the hard scowls. It'll be you. It'll be Underwood for letting you do it, and Eli's for hiring you. It'll be this team. Everybody *except* Grant's dumb ass," I explained, knowing that the best way I could advocate for Terrence wasn't to point out how *he* was affected, but how *others* might be.

Grant wasn't exactly a sympathetic character.

"Fine. So I won't make him run again. But I *damn* sure won't accept another word of disrespect or insubordination out of his mouth. I am *not* a hard person to work for – nobody is complaining, are they?"

I shook my head. "Not at all. I've heard nothing but raves. They like you a lot – and *love* what you're doing for their game."

"*Okay*! So… I don't know what Grant needs to hear from you, or Eli, or Coach Lou, whoever, but… I need him to get in formation, or as far as I'm concerned, he's eliminated. I will *not* put him in a game to embarrass this team because he thinks he knows better than everybody. I have other receivers who may not have the experience, but they damn sure have the heart and the work ethic. If he doesn't straighten up, he'll be replaced."

I nodded. "That's fair. And doesn't require the injury cart," I teased, grinning when I caught the tiniest hint of a smile at her lips. "You can't be out here trying to kill them, Coach Brooks."

"They need to know I don't fuck around. At *all*," she insisted, turning her head to hide the fact that she was smiling a bit more.

I grabbed the hem of her shirt, tugging her closer so I could wrap an arm around her waist. "Like… at all?"

"Nope."

I dropped my head, planting a kiss just behind her ear. "Like… not at *all*?"

"Uh-uh."

I moved in a little more, giving her a gentle nip to the neck that had her giggling and squirming in my grasp. "Not even now?"

"Nate, what are you doing?" she asked, even though she didn't pull away, at all.

What I was doing, was getting ready to investigate the contents of her tee shirt when the door to my office swung open, and Cole stepped inside, with a big ass donut halfway up to her mouth.

Her eyes came to me, then went to Sloane, then dropped to my arm around Sloane's waist, before I got over my surprise enough to remove it.

"*Holy shit*," Cole whispered, mouth full as Sloane sprang away from me – way too fucking late.

"I… am going to my office. Bye!"

Before I could say anything, Sloane had darted out the door, closing it behind her. Leaving me alone with my twin sister and her Cheshire-catlike grin.

"*Nigga,*" she started, eyes still wide. "I *knew* there was somebody. I even suspected it was an older woman – I *knew* it would take a certain type to pin you down. But… *Sloane Brooks*? Used to be on a poster in your room *Sloane Brooks?!* I walked in there on you without knocking and damn near lost my eyesight *Sloane Brooks?! Fine ass groundbreaking ass body goals fucking Sloane Brooks?! How dare youuuu???*" she asked, dropping her donut onto my desk and wiping her hands. "Like… when did *you* get the swag? When did *you* get the *nerve*? Like… I can't even deal with this; my mind is really blown right now. *My* brother had the juice to pull *Sloane Brooks*… I'm… proud of you."

I shook my head. "Cole, can you not—"

"No, I'm *serious!* I mean, don't get me wrong, you got ya lil money, ya lil body, lil handsome face and all that, you cute. I'm not like embarrassed to tell people you're my twin, you look *worthy* of being my brother. But I had *no* idea you were hitting it out of the park like *that*, wow!"

"*Relax.*"

"I will *not*," she insisted. "What is the *tea?*" she sat down, uninvited, and crossed her legs. "Is it serious, how long has it been going on? It can't have been long, cause you don't know you're supposed to lock the door, and get a white noise machine for in here if you're going to try to get booty at work. And get a padded mat for under the desk."

I covered my hands with my face. "*Cole…*"

"What? I'm trying to help you out, and you *still* haven't answered my questions! You know this was fate, right? You found out *my* secret from bursting into my office unannounced, and now it's how I found out yours! We're twinning right now Nate, do you feel it?"

Blowing out a sigh, I leaned on my desk. "Yeah, Cole. It's potent."

So potent, in fact, that I had no issue grabbing her donut and taking a bite before she rescued it from my hands.

"I don't even need to ask you not to tell anyone, do I?"

She scrunched her face up at me. "Hell no. But if you're careless, it won't be a secret long, and it *won't* be my fault."

"We managed to keep it under wraps four years," I admitted. "And nobody knew anything."

Cole's eyes went big. "You've been smashing Sloane Brooks for *four* years?"

"Don't… say it like that," I asked, that characterization feeling almost like an insult. "It's more than that. Or at least… it is now."

Which is why it was becoming harder to keep this under wraps. When we were just sleeping together, keeping it quiet was nothing. But now that things were deeper, we wanted to be around each other, and hiding it was already old as fuck to me.

I really didn't give a shit what anybody else thought.

"Oh, so it's… *serious,*" Cole realized, sitting up. "You didn't just *pull* Sloane. You've… *cuffed* her."

I shrugged. "Something like that."

"Wow," she nodded. "This really is… mind-blowing. I mean… what's the end game? I know you've talked about not settling down, not having babies… it seems like only one of those is true now?"

"Yeah… it does. And as far as the end game… I don't know. I just know we make each other happy, and that's what we'll keep doing until… I guess until we don't anymore."

"As long as you're happy," Cole agreed, breaking into a smile. "And if you ever decide you're not… you better figure out how to break it to her easy, cause I can't fight her. Pregnant or not, Sloane would beat my ass.

I laughed, shaking my head. "Nah, it's not like that. I don't anticipate that happening any time soon. But um… how can I help you?"

"Scuse me?" Cole asked, her mouth full of donut again. She was approaching nine weeks now, and claimed she hadn't noticed any symptoms so far, even though her pregnancy had been confirmed, and according to her doctor seemed to be progressing fine. But every time I saw her lately, she was eating.

My eyebrow lifted. "You needed something, right? That's why you came to my office…"

"Oh! I wasn't looking for you. I was looking for Sloane, and somebody told me she was up here, but there was nobody at the reception desk, so I came in, cause I knew you were just fussing at her about Terrence's bitch ass."

"*Hey.*"

She shrugged. "What? He's not *my* player, and he gets on my husband's nerves. I'll call him what I want."

"Okay," I laughed. "So why were you looking for Sloane?"

"Well, if you hadn't been playing grab-ass when I walked in, you'd know, because I would've just talked to both of you. But now," she said, pulling herself up from the chair. "I'm just gonna talk to her. Bye."

"Don't ask her anything about us."

Cole scoffed as she made her way to the door. "Yeah, I'm *definitely* not making that promise. Do you know me at all?"

"That's why I'm asking you not to. As a matter of fact, don't *tell* her anything either."

"Fun-killer," she whined. "You mean I can't *ask* her why the hell she's settling for you, and *tell* her she could do so much better? You're not even going to have a job next season if you keep stressing Daddy out."

I sucked my teeth. "Man, tell your Daddy to quit stressing *me* out," I countered. "I'm good over here. I have a meeting about league certification tomorrow. You coming or not?"

"You know I am. Send the information to my calendar. Thank you, for not putting me on blast at dinner the other night. Cause I would've yelled, "*Jordan got Cole pregnant*" to get the heat off my ass. You're a real one."

Smirking, I lifted my fist for her to tap with her own. "You know I couldn't sell you out like that. Besides – you're his baby girl anyway, he would've been cool."

"Nah, that's Emma now," Cole laughed. "But I can't blame him, with those little cheeks of hers. She got mad at him when you left, you know."

"Emma? Or Mel?"

"*Both*," Cole said, shaking her head. "Anyway, like I said – count me in for that meeting tomorrow. This pregnancy won't stop anything. I won't let it."

We parted ways, with me feeling surprisingly okay with Cole knowing about me and Sloane. It wasn't as if she didn't know how to keep a secret – she and Jordan's little reunion had been kept on the low as long as she could.

The difference was though, that my father knew, and approved.

I somehow doubted he would be quite so open to the idea of me and Sloane.

If he doesn't already know.

I shook my head, clearing it of that thought. Knowing Eli like I did, there was *no* way he'd stay quiet about it if he even had an inkling. Hell, he'd tried to intervene with Amare and Parker, and neither of them was even family.

He just couldn't help himself.

Taking a seat at my desk, I did as Cole asked, forwarding the meeting information to her calendar. It wasn't that either of us was in a hurry to leave, but if we didn't start taking the steps toward independence from the *Kings*, independence from our father… it would never happen.

And *that* wasn't an option.

My heart was still racing when the knock sounded at my door. From my seat at the desk, I looked at it, then reached for the remote to pause the TV.

"Come in!"

I was *not* expecting Nicole Richardson at my door, but there she was anyway, tall and beautiful, and striking in her similarity to her brother.

Because they're twins, fool.

"Cole... um, how can I help you?"

"I'm *not* here to talk about you and my brother," she assured, closing the door behind her when she stepped in. "But, just so you know, you don't have to worry about me telling anyone. The secret is safe with me. Just... don't break his heart? Please?"

I grinned, pushing out a sigh. "Um... I kinda already tried. Tried to get rid of him, and he wouldn't let me."

"Yeah," Cole smiled back. "He probably never told you this, but whenever all our cousins and stuff got together for pickup games, Nate played defense. He's *always* been good at pass interference."

"Sounds about right. But... you said you *weren't* here to talk about Nate. So how can I help you?"

She pushed out a breath, then sat down across from my desk. "Before I say what I have to say... I need you to promise me that you won't mention this to Jordan. *Ever.* I know it's unconventional, and probably breaking a few rules, but... I'm desperate."

My brows wrinkled in concern as I leaned forward, elbows propped on the desk. "I... sure, Nicole. If you tell me something that I need to act on, I will, but this conversation can absolutely remain confidential. What's going on?"

She swallowed, hard, staring into space for a moment before she met my eyes. "His shoulder. I know the team doctor says it's fine, and I know *he* says it's fine, but what my eyes see is him icing it every night. Asking me to rub it down. They won't give him an MRI. Because they *know* something is wrong, but they also know he's needed on that field. And he won't push, because he…," she stopped for a moment, her voice choked. "He *loves* this game. He *loves* this team. But… I don't want him to not be able to hold our baby next year because he was trying to catch a fucking *ball*."

My breath caught in my chest, as conflicting emotions dueled for control over my mouth. I empathized with her, God knows I did, but at the same time… "Whatever team I'm coaching, no matter where I am – I always try to act in its' best interest. Full stop, no matter my personal feelings… I would *never, ever* put in a player who I knew wasn't healthy enough to play. If I even think it, he's sitting his ass on the bench, because the health of these guys is absolutely within the team's best interest."

"I believe you, Sloane. But you must know that not everybody is operating with the same integrity. In a lot of ways, this team is progressive, and innovative, but in other ways… it is *just* like the rest of the league. How else do you explain the team doctor writing him a goddamn hydrocodone script, and sending him on his way, saying he's fine. Why a *narcotic painkiller* if everything is fine?!"

I pushed out a sigh. "Because it's not." I sat back, looking up toward the ceiling to organize my thoughts before I spoke again. "But my hands are tied here, Cole. As much as I want to take your word for it, if the doctor says he's fine, and Jordan says he's fine, and I don't *see* anything… I cannot justify keeping our star wide-receiver off the field. I'm going to be honest with you – I noticed him favoring his other side, before the season started. I talked to him, he said he would rest it. I have *not* seen a problem since then."

"Because he's gotten better at hiding it!"

"I *believe* you," I told her. "I honestly do. But the only thing I can promise is that if I see even the slightest indication that he's having trouble, I *will* pull him. You know how this works, my say isn't final on that field, I am *not* the head coach."

She nodded. "I understand. But you're the only one I can say this to. I know you care about him, you've cared since BSU. I know I can trust you with him."

I smiled. "Yes. You can. And... a *baby*? Did I hear that right?"

She sniffled, pulling her emotions into check as she smiled. "Yes. I would say I'm surprised Nate didn't tell you, but... no I'm not."

"He's very good at keeping things to himself," I agreed. "But in any case, *congratulations*. Babies are wonderful."

"Thank you," she gushed, then shook her head. "Although... part of me wonders if I would have *ever* dared to approach you about this if it wasn't for these... damn pregnancy hormones. This is *really* out of line."

I shrugged. "Sometimes that's what it takes. Jordan is your *husband*, and you want to protect him. I completely get that. More than you know. You know who my ex-husband is?"

"Of course. Garrett Brooks."

I nodded. "Yeah. Garrett developed *horrible* knees. So bad we actually went to an outside doctor who told us he was at risk to never walk again." I shook my head. "But the team? Swore he was fine. And he was under contract, and I... was pregnant. I went to his coach – his *head* coach, because they were spouting that shit about the Kings being a family. So I went to my *family* for help, and they laughed in my face, and… that was Garrett's last season on the field. It took *years* of physical therapy for him to not have a limp. But this was before Eli took over. *Right* before Eli took over. And he's turned a *lot* of things around, but some things… like you said, are just a plague on the league itself. I don't know what it will take to get it turned around."

"Me either," Cole whispered, staring into space again for a moment before she seemed to snap back into reality. "Anyway… *thank you*, for hearing me out."

I stood when she did, accepting her hand when she offered it across the desk. "No need to thank me, at all. Thank *you* for trusting me enough to bring this to me. I will be watching him like a hawk."

"I appreciate that, so much. And um… if you and Nate ever want company… Jordan and I are available. I know how lonely it can feel, even when you're together, to have to always be behind closed doors to protect your privacy. We *love* a good double date."

My lips parted. "I… wow. I *really* appreciate that. And I'd love to get to know you better, especially since…"

"You're coaching my husband, dating my brother, working for my father. All the men in my life have their own separate piece of Sloane Brooks, and *damn it* I want in on that action," she laughed, and I came around the desk, abandoning the shaking of hands to give her a hug.

Once she was gone, I let out a deep breath, suddenly drained.

From that horrible practice with Terrence, to the shock of her walking in on us, to her emotional appeal, and then on to the memory of damn near the same thing with me and Garrett… I was *wiped*.

A knock sounded at my door again, even though it was still open. I looked up to find Nate standing there, his eyes looking nearly as tired as I felt.

"Your place or mine?" he asked – a simple question full of more comfort and warmth than I could describe.

A quiet, contented sigh pressed through my lips, and I smiled.

"Yours is closer."

Fourteen

"Get back to the kitchen, bitch!"

"Nice tits!"

"You belong on a field, nigger! Welcome back!"

I heard it all, but tuned it all out.

Even the positive affirmations that were more plentiful than the others, but never rang quite as loud. Ignoring *all* of it was vital, if I wanted to keep my head in the game.

We'd just returned from halftime, and the crowd was antsy because of the tied score. Tensions were high – this was an away game for us, and of course the other team's fans didn't want to lose.

But obviously… neither did we.

And we weren't going to.

The strategy moving forward had already been discussed. It was our ball, and we had every intention of dominating the next plays with an aggressive offense. Coach Lou was sharing his last few words at the sideline before we headed to the field when I saw it.

Jordan Johnson winced, hard, as one of his teammates brushed past, accidentally bumping his shoulder, even through all that padding. He was quick to fix his face though, his eyes darting around to see if anyone else had noticed. These guys played through pain all the time, and mostly considered it no big deal. But knowing what I did about his previous injury – one that had required a surgery to fix – there was no way I was just letting this go.

Especially after that conversation with Cole.

Using my headset, I connected privately to Underwood, who was already up in the press box for a better view of the field as we resumed play.

"We need to pull Jordan," I spoke into my earpiece, using my hand to cover the movements of my lips from any nosy cameras. "Something is up with his shoulder."

"He complaining?" Underwood asked – a question I'd already known was coming.

"No. But—"

"We need him in this half, to put this pressure on. Didn't the doctor say he was fine?"

I huffed. "Underwood, I *know* what I'm seeing, and he should not be out there."

"We have to trust the professionals on this, you know that," Underwood replied, not unkindly, but still. "If he's not complaining, I can't just go with your eyes. Let's get through this next quarter, then re-evaluate. Best I can offer."

Shit.

"Fine," I told him, then disconnected. I rushed over to where players who were headed to the field were breaking from their huddle, stopping Jordan to ask, as low as I could, "Are you good?"

Instantly, he hit me with that dazzling smile of his, full dimples and all, even though that same confidence didn't quite reach his eyes. "I'm *good* Coach B. Watch me run this ball."

"*Jordan*," I insisted, helplessly, as he jogged away from me, onto to the field. I stepped back, watching him like a hawk, with a sick feeling.

Relax, Sloane.

The most likely worst thing to happen was he simply didn't catch the ball – there was no need to imagine the less likely, but worse, alternatives.

Apparently, the other team had gotten a little pep talk too, because they came out of the gate strong with the defense. For one reason or another, we couldn't get any real movement with the ball, and before I knew it, we were on a third down with five yards to go.

Obviously, my eyes were on Jordan as the play began – for him, a slant route, that he'd done a billion times, and had perfected. He was good – hands up, ready for the ball, perfect, precise foot placement, nicely angled, and so fast that he easily shook his defender off.

The problem was, the other defenders got after Bailey, the quarterback, so fast that he had to launch the ball at a less than perfect angle, sending it soaring high.

Jordan was a pro at this though, and he adjusted quickly.

Those basketball drills I'd had them doing came in handy as he sprung upward, leaping for the ball and catching it securely in his hands. My heart jumped into my throat as he clutched it firmly against his chest, ready to take off toward the end zone as soon as his feet hit the ground again.

Only…that didn't happen.

"*No!*" I screamed, as a safety came out of nowhere, taking Jordan out at the legs. My eyes opened wide, horrified, as he hit the ground, hard, taking the brunt of it with his elbow and shoulder.

"No. *No, no, no,*" I whispered to myself when he didn't immediately get up. He was quickly surrounded by his teammates, and my heart dropped from my throat all the way down to my feet when the nearest ref started signaling and calling for a medic.

The crowd was… quiet.

Of course not completely silent, but competition or not, no one liked seeing players get hurt. A knot of tension twisted in my stomach as I waited for the crowd to part, waited to see Jordan's teammates help him off the field.

I waited.

And waited.

And *waited.*

Then, finally, I gave up trying to not just be one more body in the way on the field, and headed out there myself with Coach Underwood at my heels, having rushed down from the press box. We were almost there when the crowd broke, and instead of seeing Jordan on his feet, he was strapped to the injury cart, wearing a precautionary neck brace and a pained expression.

Still, he lifted a hand to the crowd, a sign that was supposed to show that he was okay. I caught Coach Lou's eyes long enough for him to give me the slightest shake of his head, refuting the insinuation of that hand signal.

He was *not* okay.

My hands were shaking as the cart rushed past, into the tunnel, and both Lou and Underwood converged on me.

"Brooks – we have to make a decision. We're keeping Reyes in the slot position, but we need another receiver out there. Who you got?"

*Oh **now** you want my opinion?*

I bit my tongue rather than saying what was really on my mind, and instead glanced back at my players. The obvious choice was Grant, who had the most experience, but then my eyes fell on Amare, who between the two of them, was more consistent.

"Amare!" I called, not bothering to consult with Underwood first. "You're in." I turned to my superiors, giving them a nod. "He's your guy. He can do this. Now… can I go check on my other receiver?"

Lou nodded. "Go. Keep us updated."

By the time I made it to the back, they'd already stripped off his pads to do the mobile imaging on his shoulder. It took everything in me not to wring our team doctor's neck, knowing how insistent he'd been that there was nothing wrong when there obviously *had* been.

But I had to hold it together in front of company.

"Coach B!" Jordan called, good-natured even when he was in obvious pain. I went to his side, shaking my head as I looked down at him.

"I could really go upside your head right now," I told him in a low voice, looking frantically at the monitor they'd connected the cart to now. There were too many people in here, which I mentioned, loud enough that one of the coaching assistants immediately went to work, clearing everybody out except the essential staff.

"I can't help getting tackled," He defended himself. "I mean, I can, but… you know what I mean. That was a pretty ass catch though, wasn't it?"

I narrowed my eyes at him. "Boy ain't nobody worried about that damn *catch*. You swore there was nothing wrong with your shoulder."

"There *wasn't*… until I fell on it. Tell her, doc!"

"You shut the fuck up!" I shot immediately at our team doctor, holding a finger up at him. I turned to the stadium doctor, who was peering at the image he'd managed to pull up on the screen. "I want to hear it from *you*."

He glanced awkwardly at our doctor, then back to me. "Well, he needs an MRI to be sure of anything – we only have x-ray capability here, which won't show me any soft tissue. There aren't any bone injuries though, which is good news."

"So what is the *problem*?" I asked, prompting him to shake his head.

"Without the MRI, I c—"

"In your *opinion*," I insisted, just as Cole came rushing through the door.

He pushed out a sigh. "In my opinion, based on his history, the pain level he's in, very low range of motion… I think the rotator cuff is torn again. Probably full separation."

My mouth fell open. "Full tear? That's…"

"A season ender," Jordan finished, with none of the bravado from before. "In fucking *September.*"

"Because you just *couldn't* listen to me," Cole said, speaking up for the first time. "I *begged* you to—"

"*Not right now*," I whispered to her, with a hand at her elbow. "Not in front of these people, and not before you know exactly what's wrong. Wait for privacy. *Then* get in his ass about it."

She let out a harsh sigh, but held her tongue as the medical team prepared Jordan for his trip to the hospital, and possible emergency surgery.

Knowing there was nothing I could do back here, I headed for the door to update Underwood and Lou, only to get stopped by Cole before I could leave.

"Hey," she started, wearing the unmistakable stress of Jordan's injury in her eyes. "I saw you try to stop him before he went on the field before that play. It was about his shoulder, wasn't it?"

I nodded. "I didn't want him out there. Underwood wouldn't listen."

"Thank you anyway," she said, squeezing my hand. "For trying."

Squeezing back, I gave her another nod. "Woman of my word."

After that, I left, taking the long trip down the tunnel back to the sideline, carrying the weight of news that had the potential to derail our entire season.

The plane ride back home was going to be a quiet one.

Oct 2018

I took the stairs down two at a time, rushing to get to the door. Today was the day I was supposed to start running again, after a long five months of slowly rebuilding stamina with walking, then jogging.

I was *ready* for it.

And glad that Nate would be with me.

I didn't even bother checking the peephole before I pulled the door open, a big smile already on my face.

The scowl on Garrett's face quickly wiped mine away though.

"Well, hello to you too," I said, frowning when he brushed past me, stepping uninvited into the house. I closed the door, turning to him with crossed arms. "Uh, how can I help your bold ass today?"

For a minute, he simply stared, then pushed out a stream of air through his nose before he spoke. "Nate Richardson? *Seriously*?"

"Excuse me?"

"Don't you *dare* act like you don't know what I'm talking about!" he growled, getting right in my face. "Why the fuck do I have to overhear *my daughter* talking about telling him how her classes are going to find out you've had some nigga around her, huh?! Are you fucking this little boy?!"

I ran my tongue over my lips, mentally urging myself to calm down before I responded.

"Garrett… honestly, you have every right to be upset that I had another man around her, without you being part of the decision. It wasn't cool – I acknowledge that, and I'm sorry."

"I don't fucking accept it," he barked, towering over me, but I held my ground, looking him right in the eyes.

"Which is your right. You don't have to. So where do we go from here?"

I had two reasons to force myself to keep my cool – for one, the stress wasn't good for me, and for two… I didn't blame him for being pissed. I should have told him, period.

But I hadn't.

Now what?

"*Where we go from here*, is that I don't want that motherfucker around her. *I* bought this house, and I say he isn't fucking welcome anymore. *That's* where we go."

I let out a dry laugh, shaking my head. "This is *my* home, in accordance with our divorce decree. You don't pay alimony, and you *don't* pay child support since we split custody, so there is *zero* ambiguity about whose paychecks cover the bills around here. But since you seem confused, here's a clue – *it ain't yours.* So you don't – and *won't* – tell me who the hell is welcome in my house."

"Sloane, I said what I said," he warned.

"Motherfucker so did I! Do you realize how ridiculous you sound right now? *Nate helped my daughter with some school paperwork, you keep that nigga from around her.* I'm dating a man who has no issue offering his time and support to our daughter, and you're... mad?"

"I'm *mad* because you and that little motherfucker lied to me," he bellowed. "Talking about he was here to discuss a player, leaving your house early in the fucking morning. *That was a booty call.* And I *knew* something was up when he was looking at you like he wanted to put his nose up your ass at that goddamn wedding!"

I laughed, right in his fucking face. "Congratu-*fucking*-lations, you were right! Pick your prize, baby – Get the fuck outta my house, or *get the fuck outta my house!* You decide."

"I ain't going *nowhere* until we talk about how your ass lied to my face, woman!"

"Oh you're mad that I *lied*?" I asked, rolling my eyes. "Is that *really* where you want to go, Mr. *sorry I can't celebrate your birthday because I have to meet a client but what I really mean is that I'd rather fuck somebody else*?!"

His mouth dropped, and he shook his head. "You are *always* bringing up the past to try to justify when your ass is wrong! That shit is old news!"

"And so is *this*," I argued. "I've been fucking Nate Richardson for *four years* and his young ass has been hitting and licking it better than your lying, philandering behind *ever* did. Now clock *that*," I snapped, nostrils flaring as he stepped even closer, his face set in a deep scowl.

"One of these days, that smart ass mouth is going to get you in trouble," he snarled, eyes narrowed on mine.

"And exactly what the fuck is that supposed to mean?" I asked.

"Yeah… that's what I'm trying to figure out too." The sound of Nate's voice drew both of our gazes to the door, where he was standing, fists clenched. "*You*," he raised a hand, pointing a finger in Garrett's direction. "Need to back the fuck up."

My eyes shot back to Garrett, whose shoulders had tensed immediately over Nate's presence. "*Or what*?" he asked, not moving. "What, you think I was about to put my hands on her?!"

"I don't know what the fuck you were *going* to do," Nate told him, approaching us. "But what you're *about* to do, is *back the fuck up off her.*"

Garrett *did* move away from me, but it wasn't to follow Nate's directive. It was to get in his face, which I quickly deflected by moving between them.

"Who the fuck do you think you're talking to boy?" Garrett barked over my shoulder to Nate, who frowned.

"I damn sure wasn't talking to her, so who the fuck do you think?"

"*Guys!*" I insisted, holding up my hands. "Stop, before this goes too far!"

Garrett grunted. "Nah, it's already too far, when you've got this bold motherfucker in the house I bought, thinking he's about to take over shit with my wife and daughter!"

"*Ex*-wife," I corrected. "And *nobody* is trying to take your place with your daughter!"

"But you don't deny the rest?" he asked, in a disgusted tone. "Four years, Sloane? Really? You were that desperate that you resorted to fucking a kid?!"

"Nigga didn't I already tell you to lower your voice and watch your fucking tone with her?" Nate asked, before I could respond. "Don't be mad because I stepped up to handle what you obviously couldn't."

"What the fuck did you just say to me?" Garrett growled, stepping even closer, so much that I was wedged between them, instead of the chest-thumping dick-measuring they so obviously wanted to do.

"You need your ears checked or something old man?" Nate shot back. "You had her first, but I had her better, do you need me to break it down any further than that?"

That jab was barely off Nate's lips before Garrett yanked me out of the way, easily removing me from between them. It happened so fast that I tripped over my feet, and was on the ground before I could catch myself, with a sick *smack* against the hardwood floor.

"*Fuck*," I hissed, grabbing the wrist I'd unwisely used to attempt to break my fall.

"Sloane, *shit*. Are you okay?" Garrett asked, snapping out of his anger as Nate bent to scoop me up from the floor.

"Man just get the fuck outta here and be glad I'm not kicking your ass over this," Nate barked, depositing me on the couch.

Garrett didn't even blink over Nate's threat, even once Nate straightened to full height again, his expression practically daring Garrett to do… anything except what he'd said.

After a few moments, Garrett let out a dry laugh, and shook his head, looking between me and Nate. "This conversation? It's *not* over. Believe that."

Nate didn't even give him the courtesy of keeping his eyes on him as he left. He waved Garrett off and turned back to me, kneeling to look at my wrist, which was already swelling.

"You okay?" he asked, as Garrett slammed my front door, so loud it seemed like he was trying to tear it off the hinges. "I walked up to the door, and heard raised voices. That's why I didn't knock, I just came to see what the fuck was going on."

Shaking my head, I pushed out a deep breath. "I'm fine. My wrist might not be, but… I'm good. I didn't really need rescuing though."

"I couldn't tell," Nate said, brushing aside the hair I'd left wild to answer the door, since the bell had rung before I could secure it into my standard puff. "So I just reacted. My bad."

"It's fine," I told him, gently lowering my hand to my lap. "That was bound to happen sooner or later."

Nate shrugged. "And now it's over with."

"Oh *no*," I laughed, even though it really, *really* wasn't funny. "It's *not* over. *Now* we wait and see what happens."

I didn't have to wait long.

It was that very same day that an intern came to retrieve me from the practice field, letting me know that Eli Richardson wanted to talk to me. I had no idea what the conversation would entail, but I knew it couldn't be good, especially based on the way Underwood avoided my eyes as I headed off.

More than likely, he, Garrett, and Eli had been talking.

*And people say **women** gossip too much.*

In any case, *my* head was held high as I traveled up to where his office was, wearing a wrist brace from the sprain his little friend had caused. When I arrived, his assistant sent me right in, and I found him at his huge picture window, overlooking the natural scenery behind the building.

"You wanted to see me?" I asked, already annoyed by his evident "power play" of feigning distraction when I arrived. He turned, scrutinizing my face first before his eyes fell to my injured wrist.

"What happened?"

"I think you know," I countered, not bothering to adjust the agitation out of my tone. If I'd made a mistake on the field, my energy would be entirely different. But I knew – we *both* knew – that this wasn't a business-related meeting.

It was personal.

And none of his business.

He seemed surprised by the way I'd countered him, raising an eyebrow as he moved to his desk. Once he was there, he gestured for me to have a seat, and I shook my head.

"I'd rather stand."

"You want to tell me what's going on, Ms. Brooks?" he asked, slow enough that I could tell his words were carefully measured. "You seem a bit on edge."

I shrugged. "Just staying prepared for whatever missiles you're about to launch my way."

"Missiles? What makes you say that?"

"With all due respect, Eli… we can cut right to the chase. There's no need for the games. You know what happened to my wrist – I can confirm that it was an accident. And you already know *exactly* which missiles I'm talking about."

Pushing out a sigh, Eli came around to the front of the desk, taking a seat on the edge. "Fair enough. You want to cut to the chase, we'll do it. You *will* stop dating my son."

"You have no authority over my personal life," I told him, without even giving myself a moment to think about it, because my answer wouldn't have changed.

His eyes narrowed. "You sure that's the answer you'd like to go with. You're serious about this?"

"Serious as a heart attack," I countered, pre-empting him. "Like the one your son saved me from. But I bet neither of your informants knew *that* part."

"No," he answered, with a tip of his head. "They didn't. So I see there's even more to this story to tell."

I shook my head. "Oh no, there's nothing to tell. Not to tell *you*, because again – this is my *personal* life. It has nothing to do with you, and nothing to do with this team."

"It has to do with my son, so it has *everything* to do with it."

"Eli, your son is a grown man."

"A grown man ruining his life to be with a divorcee with nothing in the way of building a legacy to offer him."

I laughed. "I will *not* sit here and be insulted. Especially not by a man who married a *divorcee* who was twenty years younger than him. The hypocrisy is *thick*."

"It was *not* the same situation," Eli answered, in a low, dangerous tone. "Mel wanted *nothing* from me."

"And what the *hell* do you think I want from Nate? Or, better question – what the hell is it that you want for Nate?"

"The absolute *best* of happiness," Eli snarled.

I raised my hands, relaxing back into my chair. "Then *congratulations.* You're looking at her. Have you even *talked* to your son about this, or did you just decide you knew better than he does for his own life?"

"*My son* is easily swayed by… attributes that don't exactly lead to a healthy future. I won't begrudge the past, but it is time for my son to settle down and find a wife who can bear his child. And I think we both know that isn't you."

I smirked. "You know what else we *both know*? That your son wants to start and build a business, and now that he's *serious* about it – he *will* do it. When is he going to have time for this wife and child you so desperately want for him?"

Of course, I left out the fact that *I* had wanted that for him too.

How much time had I wasted badgering him like his father had, to pursue something he didn't even really want?

"He will come to his senses. He will work for this team. And he will inherit this business," Eli countered, so matter-of-factly that I shook my head.

"No. If you keep this up, what's going to happen is that you'll lose your son," I warned him. "Not to me – I'm not suggesting that he'd choose me over you. But I'm *telling* you that he will absolutely choose *not* having you in his life, if you can't put your own dreams for him aside, and let him follow his own path."

His frown deepened. "Ms. Brooks, do you presume to know my son better than his own father?"

"I presume that his father may not know him very well at all," I said, with no intention of malice. Only the truth. And a deep, *deep* hope that I never felt a need to involve myself this deeply with Madison's personal life, barring evidence that she was heading into something that would bring her real harm.

Although... was *that* what Eli thought of me?

How *little* he thought of me, that I was so far from good enough for his son that he felt strongly enough to demand I leave him alone?

"I think some things need to be set straight," Eli said, veering from his course into some demanding ass tone that raised my irritation level even higher. "This conversation has turned into a back and forth, where none was required, so let me go back to my original statement. *You will stop seeing my son.* You will agree to it immediately, or you will not step back into the facility, or on the field with the *Kings* for another game."

As soon as he finished with his threat, I stood, moving to step closer. I looked him right in the face when I asked, "Do you think I *need* this job, Eli? You may want to watch your step with threats, because I do not respond well to them, and I *will* call your bluff."

"It's not a bluff."

I chuckled. "Oh, but it is. Because you see – I *know* you, Eli. And you're a better businessman than this."

"What the hell does this have to do with my business?"

"Nothing," I smiled. "Which is exactly why you firing me because I'm dating your son is going to bite you right in the ass. These wide receivers' stats are *out of this world*, and it's because of me. I tried to save your star from a season-ending injury – Lou even said it in an interview, and now it's well-reported. Even my peers who only *tolerate* me know that I am damn good at this job, so when you fire me, and I tell everybody who'll listen that it's because you simply didn't want an older woman dating your son, the media is going to eat you and this team *alive.* I will take my ass on TV and cry my pretty brown eyes out over it, and it will undo every piece of goodwill you garnered with that statement promising that your players wouldn't get in trouble for taking a knee. And the *real* kicker will be your son sitting right the fuck beside me. But if that's where you want to go, Eli... let's do it."

Eli gave me a wry smile. "I should have known just how good you were at manipulation."

I raised an eyebrow. "*Me*? I haven't manipulated *anything*, I've told you how I will respond to an unjust firing. You're the one throwing down ultimatums and threats, not me. You're the one trying to interfere in Nate's life, not me. And *you* are the one who is only going to end up hurting *him – not me.*"

"I don't understand you, Sloane," he shook his head. "Any number of other players, trainers, front office staff, coaches – you're an incredibly attractive, smart woman. Why can't you just find someone else to have your affair?"

My eyes narrowed. "Because it's *not* an affair," I hissed, surprisingly offended by that assertion. "*That's* what you think? *That's* what Garrett told you?"

"What else could it be?" he asked, seeming genuinely confused, which only heightened my frustration.

"Love." I swallowed hard after I said that word, trying to keep my composure. "Eli… I'm not just some stubborn cougar trying to corrupt your son. We… are in love." I stopped speaking, to let that sink in, then told him, "You do whatever you want with that information, okay? Fire me, try to ruin my reputation, whatever. Say whatever the hell you want, you know? And I take it back – I won't waste my time talking to the news about you. You and this team can burn, and I will be at my house, with my daughter, and with your son… living, and loving, and happy as fuck."

I turned to leave, somehow feeling lighter than I had when I walked in. I was angry at his nerve, to attempt to force me to do anything, but when I thought about the toll it would take to try to fight him… it wasn't worth it.

I didn't have to fight anything.

I didn't have to say a word.

I'd gotten hired.

I'd done my fucking job.

And I'd fallen in love.

At this point, I had *nothing* to prove.

"Are you going back down to practice?" he asked, with none of the previous disrespect in his tone. Obviously, he'd seen the light, done a bit of weighing the repercussions on his own, and decided he should reevaluate.

But I took no joy in that.

If my job was going to be threatened over some *bullshit*… I wasn't even sure I wanted it.

"No," I answered, not turning around. "I'm going home."

Fifteen

She'd been crying, and that pissed me off.

We'd known there would be some type of blowback now that Garrett knew about us. He was too tight with exactly the right people, and I'd pissed him off too badly for there to not be a reaction. Now, between the brace on her wrist, her red eyes, and the whispers I'd heard of her storming out of my father's office, I found myself wishing I'd just socked that motherfucker in the face and called it a day.

Just to make the point, very clearly, that I didn't fuck around when it came to Sloane.

"You have to eat something," I urged, running a hand over her back. She was draped across my lap, in the same position she'd been in for hours, staring absently at some ridiculous show about six black friends living in Detroit.

Instead of a verbal answer, she just shook her head, but now she'd declined one too many times. I hooked her under the arms, pulling her upright.

"Hey babe… you have to eat, so you can take your medicine."

She let out a sigh, and turned to look me in the face. "*Always* the right thing to say with you, isn't it?"

I raised a hand, stroking her cheek. "You already know. Now… why don't you tell me what happened today with you and my father?"

"I thought I was supposed to be eating. *Not* rehashing pointless conversations."

"If that's your way of deflecting, it's not going to work. What is it that's so bad that you don't want to say anything? You know you can tell me anything, right?"

She gave me a wry smile. "I do. But… it got a little ugly between me and Eli, honestly. And I am *so* far from interested in even the appearance of coming between you and your father. You want to know what happened, you talk to *him*."

"Right now, I'm talking to *you*," I insisted. "You left practice today, which is completely unlike you, and I know you've been crying – I see it. All you have to do is tell the truth."

"The truth is that your father threatened to fire me if I didn't stop seeing you. The details aren't important. I called his bluff, he backed off, and I left anyway. That's the whole story."

My eyes narrowed. "*What*? He threatened to fire you over me… but *not* about keeping the heart attack from him?"

"I'm honestly not even positive he *knows* about the heart attack. He's tight with Underwood, so I'm assuming at this point that everything is out of the bag. I'll conduct myself accordingly."

After that, she pulled herself from my lap, heading to the kitchen to grab a snack. I propped my elbows on my knees, head in my hands, trying to sort through the facts.

Not *everything* was out of the bag, but the fact that she and I were involved certainly was. It hadn't hit the internet yet, and no one had been bold enough to ask me to my face, but the undercurrent was there, and would only be stronger tomorrow as the news traveled from ear to ear.

On the surface, people knowing about us didn't bother me. It was *barely* a blip on my radar. But deeper than that, I knew it had potential repercussions for Sloane – she had a lot more to lose by publicly acknowledging our relationship than I did.

Her credibility.

Her reputation.

And her job.

Apparently, her job had already been threatened.

That was part of the story I was having trouble wrapping my head around, the fact that there had been hostility between the two, with both living to tell the tale. Sloane wasn't a woman who took kindly to threats, and Eli wasn't the type to idly give them. For him to have "backed off" as she claimed, she had to have come with heat herself. And for her to have called his bluff, when the stakes were her job – a job she cherished – there had to be a lot more to this than she was telling me.

I got up and followed her, entering the kitchen while she was ending a phone call.

"Retained Chloe McKenna… just in case," she explained, gesturing with the phone. "I don't know what's going to happen, but I do know I want to be prepared."

I nodded. "Probably a smart move, considering that he threatened you… which I'd like to get a little more detail about."

"Does it really matter?" she asked, moving to grab a bowl of sliced cucumbers from her fridge. "What does having the details change?"

"Just indulge me."

With her mouth full of cucumber, she shrugged. "Fine. What do you want to know?"

"I want to know what he said to you."

"That his son needed a woman who could bear his children, so I needed to find someone else for my little affair. That he would fire me if I didn't."

I closed my eyes, trying my best to check the rush of anger that washed over me. But Sloane wasn't finished speaking.

"And I... dared him to do it, basically. I reminded him of the shit storm that would follow, and threatened to talk to the media. And I told him... that you wouldn't be happy with him, for doing something like that over you. That, out of anger, you'd probably be by *my* side during the interviews. Which wasn't cool, because I don't speak for you."

"That doesn't make it less true."

"But still. In any case, I walked it all back anyway, because if he wants to fire me, whatever. My life is full, and beautiful, and no *job* is going to change that. I refuse to let anybody have that kind of power over me. Any job that can be snatched away because of who I love isn't a job I need."

"Snatched away because of... what?" I asked, not sure if I'd heard that correctly, and knowing that I *needed* clarity there.

Sloane's gaze dropped to those cucumbers, resting there before she lifted her head again. "You heard me. Because of who I... love. But don't worry, I'm not looking for—"

She didn't get a chance to finish whatever bullshit minimizing tactic she was about to employ, because I'd rounded the corner to sweep her into my arms, muffling the words with a kiss. She melted right into me, arms around me, eyes closed, just... reveling in it.

When we pulled back, there was no mistaking the happiness in her eyes, though she tried to hide it by making a big deal of getting back to her cucumbers. I let her do it, taking the opportunity to gather my thoughts for a bit before I spoke again.

"I'm going to talk to my father," I told her, and she lifted her eyes from the bowl. "He went too far, and I... can't let this ride."

Sloane shook her head. "Nate, I'm *fine*. Underwood texted me, and Coach Lou *called*, making sure I'll be back at practice tomorrow. As long as nobody fucks with me, I'm good, and even then... I'm still good. I don't bow my head to anyone."

"It's not just that. He's getting more and more aggressive with this director role in my life, and I can't just let that ride, or he'll never stop. The conversation is overdue."

"I understand. I... can't bring myself to offer much in the way of defending him after the way he treated me today, and I have no idea what he's going through, but... just keep in mind that this is all because he loves you."

I nodded. "Yeah. We're going to have to do some fine-tuning on the way he shows it."

"If *anybody* can handle it, I know you can." She leaned in, pressing a kiss to my lips before she replaced the top on the bowl she'd been eating from, and put it away. "It has been a long ass day, and I'm tired. I'm taking my medicine and going to bed. You coming?"

"Wouldn't miss it," I grinned. "I'm just going to straighten up down here, and then I'll be up to join you."

"Okay."

I followed her back out to the living room, where she headed for the stairs, and I moved to clear the glasses we'd used while we were sitting out there watching TV. She was halfway up the stairs when I looked up, feeling the sudden need to stop her.

"Sloane!"

She turned to look at me, her pretty face caught in a wondering expression that made me smile. A face, a smile... a *woman* I could never see myself growing tired of.

"I love you too."

He was avoiding the office.

That was the only conclusion I could come to when, days after my father's so-called confrontation with Sloane, I still hadn't been able to pin him down.

Seeking him at the office had been a courtesy. Neutral ground for the conversation we *had* to have, with relative privacy. But since he'd removed that as an option, I went to where he'd have no choice but to engage.

I went to his house.

The silver lining of this delay lied in the fact that now, I was considerably calmer. The day of, when Sloane was so obviously hurt, the likelihood of me crossing a line was high. Now a few days had passed. Sloane had gone back to practice with no ugliness, and I'd had time to really shuffle through my thoughts.

This was better.

I found him in his home office, deeply engaged in whatever documents he had spread across his desk.

"Knock-knock," I called, not crossing the threshold of the open doorway until he looked up, urging me to come in.

"Let me guess," he started, stacking the documents and putting them away in a folder, which he moved to the side. "You're here to defend Ms. Brooks' honor."

I chuckled, taking a seat in front of the desk. "I doubt she needs it. If I know her like I think I do, I'm sure she defended herself quite well."

"Indeed," he nodded, then stared at me, chin in hand, for several seconds before he pulled himself from his chair. "Come walk with me."

I followed him out to the tree-lined backyard, where winding pathways led through huge maples that had been there since before I was born. My father said nothing, and neither did I. As much time as I'd spent mulling this whole thing over... I didn't really know *what* to say.

Wrong or not... he was still my father.

"Emma loves it out here," he finally spoke up, stopping underneath a tree Cole and I had carved our initials into, more than twenty years ago. "Especially now that the leaves have changed colors. She's very, *very* concerned that they're "on fire"."

I grinned. "And I'm sure, of course, she's tasted a few."

"Of course. Shoving fistfuls in her mouth, and then crying for somebody to get the crunchy pieces off her tongue."

Again, neither of us said anything. But then...

"Seems like you would be too busy keeping up with, molding her, to have time to micromanage me."

Eli pushed out a long, deep sigh. "Ah. Here it is."

"Yes," I answered. "Here it is. I'm sure I don't even really need to explain how flat out wrong you are."

"For wanting the best for you?"

"For feeling like it's up to you decide what that is," I countered. "I will *never* fault you for being an involved father – can't ever repay you for it either. I have no desire to minimize the fact that I wouldn't be where I am now if it weren't for you, but you have to understand that my gratefulness does not mean I'm going to simply fall in line with what you want me to do."

"You act as if I'm trying to dictate what you wear, what you eat for breakfast. I'm simply trying to mold you into a success story for your grandchildren, like I hope to be for mine."

I smiled. "And see, if it stopped at advice, or input, that would be one thing. But when you start tearing down the idea of me building something for myself, threatening the livelihood of a woman I deeply care about, all because it doesn't fit into *your* ideal of what you think my life should be… you're taking it too far. *Way* too far, and I know you understand that."

"I don't want you choosing a harder path than you have to."

"And *my* life cannot be about *your* wants. I'm sorry if that's disappointing for you, but… I *will* be pursuing sports management. And I'm going to do it with Sloane Brooks by my side. Neither of us is interested in the baby thing, but Sloane already has a sixteen-year-old daughter, who is an amazing kid – you'd like her. My life may not look like what you planned or dreamed for me, but that doesn't make it any less worthy of pride. And it doesn't mean I think you're any less worthy of admiration. I hope you can see that."

Eli chuckled about that, reaching out to touch the names carved into the tree. "I never thought, after all I've done to ensure their future, my children would find accepting their legacy too heavy a burden to bear. You'll have to forgive me if this whole conversation feels like a slap in the face."

"You're moving the goalposts now," I defended. "Your problem with me right now, today, is that I'm dating a woman with no interest in marriage or children, and that I want to start a business of my own. That's not the same as refusing your legacy. The *Kings* are your crown jewel, and you enjoy the hell out of that throne. And we both know you aren't interested in relinquishing your crown any time soon."

He pulled in a breath, then let it out through his nose. "Interested? No. I have every intention of running this team for many more years to come, but… you know what they say about making plans, don't you son?"

"We make them, and God laughs at our dumb asses?"

He nodded. "And I'm afraid that our maker is having himself a really good time at your old man's expense."

Turning to him, I frowned. "Meaning what?"

"Meaning… you remember Jimmy, don't you?"

"Jimmy Wright? The Boulder? Yeah, why wouldn't I? He *just* died, like a month ago."

"Yes, exactly," my father grunted, pointing a finger for emphasis. "He gets sick, and within a few years… completely wasted away. Survived by who? Children who left him to be cared for by a woman he barely knew – but did more for him than they *ever* did. There are no… charities, no scholarships, no… *anything* left from him. I've half a mind to fire that no good son of his who works in the front office. It's *shameful*."

"And that's what you think Cole and I are going to do? You think Mel is going to let that happen? Emma's still a baby, but by the time she's grown—"

"*I might not be here*," Eli growled, stunning me into silence. "You think I don't want to see my baby girl… go to kindergarten? College? You think I don't have plans for all of that?"

"Dad—"

"I *told you*. God is laughing at all my grand plans, and it is time for me to get my affairs in order. *Of course* I want to see you build a business, and make it your own, but… son… I may not have *time*."

"What are you *talking about*?!" I yelled, grabbing him by the shoulders to make him look at me. "Why the hell wouldn't you have time?"

"Because I have cancer."

My mouth dropped open. "You… *what*?"

"You heard me right," he sighed, then turned back to the path to start walking again, leaving me to fall in step beside him as he continued. "Prostate. Found during a routine checkup. Biopsied and confirmed a few months ago."

"*Months*?! And you're just now sharing this?! Does Mel know?"

He gave a deep nod. "Yes. And she's been like a mother hen ever since. Every little bit of peace I have comes in small pockets. I didn't even want to imagine what would come of my life once anyone else knew. Once the world knew. No peace at all."

That sort of reasoning sounds familiar.

"What's the prognosis?" I asked, disinterested in dwelling on the fine details of how and when he'd told me. "What are the doctors saying?"

"They're saying that we found it before it spread anywhere else, so the outlook is good. No treatment for now, just watching and waiting for any signs of spreading. If it gets more aggressive, then they'll move forward with treatment."

"Wait, *what*? No treatment? Why the fuck not?!"

"I'm an old man, son. If they rush in doing things just because, those complications could kill me before the cancer does. That's why they wait, and see. That's the approach they think is best."

My eyebrows went up. "That… has to be a hard pill to swallow."

"Very," he agreed. "No one wants to walk around with a ticking time bomb in their body, just waiting for the blowback to happen. They can offer all the assurances they'd like, but the bottom line is that it *feels* like my time here is winding down."

I nodded. "And *that's* why you're all over me about my future. You've been reminded that you're not immortal."

"Can't say I ever thought *that*," he chuckled. "But… I certainly wasn't expecting *this*." He stopped walking to take a seat at the bench near the playground area he'd installed for Cole and me as small kids, and recently refurbished for Emma. "I won't apologize for trying to guide you, because that's my job. No matter how old you get, that will always be my job. My methods, however… I won't lie and tell you that I don't see my error."

"I'm not here looking for an apology, man. At least… not for myself. I'm good, and as far as I'm concerned, *we're* good… but that shit you tried to pull with Sloane was flat out foul. She makes me happy as hell, and she's not going anywhere any time soon. I need you to make it right with her."

He smirked. "It's already in process, after a nice scolding from Nyree," he said, referencing his executive assistant. "*Smooth it over before she sues this team – and wins,*" he said, mimicking the higher pitch of her voice. "Before this London game, I'll make a point of speaking to her personally – and not just for the sake of avoiding legal action. But… because I crossed a line."

"And because you don't want any smoke with Mel. I *know* she was heated, wasn't she?"

"Why do you think I sent her and Emma out shopping?" he laughed. "Between the two of them, I wasn't sure I was safe around here. You know that woman said to me, "*You sure your dick is the problem, cause it seems like your brain to me.*" Can you believe that?!"

I snickered. "Damn, that's cold."

"Then why are you laughing?"

"Because there's some basis in the truth. You've been wildin' a little… a lot."

He pushed out a deep sigh. "Just an old man grasping at anything to make sure my family will be okay without me."

"That's already a done deal. So… relax. Focus on eating well, and staying active, and giving Emma and Mel as much time as you can. This other stuff you've been on? You're not doing anything but pushing me away."

"Understood."

We stayed like that for several moments, enjoying the quiet until Emma came bouncing outside, obviously back from her trip with Mel. Her tiny feet moved across the grass with purpose, sprinting until she flung herself at me for a big hug, then reached for our father.

While he was occupied with the kisses she demanded, I looked up at the glass doors to find Mel standing there, observing. She lifted an eyebrow – nonverbally asking a question to which I nodded in answer, then gave her a thumbs up gesture that made her smile, and nod back before she moved on.

For now at least, we were good.

I just hoped it could remain that way.

"How's the wrist?"

I stopped what I was doing – packing for the team's international game in London – to look at Garrett face to face for the first time in two weeks. I couldn't keep the immediate frown from my face – didn't even try.

"What the hell are you doing in my house?"

He at least had the decency to looked ashamed of himself, leaning into the doorway with a shrug. "Mads let me in. When I told her why I was here."

"Which is…?"

"To apologize."

Hm.

Lately, there was a *lot* of that going around.

Eli had sent a bouquet, and then brought a second one to my office himself, sitting down for a one on one apology that helped me feel a lot more settled. Underwood apologized for not giving me a heads up that Eli knew about me and Nate, but it turned out that he'd kept his word about not saying anything about the heart attack, to Eli *or* Garrett.

And now, here was my ex-husband himself.

I cleared a space on my bed and sat down, arms crossed. "I'm listening."

His face pulled into a slight frown on concentration, like he was working through what he wanted to say before he opened his mouth again.

"I've… loved you for a long time, Sloane," he started, making me immediately roll my eyes. If this was about to turn into another attempt to get me back… "You're the only woman I've ever really given my heart to. And I know the same was true for you. *Was.* And I can't lie… it's a hard thing to accept. Hard as fuck. You were *it* for me, and I fucked it up, and I don't want you to be *it* for another nigga. Just… *honestly.*"

I nodded. "Trust me, I get it… sort of. See, I had to go through the realization that you weren't just mine *while we were married.* I don't know if there was ever a time that I had my husband to myself, so… if this is supposed to make me sympathize with you—"

"It's not, I swear," he explained. "I'm just trying to explain where I'm coming from. When I heard my kid talking about Nate, it's like something snapped. Cause in my head, it's like… if you had him around her, you had to have been involved with him for a while. You had to trust him… maybe *love* him, and that shit is hard to get my head around. Like… some lil dude that probably still has milk on his breath, and you want *him* over *me?*"

I smiled. "*He* has my trust. You don't. And on a romantic level, I don't believe you ever will, just based on our history. You're the father of my child -we'll always be connected. But you must accept that it is time for you to step aside. You've had girlfriends, you've had women around my daughter, and as long as they were respectful, and kind to Mads, I never said *shit* to you about it. But you thought it was cool to run up in *my* home beating your chest over it. And who ended up paying for it?" I asked, holding up my wrist, which was still strapped into a brace.

"Wait now, that's *his* fault. He wanted to run in playing Captain Save-A-Sloane, escalating shit!"

"Defending me," I countered. "He walked in here, saw you in my face, and did exactly what he was supposed to do. You're lucky he didn't punch your ass."

Garrett sucked his teeth. "Man, I'on know about all *that*. But. I'll give it to him – he has heart. Defended you without a second thought, like I wouldn't snap his ass in half."

"He is nearly twenty years younger than you. You'd break a hip calling yourself fighting him."

"I can't think of a better way to go," Garrett teased, making me laugh.

"You are really a damn mess, you know that right?"

He shrugged. "I try to keep things interesting, you know? But… anyway. I'm sorry for flipping on you like that."

"And for trying to get me fired?"

"Wait, *hollld up*," he countered, lifting his hands. "That is *not* where I was coming from with that. I approached Eli on some "Get your son cause I'ma kill his ass over my wife" type of energy. It was *not* about taking anything from you, at all. I know what this job means to you, and I don't care how mad I get – I'd never do you like that."

I shook my head. "I believe you, but… that's *exactly* how it ended up. You couldn't have thought that running to Eli wouldn't have negative consequences for *me*."

"I wasn't thinking at all. I was just fucking angry. But – I *am* sorry about jeopardizing your job too. And adding undue stress to your life. You know… with… your heart issues. Madison told me."

"I appreciate that. And… I accept your apologies. I'm still not really trying to look at you for another week or so though."

He chuckled. "Fair enough. I was just trying to catch you before you went to the airport. Didn't want you all the way in London still mad at me."

"I didn't say anything about not being mad anymore."

"You know you can't stay mad at this face," he joked, putting on a fake ass puppy-eyed expression.

"You look just like your child when I won't let her in my closet." I laughed, pulling myself up. "She still in the driveway washing Baby T?" I asked, referring to the bright orange Tiguan we'd settled on for her, months ago.

"Polishing the rims, just like I taught her. I should probably go down and confirm that you didn't kill me."

"Maybe so," I told him, following when he turned to go down the stairs, leading outside. What was supposed to be a light moment quickly shifted to making me anxious when I stepped out to find Nate's car in the circular driveway as well, parked right next to Garrett's.

The man himself was talking to Madison, presumably about her car from the way she was gesturing at it as she spoke.

I could feel the sudden tension from Garrett, and pushed out a sigh, already mentally preparing myself for this to become a problem. Especially when Garrett stepped right up to Nate, saying something I couldn't hear over Madison's mumble-rap music thumping from her speakers.

Whatever it was, Nate nodded, allowing Garrett to pull him aside so they could speak.

"What do you think they're talking about?" Mads asked, moving to stand next to me, still holding the garden hose in her hand. "They're not about to like… cage fight or anything are they?"

"I don't think so. They're actually… are they… are they *shaking hands*?"

Sure enough, they were, and after parting ways, Nate came to me, while Garrett retrieved Madison, talking to her about something as she walked him to his car.

"What was all that about?" I asked Nate, dying to know what their conversation had consisted of.

He smirked. "None of your business, nosy."

"Oh it's definitely my business," I countered, looking up as Garrett drove off. "What did he say to you?"

"Nothing to worry about. Everything is cool, everybody is cool. He even offered to share some resources about getting into sports management – which I'm going to assume he knows about from my father."

My eyes went wide. "*Wow*! Seriously? No… no cage match?"

"Nah," he laughed. "He *did* threaten to make sure my body was never found if I hurt you or Madison, but I mean… I feel like that's fair."

"True," I nodded. "But overall… we've gotten off pretty easy with this, huh?"

He grinned. "I told you, you were making it bigger in your head than it had to be."

"I don't think so – social media hasn't gotten ahold of this news yet, but it's coming."

"You say that like you actually care," he countered, putting his hands at my waist. "When we both know that beyond the shallow part, the not wanting people to have anything negative to say about your relationship… you don't give a fuck."

I sucked my teeth. "Who asked you though?"

"Yeah, that's what I thought."

He dropped his lips to mine, and I was completely ready to get lost in the kiss, lost in him, until I heard a throat clear behind me, reminding me of Madison's presence. Laughing, I turned to find her wearing a pained, disgusted expression.

"Can y'all get a room?"

Sixteen

"I want to take you on a date."

That was Nate's greeting when I opened my hotel room door, after a long ass day.

A *good* day, but long nonetheless.

The time difference between Connecticut and England had done a number on me, but the *Kings* seemed to have adapted fine. They practiced, and did the photo ops and played to win – *did* win – and my receivers made mama proud. We had a *bye* week after this, and they were all off to vacation, with France seeming to be the place to be.

All I wanted to do was go home.

But there Nate was, at my door.

"A… date?" I asked, stepping aside to let him in. "What are you doing here anyway?"

Leading all the way up to this trip, Nate had been very clear about his disinterest in going. He didn't do well on trans-Atlantic flights, or something like that, and I hadn't questioned it, because hell, neither did I.

And yet… here he was.

"I'm here… to take my lady on a date. Outside."

I smiled. "That's what I am? Your *lady*?" I teased, biting my lip as he wrapped his arms around my waist, pulling me close.

"You know good and goddamn well this is *all* me." His hands slipped lower, grabbing handfuls of ass. "Thank you for keeping my pussy warm all the way over here."

"Damn fool," I squealed, giggling as his mouth moved to my neck, licking and biting me there. "I thought you were here to take me out, not play grab-ass."

He groaned. "I am. You're right. So get dressed."

"Dressed how? Where are you trying to take me?"

"Brixton. Take us about an hour to get there. Dress… to dance."

My eyes went wide. "To… *dance*? We've never *danced*."

"But I've definitely seen these hips in action."

He smacked my ass, then pressed a quick kiss to my lips before he stepped back, grabbing the remote before he sprawled across my bed, flipping the TV on.

"Put ya' backside in motion woman. Get dressed."

I rolled my eyes at his demand, but did what he asked, going to my suitcase to see what I could put together. I hadn't really planned for a night spent clubbing, but I found leggings and a light, oversized sweater which I layered over a tank in case I got hot. I left my hair in the goddess braid it had been in since this morning, only taking time to touch up my edges before putting on a quick face and tossed on earrings, then stepped back into the main part of the hotel room, where Nate was waiting.

"Damn," he grunted, sitting up as I took a seat on the end of the bed to pull on my boots. "Might not take your fine ass anywhere."

"Think again," I scolded, shying away when he tried to put his face in my neck.

"Fine." He pulled out his phone, and I glanced at the screen to see that he was calling a car for us. "But afterward, I'm wearing you out... if this date doesn't."

My eyebrow lifted as he stood up, extending a hand to help me. "Where did you say you were taking me again?"

"Brixton? As in... the Brixton riots?"

"As in, the Black British mecca. Now come on. Let's go."

It was simultaneously terrifying and exhilarating to walk out of my hotel room with my fingers intertwined with Nate's. Even though several key people on the team knew about us, we'd kept a low profile, still hadn't been out together in public.

Here, no one except those who were *Kings* affiliated knew who the hell we were.

There was freedom in not being recognized.

Because of what he'd said about Brixton, we spent the hour-long car ride Googling and telling each other what we'd found – including the fact that police brutality and the subsequent protests and abuse and rioting were far from an exclusively American problem. To a degree, I'd felt somewhat sheltered from that, but now realized how naïve it was. By the time we pulled up at our destination, I was wishing I'd given all those young Black men on the team a warning before they went out celebrating their win.

They weren't safe *here* either.

But it was hard to remain somber as I breathed in the sights and smells of *Brixton Village*. It was an eclectic mix of shopping center, farmer's market, swap meet and restaurants, with flags and fabrics and cuisines from all around the world represented.

"I'll bring you back tomorrow if you want to shop or something," Nate spoke into my ear, obviously noting my desire to stop and look at everything. "But we only have one destination here for now."

I turned to him, smiling. "Lead the way."

The way turned out to not be very far, to a little storefront with a red canopy and a bright yellow, hand-painted sign declaring itself *Fish, Wings, and Tings.* We made our way through a thick throng of people to get inside, ordering roti and prawns and jerk chicken and curry and *Carib* beers, all of which were delivered to us on bright teal, picnic style tables inside.

The food was amazing, but Nate's company was better. We were so busy flirting and exchanging kisses that it took us way too long to finish our food.

Once we left there, I declared that I wanted to *experience London*, whatever the hell that meant, so we walked to the nearest public transit and used that, laughing and getting lost a few times as we hopped from stop to stop, changing trains until we made it to Shoreditch. Our destination, *Queen of Hoxton*, was a building covered in painted-on vines, with a bright neon sign announcing its' name.

Outside, signs advertised *Old Skool Sundays*, which worried me a little, but inside… was, as Madison would say, "a vibe". The music wasn't remotely what *I* would consider "old school" – this particular night was "Drake night" but it was a walk down memory lane.

As promised, we danced, we sang along with the hip-hop, R&B, and soul pumping from the speakers, we played ping-pong and Jenga and danced off any heaviness from our late dinner.

The whole thing shut down at midnight, which was honestly relieving – my feet were killing me, even though I'd had a great time. I was further relieved when instead of pulling me back onto public transit, Nate had the foresight to call a car, allowing us to spend the ride back to the hotel in relative privacy and comfort.

"You know," I told him, with my head propped on his shoulder in the backseat of the car. "If this were a real first date, you'd get major points. This was a lot of fun."

He shifted, pressing his lips to my forehead. "You know… it *is* our first real date though. When you think about it."

"It is, huh?" I smiled, turning to meet his eyes. "You *finally* brought me out in public."

"Nah, chill," he laughed. "We *both* know you're the one who wanted to keep it all on the low. I would've *proudly* walked you out of the party in Vegas on my arm. That very first night."

With *everything* that had happened since then, somehow that memory still made me blush. If he'd never approached me that night…

"Where do you think we'd be now if… you know…" I started, unsure of how to phrase my question, but Nate grinned.

"If you'd responded to any of my *"this could be us but you playing"* messages?"

"Yes. That. If… two years ago, we'd said *fuck it*, and decided to do more than screw each other's brains out… you think we'd even still like each other by now?"

"I think you'd be Sloane Richardson by now. Gotta get rid of the *Brooks* shit."

I laughed, *loud*. "Wooow. I've become quite accustomed to *Brooks* now – why do you think I kept it, even after I dropped the husband?

"Sloane Brooks sounds better than Sloane Charles, which sounds like a small town from a *Lifetime* movie, so I get it."

"So you're just gonna completely roast my maiden name? That's what we're doing now?"

"I'm just saying…"

"Mmm*hmm*," I hummed. "And besides that, um… I could've sworn getting married wasn't even on your radar, but now you're telling me you would've changed my last name?"

"You asked a question baby, and I answered it."

"Yes, and now I'm asking what changed?"

He shrugged. "We changed. You changed. I changed. Four years is a long time to do anything with one person."

I sucked my teeth. "You know *goddamn well…*"

"Okay," he grinned. "A lot changed in… like a year and a half?"

Yep.

That was about when I noticed the shift, and started trying to push him away… obviously, I'd failed at that.

"That's when you dropped all your hoes for me?"

"Nah, the real question is when did *you* drop *your* hoes for *me*?"

I smirked. "Who says I have?"

"You're trying to get some motherfucker killed, aren't you?" he asked, dropping his head to kiss me behind the ear. "I told you whose pussy you were carrying around, didn't I? I know you're not letting anybody else get it."

"They can't even get close," I assured, prompting him to grab me under the chin, turning my face toward his.

"Why not?" he asked, instead of kissing me, which was what I'd expected.

"Certainty."

I knew, from the way his expression shifted, that he knew exactly what I was talking about – knew exactly the conversation I was referencing. I'd been the doting wife and young mother, had already gotten my fill of that phase. I wasn't opposed to being married again but certainly wasn't craving it. My life was in a very specific place, with a very specific need.

Certainty.

I'd told Nate before that he'd turned me into a liar when it came to that specific topic, and that was still true. He was offering exactly what I needed.

"I love you," he told me, as we pulled up to the hotel, and all I could do in return was grin.

"The feeling is so, *so* mutual."

Nov 2018

I was only a *little* nervous.

Despite the post-game interviews, and our short session after training camp, the thought of talking to Wil Cunningham-Bishop in a longer format had my stomach flipping a little. Through the season, as my profile lifted, I'd been offered plenty of opportunities to speak with the media, and declined every one, preferring to focus.

The season was halfway done now though.

As was her standard, Wil and her crew had come into my home, taking over my living room for the interview. We sat together on the couch, both dressed down, in designer athleisure, giving the appearance of simply talking with a girlfriend. I wanted to focus in on that, to meet her halfway with that friendly vibe. But, she'd asked me before we started if there was any topic off-limits for our conversation. Without thinking, I'd said no.

Now, I was second-guessing that.

She started with the easy questions – how it felt to be first, if I'd faced any backlash, how I handled it, and all that. Those inquiries settled me, and helped me feel a little more comfortable with what I knew was coming.

"So... we're halfway through football season now, and the Kings... are doing okay. Not *great*, but not bad either – you're 6-3 so far, with seven more games on the table. What do you say to critics who feel like, with those numbers, your hiring was overhyped, that you've dropped the ball?"

"I'd say I don't know what they're talking about when they say I've dropped the ball – the *Kings* have the lowest fumble stats in the league this year," I laughed, shaking my head. "But no, honestly... I've had to tune out the critics. Football isn't the type of thing where the public's opinion is something to take into consideration. It's a game, with very specific rules, very specific – yet unpredictable – moves to follow if you want to win. There's nothing a commentator, opponent, or fan can *say* that's going to make you better at this, whether you're coaching or playing. In this game, focus is very important, so I choose to focus on what matters – helping those guys in uniform play the best they possibly can. That's it."

Wil grinned. "So... you're saying you *wouldn't* point them to the difference between last year's receiver stats and what they've done since you took on the wide receiver position?"

"I ain't say all *that* now," I laughed. "On a surface level, there's the urge to point out what you've been doing well, but like you said... the *team* hasn't had a *great* season. Last year they did, and the year before that, once Trent Bailey came back. Hiring me hasn't been the only development for the *Kings* this season, but it's significant. Even though my receivers have been doing well, I don't get to dust my hands of responsibility. We're a team. A unit. I have a duty to tailor what the receivers are doing in a way that complements the *whole* team. It's something to work on, and I'm confident in the *Kings* moving into the next seven games."

"Speaking of confidence," Wil started, with a grin that made me wonder what was coming. "A few weeks ago, I had a conversation that you've probably seen, with Mr. Rutledge Kadar Amare – a rookie with the confidence of a ten-year vet. He credited *you*, by name, with making him a better player."

"Yes, I *did* see that interview, and I'm... honestly blown away by that young man. Our very first encounter was *rough* to say the least, but ever since then, he has consistently impressed me. In a really short time, he has grown up so much, and become an asset to this team."

Wil nodded. "Is that why you chose to put him in, instead of Terrence Grant, after that cringe-worthy play that took Jordan Johnson out for the season?"

"It is," I confirmed. "Amare has major potential, he just needs experience. And he's responded very well to having this spotlight thrust on him. I won't pretend that Johnson's presence isn't missed on the field, but Amare has more than proven himself worthy to stand in the gap."

"And how is Jordan Johnson doing? His serious rotator cuff repair was confirmed, he's already had the surgery... what impact has it had on him as a player, and on the team as a whole?"

"As mentioned, he's missed, but only on the game day field. Jordan is very much still present with us, at team activities, and practices, and with his usual infectious energy. He's only missed one or two weeks, right after he was injured, and that was only because he was recovering. He's already started the rehab he'll need to be back on the field with us next season, but we're making sure he takes it slow."

"Something I'm sure his new wife appreciates."

"Oh of course."

"While we're on the topic of the Richardson family," Wil started, and I rolled my eyes.

"Oh *God*, here we go," I groaned, making Wil laugh.

"Come on, Sloane. You knew it was coming."

I pushed out a sigh. "I did."

"For the viewers and listeners who may not know what's going on, we're referring to Sloane's relationship with Nathan Richardson, Nicole's twin brother. Now… pictures of the two of you looking *quite* cozy first popped up in London, after the international game, and had the internet buzzing like crazy for multiple reasons. I'm going to be real with you Sloane – after my own experience with invaded privacy, pictures on the internet, all that, I was torn over whether I'd bring this up or not. But… it doesn't appear that you and Nate are hiding, because since London, you've been seen together several times. Do you care to make an official announcement?"

"Absolutely not," I laughed. "I'll say that my life is great right now."

"Now you already know I have to dig deeper than that, miss lady," Wil giggled. "Nate Richardson is not only the son of *Kings'* owner, Eli Richardson, but he holds an executive position in the *Kings* front office. *And*, he's thirteen years younger than you. Is there *anything* you're willing to give us about this whole older-woman younger-man workplace romance thing the two of you have going?"

"Very little," I answered, making her laugh harder. "Other than clarifying that he and I were involved well before I became a *Kings* employee, and the relationship had absolutely no bearing on my being hired."

Wil nodded. "There has definitely been some ugly speculation surrounded that..."

"There has, and just like with coaching, I had to tune it out, because my relationship is yet another thing that public opinion should have no sway over. But even understanding that, there's a real difficulty in deciding not to let it affect you when people are using your love life and other personal things to discredit you. Such as saying I was only hired because I was sleeping with the bosses' son, and it's like... honey, if you only *knew*... that definitely wasn't the energy I got. It's insulting to the team, to suggest they'd hire me because of that. I was hired because of my resume, and I do my job damn well."

"And your ability is *obvious*. Which makes it insulting to you as well."

"And insulting to him. As if access to the *Kings* is the only thing he has to offer, which is far from the truth."

A smile crept onto Wil's face. "Dare I ask what else?"

"Well, he saved my life, for starters," I answered, smiling too when I realized what had prompted Wil to ask that question. Nate had shown up, and as hard as he was trying to stay near the back, out of sight, his presence was obvious. "About six months ago, I had a minor heart attack, and went into cardiac arrest. Nate happened to be there when it happened, and he saved my life."

"Okay so you just dropped about fifteen different bombs just now, wow."

"*Sorry*," I laughed. "I just need it to be clear, that this thing isn't for convenience or show. It's *real*. And no amount of speculation will change that."

She gave me a deep nod. "I know that's right! So with *that* settled… let's talk about this heart attack, if that's okay with you?"

"Yes, it is," I agreed.

So we talked about it.

And then conversation came back around to football, and my experience on the team, and all those other things. And the interview was over, and Wil was hugging and thanking me, and then her team packed up to leave.

And then it was just me and Nate.

"Wasn't expecting you today," I told him, frowning over the lack of the usual enthusiasm in his embrace. "What's wrong? Did something happen?"

"Uh… kind of? Got some not-that-great news about my father, and I'm… honestly a little dazed. He's trying to pretend the shit isn't happening, Cole is trying not to stress about it because of the baby, Mel is… her head is fucked up, but *she's* trying to keep a brave face for Emma, and it's just… it's a lot," he admitted, the stress of it all clear in his voice.

"Okay. Okay, um… come here, to the kitchen. Let me fix you some tea, okay?"

Absently, he nodded, and I pulled him along, getting him situated at the counter while I brewed cups of loose leaf for both of us. I already knew about Eli's cancer diagnosis – he'd told me about it himself, during his apology, and he'd seemed optimistic, even though there was obvious, understandable anxiety.

The new development that Nate revealed, while not touching his tea, was that the tumor they'd found was growing, and rapidly. At what was referred to as, "an alarming rate."

"But his prognosis is still good though… right?"

Nate nodded. "Yeah. Which helps. But this development means that they aren't just watching it anymore, now it's moving into treatment. They have him scheduled for surgery. *Next week*. And then talking about chemo for a short period after that. Which… he's not a young man anymore. There are side effects, and complications, and all that, and… I don't know how to fucking deal."

"Yes, you do," I told him, cupping his face in my hands. He was seated, but I was still standing, which put us closer to eye level than usual. "I know for a fact that you know how to take care of someone, even when it's scary. Obviously, cancer is different, and they're talking about chemotherapy, and surgery, but… you've had practice. You got me up and about, you talked to me, made sure I was taking my medicine and all that, but most of all… you were *there*. And I knew that if I needed you, all I had to do was call, and that was *the* most valuable thing. Offer that same big heart to your family."

Nate wrapped his arms around my waist, pulling me close. It tugged at me when he dropped his face to my neck, clearly seeking comfort that I was more than willing to give, hooking my arms around him to deepen the embrace.

"I canceled my licensing exam," he told me, seemingly out of the blue, after we'd been like that for a few moments. "I need to focus on my family, and Cole is going to want time to just be with the baby, so…"

"You're putting a pin it," I finished for him, when he didn't complete the statement. I pulled back, so I could see his face – or more so he could see mine, see that I wasn't just saying what I thought he needed to hear. "Another year or so won't hurt anything, and that licensure isn't going anywhere. You'll get it when it's time."

A hint of a smile came to his face. "Look who is saying exactly the right thing *now*."

"Well you know… *I try*," I teased, pulling a little more of a curve to the corners of his mouth. "Drink this," I insisted, pointing at the tea. "It'll help, seriously. You can bring it with you. Let's go lay down."

He stood to follow me upstairs, but I could tell there was something else still weighing heavily on his mind.

"What is it?" I asked, stopping him on the stairs. "There's more… isn't there?"

He shook his head. "Not exactly. It's just fucked up to find this all out right now. Surgery the week before Thanksgiving, which is like… his *favorite* time. He's always in the kitchen with Mel, doing the big meal and all that, and now…"

"That doesn't have to change," I offered. "Well… not completely. You already invited me and Madison for the holiday, so… maybe I'll help Mel. It's been a long time since I've cooked for a bunch of people, since we usually go visit family around this time. But if Mel will have me, and she's feeling up to it, I'm sure between the two of us we can make it happen."

"If I know Mel like I think I do, she'd definitely be into it. She'd *love* that."

I smiled. "Then it's settled," I told him, grabbing his hand to pull him the rest of the way up the stairs. "I'll even make my mother's sweet potato pie."

Seventeen

Whole cranberries

~~Butter~~

~~Brandy   (top shelf)~~

Exactly what the hell are they making?

I looked up from the list I'd been sent to the store with, scanning the produce aisle for whole cranberries – some shit I'd never even seen before. My eyes landed on a display that held one lonely bag.

Probably the *last* bag, considering it was Thanksgiving Day.

With a relieved sigh, I put a little extra pep in my step so I could grab it and get back to my parent's house. Back to the couch, back to the TV, back to dark liquor in a short glass and delicious smells coming from the kitchen.

But apparently, I wasn't the only one who needed them.

The bag was in my sights, almost in my grip, and my gaze was already turned toward my hand basket, assessing where I'd put it. However, as soon as I grabbed it, I felt a tug. With the way the display was set up, the signage advertising the cranberries blocked the view of the other side, so whoever was trying to get it probably hadn't seen me.

Which was fine.

Those cranberries were still coming home with me.

I gave a firm tug, effectively claiming the bag for myself, and would've been unfazed by the feminine *"Hey!"* that came from the other side of the display if it hadn't sounded so damn familiar. Frowning, I peeked around the signage at the same time my cranberry-sparring partner stepped to my side, pretty face set in a deep scowl.

Leya.

"Seriously, Nate?" she asked, her expression easily shifting into a smile once she realized it was me. "See what happens when you quit me? Found yourself stealing cranberries from helpless women on Thanksgiving Day. You've fallen *so* far."

I laughed, feeling adequately ashamed of myself, but hey, "I'm actually stealing them *for* a woman, so I feel like it's justified. For a good cause."

"The cause being… filling your belly while you watch the game?" she asked, stuffing her own handwritten list into the pocket of her coat. "Are you having Thanksgiving dinner with *Sloane?*"

"With my family and a couple of friends too, but yeah. She's helping my sister and my father's wife with dinner as we speak."

Leya nodded. "And *you* got the lovely task of the *all the shit we forgot* run," she correctly deduced, peeking into my basket. "You forgot the foil."

I glanced at my list. "It's not on there though…"

"No, trust me," she laughed. "You should get it. There's never enough on Thanksgiving."

"You know what… I think I will. Never can have too much, right?"

"I know from experience," she nodded. "Should get you a few points… not that you need them, I mean… *Sloane Brooks*? When I saw those pictures of you two in London, and realized *she* must be the one things were "complicated" with for you? Any residual saltiness I felt over us not going anywhere, eliminated instantly. I would've dropped me for her too. Sloane is fucking *fine*, Nate."

I chuckled. "Yeah, she's… I'm a very lucky man."

"You sure as hell are," she agreed. "So lucky that you could probably spare those cranberries so I can make an old lady smile, right?"

"Not a chance," I told her, shaking my head. "These cranberries were the *don't come back without them* item on the list. I can't let them go."

"*Ugggh*," she exclaimed, halfheartedly, before her smile came back. "I had to at least try. I'll just dump the canned stuff in a bowl and chop it up. My folks won't even realize a difference."

"So we're good then?" I asked, prompting her to laugh.

"Of course, I could never stay mad at this face," she teased. "Anyway, it was good to… wrestle over a bag of cranberries with you."

I extended my arms, pulling her into what I intended to be a quick hug. But, just as we were getting ready to pull away, a male voice said, "Leya?" and her one-armed grip around my waist tightened.

"*Please just play along,*" she hissed into my ear, before she turned to look at the guy who'd approached us, pushing a shopping cart. "Shawn, *hey*! Look who I ran into," she gushed, practically draping herself over me, and putting a hand to my chest. "You remember me telling you about Nate, right? Nate, this is Shawn… my best and oldest friend. Our families are having Thanksgiving together this year."

Oh.

Ohhhh!

So *that's* why this nigga was looking like he wanted to tear me in half. A big ass vein appeared at his temple, and he swallowed before he gave the vaguest of nods.

"Yeah. I remember."

Leya grinned, eyes wide as she looked up at me – she still had herself pressed against my side. "He remembers. Do you remember me telling you about Shawn?"

Yeah.

I did.

"Of course. Your bestie. How you doing, man?" I asked, extending a hand in his direction. He looked at it, probably debating if he wanted to crush it or smack it away, but in front of her, he wasn't about to do either one. He accepted it, giving a too-firm handshake – energy he probably wasn't expecting me to give right back, but I did.

"Can't complain," he answered, once we'd pulled back. He was salty as hell, trying not to scowl, so I decided to put him out of his misery.

"I need to get back with these groceries, so I'm going to head out," I told Leya. "Again, it was good to see you."

"Likewise," she answered, pushing up to plant a kiss on my cheek. When she did, I pulled my arms around her again, giving me a chance to speak quickly into her ear.

"*That nigga likes you back, just talk to him,*" I told her, nodding at the "*are you sure?*" look she gave me when we pulled apart.

Hell yes I was sure that Shawn who almost certainly had only agreed to go to the grocery store for a chance to be alone with her today, and who was definitely buying into her attempt to make him jealous by being overly-familiar with me, liked her back.

In less than two minutes with them, there was no doubt in my mind.

I left them there to not tell each other how they felt and took myself home, dropping off the bag in the kitchen with Sloane, Mel, Cole, Jordan's sister, Jess, Madison and Emma. They were talking and laughing, having a great time, all of which stopped when I entered, pretty much letting me know I'd been the subject of the conversation. With my hands up, I backed out, confident that it couldn't be *too* rowdy, not with Madison and Emma in there, and went to look for Eli and Jordan.

When I found them, they were embroiled in an intense game of dominoes along with the boyfriend Jess had brought with her. The TV was on, and the liquor was flowing freely, so I found my place and fit right in.

As it got closer to dinner time, our crowd grew – Sloane's friend Joan and her husband, Miles and their kids, plus Garrett and his date, and Kyle Underwood and his wife and kids, since they were all buddies with my father. Garrett and I had already had a discussion, right after Eli's surgery, and then I talked it over with Sloane, who hadn't wanted to make Madison choose who to spend the holiday with.

Everybody was cool.

Not besties, but we didn't need all that.

All we needed was to be able to enjoy a meal together, and we pulled that off with no issues – mostly because we were too busy stuffing our faces. At the big dining table, Sloane ended up between Madison and Joan instead of next to me, which was fine. It gave me a chance to watch her as she watched everyone else – gave me a chance to see the deep, joyful peace in her eyes as she observed the happiness of her family.

I didn't even mind it when Cole, seated beside me, made a point of nudging me to ask, "Dude, could you *be* any more in love with her?"

I… wasn't sure.

But I was willing to find out.

After dinner, the men oversaw cleaning up and distributing plates and all that, since the ladies had done all the preparing. When we were done, I went searching for Sloane. I found Madison with Joan's kids and Emma, giving my baby sister the time of her life with a dress-up party. I asked Mads where her mother was, and was pointed outside, where she'd gone to "get some air".

Something about that didn't strike me quite right.

I *did* find Sloane outside, strolling the same path I'd taken with my father a few months before. She was coming toward the house instead of heading away from it, which told me she was probably at the end of her walk.

When she noticed me walking in her direction, a grin spread across her face, but I immediately noticed that it didn't quite reach her eyes. Once I was close enough, I grabbed her hand, squeezing as I pulled her into my open arms.

"What's wrong?" I asked her, tilting her chin up.

"You mean outside of being intensely tired, and my feet hurting, and my back hurting…"

I could tell she intended for me to stop right there, too distracted by that stuff to interrogate further. But I'd seen tired Sloane, seen *in-desperate-need-of-a-massage* Sloane, and all sorts of in-between. This was… something else.

"Yes," I told her. "Besides that."

She met my eyes, and let out a deep sigh. "Do we have to? It's Thanksgiving, and I'm still processing my… I don't even want to call it an issue, because it's not an issue."

"It's forty degrees out here."

"I know, I just needed a breather after being in the kitchen all morning, and then dinner, and then…"

"And then… what?"

Sloane let out a breath, then reached into the pocket of her coat, pulling out her phone. "So… I get my phone to respond to Thanksgiving texts from friends, family, players, whatever, right? But while I'm there, I notice I'm tagged a bunch of times in something on social media. I wasn't thinking much of it, like one of the players maybe tagged everybody, but then… I get there, and I see… *this*."

She held up the phone, and my heart dropped at the collage of images, posted by some gossip site. Images of me and Leya –

embracing, her kissing my cheek, her draped against my side, me speaking into her ear. And the damn caption…

Just last week, soon to be senior citizen Sloane Brooks was bragging about her young boy toy Nate Richardson in an interview… but looks to us like he snuck away from Grandma's table to meet up with a prime cut who's a little less… dry aged. We have the tea on Ms. Honey in these flix. Just hit the link!

"Sloane, this is—"

"Not what it looks like," she finished for me, tucking the phone back into her pocket. "I know that, which is why, like I said… I was just processing. I know you didn't leave here to go meet her. I knew that as soon as I saw the pictures. But even knowing the truth, it still doesn't feel good, Nate. I'm not holding it against you, I know it's not your fault, but… it's shitty. So I came out here to take a second."

"And that's understandable. I do want to make clear that I ran into her completely by chance – and she was with a guy who she *wants* to be with. She was putting on a show for his benefit, trying to get a reaction out of him. That's all."

"I believe you," she assured, immediately. "This is not an *us* issue, it's a *me* issue."

I shook my head. "Nah, there's no such thing. I have to be mindful – even when it's innocent to me, it's not a good look, and I have to be cognizant of that. You have the higher profile here, and there are people who… just want to tear shit down. I'm not interested in giving fuel to that fire."

"I appreciate that," she nodded. "Especially after… you know. What I went through with Garrett. Being in a position where I'm getting *constantly* embarrassed by someone who claims to love me… it's not something I want to do again. So that means a lot to me."

"And *you* mean a lot to me," I told her, wrapping my arms around her shoulders to pull her in close. "Were you really not going to bring this shit up to me?"

She laughed. "While we were here? Hell no. Later? Probably. Like I said, I just had to sort through my thoughts first. Especially since *I* was the one who pushed the whole Leya thing, so…"

"Nah, man," I chuckled. "If we're going to be non-traditional, let's do it. Instead of letting shit fester, let's just talk about it. What the fuck am I gonna do, break up with you?"

Grinning, she shook her head. "You worked way too hard for this position to walk away from it. You're not going anywhere."

"Exactly. So… you don't ever have to suffer in silence, or process *shit* that makes you feel unsure, or whatever. However long this thing between us is going to last, the end isn't going to be because of a conversation. Okay?"

She let out another sigh – a deep, contented one this time. "Okay."

"Alright. Now… let's get in here and find Garrett and his date, and whoop their ass in spades."

"*Oooh*," she groaned, reaching to kiss me. "I *love* the way you think."

"You ready to call it a night, old man?" I asked my father, after walking the last of the non-family guests to the door. Madison had gone with Garrett, and Sloane had passed out asleep in my old room, so I was taking advantage of the time with my father.

He answered with just an affirmative grunt, letting me know just how tired he was. It wasn't often that my father didn't have much to say, but I took it as a sign to help him to the room he and Mel had moved to downstairs, while he was recovering from the surgery.

Mel was already there, carefully cleaning makeup off Emma's face in the bathroom mirror. While I was getting my father settled, she switched gears to give baby girl a bath. Since she was occupied, I opted to sit with my father.

"Pretty nice turnout, huh?" he asked, sleepily. I was seated in a chair beside the bed, and grinned.

"Yeah, it was. You enjoyed yourself?"

"Yessir. That Sloane – she sure can make a sweet potato pie."

"She left a whole one just for you," I chuckled. "When I told her it was your favorite. And she didn't poison it or anything."

Eli laughed, cringing over the obvious stress it put on his body. "Thank you for that. I am truly grateful for the power of forgiveness."

"Well, she wasn't interested in holding a grudge, you know?"

He nodded. "She's a good woman."

"Oh, *now* you know that?"

"Knew it before you knew it," he countered, eyes half open. "I just… lost my head a little bit. You know that. You called it. I'm getting to be an old man, son."

"Getting to be?"

He smirked. "Don't come after me too hard – if I'm getting old, means you're getting old too. Before you know it, you're going to start finding grays everywhere."

"Ladies love a little salt-and-pepper seasoning," I replied. "I welcome it with open arms."

"So you say now."

He barely got that out before his eyes were completely closed, and I pulled his covers up, turning off the lamp at his bedside. I peeked into where Mel had Emma in her jammies, and was brushing her hair before she covered it with a kid-sized satin bonnet.

"He's out cold," I told her, scooping Emma up, to take her off her mother's hands. "I'll drop baby girl in her room. I know you're probably exhausted."

She smiled, but her eyes spoke to her level of fatigue, and she gave me a grateful arm squeeze. "Not even going to front – I definitely am. So thank you. She's barely keeping her eyes open, so she shouldn't be much trouble."

More like *no* trouble – Emma had already rested her head on my shoulder, and was quietly keeping herself occupied by running her hands over my facial hair, with closed eyes.

"Yeah," I laughed. "I'm thinking she won't be either."

"You look good with a baby in your arms," Mel teased. "You and Sloane…?"

I shook my head. "Nah. I get to be a big brother and an uncle and…"

"Maybe someday a stepfather?" she finished for me, since for some reason I had trouble verbalizing what I'd already teased Sloane with.

I smiled, and nodded. "Yeah. Maybe."

With Emma in my arms, I headed up the stairs, dropping her off in her gray and yellow, elephant themed room. As expected, she was so tired from all the activity of the day, plus the nap she'd refused earlier, that she barely stirred when I tucked her into her little bed.

I found Sloane still asleep in my room, and didn't bother to wake her. Instead, I took my own shower and then settled into the bed beside her, smiling when she immediately adjusted, tucking herself into my side.

A blinking light from my phone at the bedside got my attention, so I picked it up, surprised to see a text from Leya.

"I am soooo sorry about those pictures, Nate. I was just trying to make Shawn jealous – no idea that some weirdo would be taking pictures. I hope I didn't get you in trouble at all! I'll talk to her if you need me too. I am SO sorry. – Leya."

I shook my head, then typed out a response.

"Nah, it's fine. Sloane wasn't tripping about it, but I appreciate you trying to smooth it over. Did you tell him?"

"Well, after I saw what happened with the pictures… yeah. Figured I should at least make it worth it. – Leya."

"And?"

"And… we're meeting for drinks tonight, to talk about it. At his place. Alone. So basically, I'm getting that dick tuh-night!!!! – Leya."

I covered my mouth to keep from waking Sloane as I laughed. **"Congratulations I think? And Happy Thanksgiving."**

"Happy Thanksgiving Nate! – Leya."

I put the phone down beside the bed and turned to watch the rise and fall of Sloane's chest as she slept. She had an arm around my waist, and the warmth of her body, the faint scent of sweet potato pie – probably in her hair – had me more than a little turned on… and ready to make some of the fantasies I'd had about her in the room reality.

Gently, I ran a hand up her bare arm, trying to rouse her from her sleep. She groaned a little as my touch grew more firm, moving down to grip a handful of her ass.

Sleepily, she peeled her eyes open, looking up at me with a grin.

"What, Nate?" she asked, barely awake. "You want me to give you the hand job of your teenage fantasies, don't you? Maybe a little mouth action? Make the dream complete?"

I groaned just thinking about it. "I mean… Thanksgiving is all about gratefulness, right? I'm definitely down for some giving and receiving."

"In your parents' house? Really?"

I smirked. "Sloane… baby… trust me. This wouldn't remotely be the first time you made me cum in this house."

"*Ewww,*" she said, wrinkling her nose at me. "You're so nasty."

"Tell me you don't like it."

"That would be a lie," she purred, closing her eyes as she snuggled even closer to me. "Just give me like… ten more minutes of sleep?"

"Of course," I told her, closing my eyes too, even if it was just for a few minutes.

I'd never had a problem with her making me wait.

The end.

Jan 2019

Sloane

"You sit out here too much longer, they might call the people on you."

I smiled, but didn't take my eyes off the field. "The people?"

"The folks. The looney bin or whatever."

"Why? I'm not doing anything."

"That's my whole fuckin' point."

Finally, I turned to where Rutledge Amare was standing, in the aisle, several seats down from where I'd posted up in the bleachers. It was after our last game – a home game, which we'd won.

The win hadn't been enough though.

Not that I didn't already know that – our fate was already secured, before this last game even kicked off. The *Kings* were in transition, and that had been a common refrain all year. No one, not even the media honestly, was harping too much on the fact that we hadn't made it past the championships. We'd been all the way to the top, two years in a row, which was special. A season off didn't take away any of credibility.

For me though… it stung.

"We didn't get our rings," I said, returning my eyes to the empty field. "We were supposed to shut this shit down. Prove all the haters wrong."

"And you think we didn't?"

I held up my hands, gesturing at the field. "We're here, instead of celebrating. So you tell me."

"I can't tell you shit, but to speak for yourself. I shut *all* my haters up," Amare laughed. Again, I smiled, but my eyes stayed on the field as I felt the shift in energy of him moving to sit beside me. "Including the one that's about to have this drink with me."

My eyebrows went up, and I turned to see him holding out two empty glasses that he must've had in his hands already. I accepted one as he pulled a bottle of *Mauve* from the pocket of his coat.

"I have heart disease, Amare. Not supposed to be drinking hard liquor."

He smacked his lips. "You can have a lil' taste with me at least, right? Celebrate how far we've come?"

I smirked, then nodded. "You know… actually, I *will* drink to that. It's the least I can do, after you've sent me flowers and shit, right?"

"According to y'alls feminist shit, I wasn't supposed to expect anything in return, but…" he shrugged, laughing, and I held out my glass for him to pour just enough for a sip.

"I saw your interview, you know?" I asked him. "With Wil Cunningham-Bishop. It was a great showing of how much you've matured."

He scoffed. "Yeah, and I saw *your* interview with her too – great showing of you fucking the owner's son. You wild, Coach Brooks. I ain't think you had something like that in you."

I chuckled as he poured his own glass, then held mine up. "In that case... here's to subverting expectations."

"Fa sho'."

I took a sip – well, *the* sip – from the glass, letting the smooth liquor warm me against the frigid cold outside. I knew it probably looked a little crazy, me making my way back to the empty stadium for this moment of clarity and reflection, but... I was okay with that.

I was looking for the last little bit of peace I needed to move forward, and I'd found it.

"You'll be here next season?"

I wasn't surprised by the question, not after the little battle I'd had with Eli once he'd found out about Nate and me. The details of the conversation weren't something I'd been privy to, but when Nate said he'd handled it, I looked for clues that backed that up – my acceptance into the Richardson family fold had been a major one.

"Yep," I nodded, stifling a smile over the hopefulness I knew Amare didn't realize was in his tone. "Already signed my paperwork, actually. Are your people working out something better for you? Better money?"

Amare shook his head. "Can't talk about that with you. You sleepin' with the... well, I can't call Nate the enemy, but you feel me."

"I do," I laughed. "And I respect it. But however it goes... next season... we kickin' ass, right?"

He held out his fist, and I tapped it with mine. "You already know."

Before I could say anything else, my phone started vibrating. I pulled it from my pocket to see Nate's name on the screen, along with a few other calls I must have missed while I was zoned out, before Amare showed up.

"Hey," I answered, gesturing to Amare to give me a second. "Is everything okay?"

The slight pause before he answered told me everything. "Uh… it's about Cole. We're at the hospital."

My breath caught in my throat. "Okay. I'm on my way."

I said quick goodbyes to Amare, rushing out of the stadium to get to my car, and then to the hospital where the Richardson family had gathered. I hadn't gathered details over the phone, so by the time I stepped into the waiting room, I had several nightmare scenarios in my head, all of which I was hoping were wrong.

Nate was the first to approach me, pulling me into a hug.

"What's wrong?" I asked, when we stepped back. "Is she okay?"

Nate sighed. "Uh… early labor, they think. Maybe. Very early."

My eyes went wide. "But… they can stop it, right? Remember this just happened, with Ramsey and Wil Bishop, and they were able to press pause. Their baby boy is just fine."

"Well, we can hope," Nate nodded. "Jordan is back there with her now, with the doula and midwife, talking to a doctor. I just… *fuck*," he sighed, shaking his head as he stuffed his hands into his pockets. "I had hoped my next trip to a hospital would be a happy occasion, like… when she was having the baby, when she was *supposed* to have the baby."

"I thought she wanted a home birth?"

"She does, but... shit happens, you know? I just—"

"Didn't want to see anyone else you cared about in a hospital bed?" I finished for him, and he nodded, wrapping his arms around me again.

"Right."

I settled into him, staring up to meet his eyes. "She's going to be okay. And so will your niece or nephew."

"Yeah, that's what I'm hoping." His expression shifted, like he'd suddenly remembered something. "What about you? You good? I know you said you needed a second to yourself. I hated to interrupt, but I know you would've been pissed if I hadn't."

I grinned. "You know me well. And, I'd already been interrupted, so it was totally fine."

A sudden grip around my leg made me gasp, and I looked down to see that Emma had broken free from her parents, and was now holding onto me, offering a soggy cookie.

"Oh, *thank you* sweetheart," I gushed, smiling at her. "But I've had enough cookies today already. I don't want to have a tummy ache!"

She frowned at me, then looked at the cookie, then back at me. "... no cookie?"

"I'm sorry," I told her. "But thank you so much!"

That thank you earned me exactly zero points with Emma – which I luckily didn't need, because typically, she adored me – only deepening her frown as she let me go, reaching instead for her big brother.

Nate bent down, sweeping her up into his arms, making me swoon – and gag, at the same time – as he allowed her to put that cookie in his mouth.

Watching him with her was a secret guilty pleasure of mine. Despite his continued insistence that babies weren't on his radar until after he established himself as a sports manager, I was confident that fatherhood would have been a good look on him. He wasn't letting on – and neither was I – but we were both looking forward to Cole's new addition to the family.

I wanted to see him with a *baby* baby.

We all looked up as Jordan came out of Cole's room, wearing an inscrutable expression. He stopped, propping his hands on his waist as he looked around at us, seemingly… *dazed.*

"Jordan," Eli called, standing up. "What is it? Is Cole okay?"

He nodded, still looking baffled. "Uh… yeah," he said, after several hard blinks. "She's perfectly okay. It's not labor, she's just… it's, um… holy shit, man…"

"JJ," Nate stepped in, concerned. "What aren't you telling us?"

Jordan looked up at Nate – stared at Nate – then scoffed, shaking his head. "I should've been prepared for this. We should've expected this."

"Expected what, Jordan?" Mel asked, moving toward him at the same time I did. "What's going on?"

"Twins," he answered, still wearing that dazed expression. "She… *we*… wanted to do the natural thing, so we only ever listened for a heartbeat. The midwife has been measuring her belly and all that was cool, so… we didn't think anything of it. I mean, she measured a little bigger than expected, but… I wasn't really trying to harp on that with her, but apparently… it's cause there are two babies. They're pressing on her spine, on her organs and shit. That's why she's in pain. The doctor said maybe a sudden growth spurt."

For several moments, there was silence, and then the room erupted in activity and talk and laughter. The doctor and midwife came out, and the family filed in to see Cole, but Jordan caught me, keeping me back a second to deliver a warning before he slipped back inside himself.

"Be careful, Coach B. Apparently, twins run in their family."

I hope you enjoyed Nate and Sloane's story! Please consider leaving a review. You can also reach me via my website (www.beingmrsjones.com) on facebook (www.facebook.com/beingmrsjones) on twitter (www.twitter.com/beingmrsjones) or instagram (www.instagram.com/beingmrsjones) For notifications about new releases, sales, events, or other announcements, you can subscribe to my mailing list.

Christina C. Jones is a modern romance novelist who has penned many love stories. She has earned a reputation as a storyteller who seamlessly weaves the complexities of modern life into captivating tales of black romance.

Friends & Lovers:
Finding Forever
Chasing Commitment
Strictly Professional:
Strictly Professional
Unfinished Business
Serendipitous Love:
A Crazy Little Thing Called Love
Didn't Mean To Love You
Fall In Love Again
The Way Love Goes
Love You Forever
Something Like Love
Trouble:
The Trouble With Love
The Trouble With Us
The Right Kind Of Trouble
If You Can (Romantic Suspense):
Catch Me If You Can
Release Me If You Can
Save Me If You Can
Inevitable Love:
Inevitable Conclusions
Inevitable Seductions
Inevitable Addiction
The Wright Brothers:
Getting Schooled – Jason & Reese
Pulling Doubles – Joseph & Devyn
Bending The Rules – Justin & Toni
Connecticut Kings:
CK #1 *Love in the Red Zone* — Love Belvin

37035466R00190

Made in the USA
Middletown, DE
21 February 2019